After You

A Novel

JULIE BUXBAUM

VIKING
CANADA

VIKING CANADA

Published by the Penguin Group

Penguin Group (Canada), 90 Eglinton Avenue East, Suite 700, Toronto, Ontario, Canada M4P 2Y3
(a division of Pearson Canada Inc.)

Penguin Group (USA) Inc., 375 Hudson Street, New York, New York 10014, U.S.A.
Penguin Books Ltd, 80 Strand, London WC2R 0RL, England
Penguin Ireland, 25 St Stephen's Green, Dublin 2, Ireland (a division of Penguin Books Ltd)
Penguin Group (Australia), 250 Camberwell Road, Camberwell, Victoria 3124, Australia
(a division of Pearson Australia Group Pty Ltd)
Penguin Books India Pvt Ltd, 11 Community Centre, Panchsheel Park, New Delhi – 110 017, India
Penguin Group (NZ), 67 Apollo Drive, Rosedale, North Shore 0745, Auckland, New Zealand
(a division of Pearson New Zealand Ltd)
Penguin Books (South Africa) (Pty) Ltd, 24 Sturdee Avenue, Rosebank,
Johannesburg 2196, South Africa

Penguin Books Ltd, Registered Offices: 80 Strand, London WC2R 0RL, England

Published in Canada by Penguin Group (Canada), a division of Pearson Canada Inc., 2009.
Simultaneously published in the United States by The Dial Press, an imprint of The Random
House Publishing Group, a division of Random House, Inc., New York.

1 2 3 4 5 6 7 8 9 10 (RRD)

Copyright © Julie R. Buxbaum, Inc., 2009

Publisher's note: This book is a work of fiction. Names, characters, places and incidents either are
the product of the author's imagination or are used fictitiously, and any resemblance to actual
persons living or dead, events, or locales is entirely coincidental.

Manufactured in the U.S.A.

LIBRARY AND ARCHIVES CANADA CATALOGUING IN PUBLICATION

Buxbaum, Julie
After you / Julie Buxbaum.

ISBN 978-0-670-06683-4

I. Title.

PS3602.U98A7 2009a   813'.6   C2009-902898-0

American Library of Congress Cataloging in Publication data available.

Visit the Penguin Group (Canada) website at **www.penguin.ca**

Special and corporate bulk purchase rates available; please see
www.penguin.ca/corporatesales or call 1-800-810-3104, ext. 477 or 474

For Indy, my home spot

After You

Part One

"You are going to be sent home," Basil said to her,
"at the end of the week. And we're glad of it."
"I'm glad of it, too," answered Mary. "Where is home?"
—THE SECRET GARDEN

1

Let's pretend that things are different. That in the last couple of days, I haven't become the kind of person who resorts to wishing on eyelashes, first stars of the night, and the ridiculous 11:11, both a.m. and p.m., in earnest and with my eyes closed. That Lucy and her family haven't transformed into tabloid stars with a full picture on the cover of the *Daily Mail* with the headline *Notting Hill Murdergate!*, and the lead story on the BBC evening news. Let's pretend that I am home, on the right side of the Atlantic, the one where I understand the *English* language, and that tomorrow will be just like early last week, or the week before that one, when the days were indistinguishable. That it's not necessary to resort to memories—to a time *before*—when I think of Lucy.

How about this: Let's just pretend that Lucy is not dead.

That she will not continue to be dead now, even though that's what that means—dead.

"Want some more?" I ask Sophie, Lucy's eight-year-old daughter, but she seems uninterested in the elaborate bowl of ice cream I've doused with concentric circles of whipped cream. She sits with her knees drawn to her chest and her arms wrapped around them. An upright fetal position, a pose that has been as reflexive for her as irrational wishing and pretending has been for me. Striped pastel pajamas ring her legs—pink, blue, yellow stripes—and on top, she wears a long-sleeved T-shirt with a decal of a purple horse with a silver mane. Her socks have abrasive soles that scratch and swish along the kitchen tiles, a sound I haven't heard since my own childhood and that I associate with my younger brother, Mikey, asking for a glass of water before bedtime.

She shakes her head no.

"Is it good?"

She stays noncommittal. Her tiny glasses slip down her nose and are caught by her finger, pushed back up with an efficient tap. They are tortoiseshell frames, brown on the outside, pink along the inner edges, like an eyelid, and they magnify her already large brown eyes, so that she always looks just a tiny bit moony.

Sophie has not been speaking much since the accident. That's what we've been calling it—Greg, Lucy's husband, and I—"the accident," a comforting euphemism despite the fact that there is nothing accidental about what happened. The word *homicide* is one that no eight-year-old should ever have to hear. Using *accident* makes us feel better too. As adults, we can handle an accident; that's in our repertoire.

I am not sure when Sophie last spoke out loud. She was interviewed by the police on Thursday, right afterward, and somehow Lucy's little girl found the strength to use her words and describe the unspeakable. When I arrived less than twenty-four hours later, blurry from grief and the red-eye, she said, "Hi, Auntie Ellie," before putting her arms around my waist and burying her face in my shirt. But since then, since that first greeting, spoken in her crisp

British accent, I can't remember the last time I heard her voice. Did she say good night to Greg before he went upstairs and knocked himself out with Xanax?

"Soph?"

A shrug.

"Where did you get that shirt? It's pretty. And that horse has really cool hair."

Another shrug.

"Soph, sweetheart, are you not talking?"

Sophie just looks at me, her eyes burning in a silent protest.

Shrug number three. She looks impossibly small and thin, the stringiness of her arms and legs exaggerated by the unforgiving cotton of her pajamas. I wish she'd eat more. I want to feed her cookies and sugar cereal too. Tomorrow, first thing, I'll replace their two percent milk with full fat.

My mother, a therapist, warned me this might happen to Sophie. That kids often go quiet for a while in the wake of a traumatic loss. Their only way of exerting control in a world in which they clearly have none.

It's been only twenty-nine hours since Lucy's funeral, an event so improbable that pretending still works. Surreal, too, like the news vans that are idling out front of her house, waiting for a sound bite. I want to scoop Sophie up into my arms and let her cry into my shoulder, but she is not the sort of kid you just scoop up. She would know that I was doing it more for my comfort than for hers.

"Okay," I say, as if she'd actually answered me. "It's all right if you don't want to talk for now. But not forever, right? I love that voice of yours. *Cheerio. Let's take the lift and go to the loo,*" I say in my best British impression, which used to be a surefire way to make her laugh.

"Speak like me, Mummy, Auntie Ellie!" Sophie used to demand of Lucy and me when I would come to visit, and the two of us would go back and forth, spitting out all of the British expressions we knew. Even after nearly a decade in London, and despite a husband and child whose inflections were as posh as the Queen's, Lucy's Boston accent had barely softened. She always *paa'ked her caa' in Haa'va'd Yaa'd.*

Today, Sophie ignores me and looks around like she's not sure whose kitchen this is. We are in the breakfast nook, with its Americana diner style, the sort you would see in a cornflakes commercial: two kids, two bowls of cereal, and two glasses of orange juice, with two parents—always two cheerful parents—rushing everyone out of their red pleather seats and off to school after their nutritionally balanced breakfast. I can picture Lucy deciding to put a booth in the corner, knowing that making your house look like a home is the first step.

"We're going to be okay, you know," I say, and run my fingers through Sophie's curly dirty-blond hair; they get caught on a knot. I remember the first time I held her, when she was less than a week old, bald and tiny, and how she would sleep with her mouth opening and closing against my arm, her dreams, no doubt, filled with glorious imaginary milk. She had seemed so fragile then, so far from a real person, that looking at her now, a fully formed little girl, beautiful and tough and exerting her power in the only way she can, makes me glow with a vicarious pride for Lucy. My best friend did a lot with her thirty-five years on this planet; her exposé on the corruption in the Chilean government should have won her a Pulitzer. But of one thing I am sure. Making this creature, this fierce mini-Lucy, is my favorite of all.

* * *

When did I start speaking a language I don't recognize as my own? I dismiss the stalking reporters with copied phrases I've learned from watching TV, *please respect our privacy during this very difficult time*; reassure Sophie with silly platitudes, *we are going to be okay*; lie to all the well-wishers at the funeral Greg and I hastily planned, *Lucy spoke so highly of you*. I guess when your world blows up, when you lose the person you were closest to for thirty-one years—almost my entire life—language skills are the first to go.

Here is what happened: Lucy woke up a few days ago, happy and healthy, trapped in a tent of all the clichés of a perfect modern adult life, with the international glamour of an American expat thrown in to boot, and one hour and forty-five minutes later, while walking Sophie to school, she died. Just like that. No, she didn't die, just like that. She was murdered. Apparently, there was a knife and a meth-head overly interested in her two-carat diamond ring, some idiotic resistance on Lucy's part, and then it was over.

And, yes, there is a worst part of all: Sophie saw the whole thing.

I am not surprised Lucy fought back—she's always had an inhuman amount of courage—but I am surprised she fought back for that ring. She hated that ring.

"Who buys a diamond-shaped diamond?" Lucy would say. It was one of her favorite bits when Greg wasn't around. "I mean, seriously, a diamond-shaped diamond? It's so redundant. I swear, all men think about is size."

And now I am here, in her kitchen, sitting next to her daughter—my goddaughter—trying to adjust to this new world we have entered. After Lucy. I am sipping tea because, from my experience over the last few days, that seems to be what the British do in situations like these. As if consuming mass quantities of flavored hot water with a spot of milk and sugar will make everything better. But it's too late for stopgap measures. The grief has started to burrow into my skin like a parasite, slow and steady, in inverse proportion to my disbelief.

"Soph, what do you want to do? You want me to be quiet, too, for a bit? We can just sit here." I get a nod, slow, as if she wants to say, *Yes, please*. I can tell simply by looking at her that we both want exactly the same thing. For it all to stop for a little while.

And so the two of us do the closest thing I can think of. We sit in the booth and stare straight ahead at nothing in particular. I pull her in closer, and her head rests against my shoulder.

We pass the next hour this way. Silent and watchful. Like we are waiting for a bus that may never come.

2

re you all right?" my husband, Phillip, asks over the telephone, after I have spent the last fifteen minutes rambling on about the London rain. Part of the pretend game: Let's talk about anything but why I'm here.

"I don't know. I forgot my umbrella. That's going to be a problem."

"I mean about Lucy and stuff."

"I don't know. No. Yes. No."

"Come home."

"Not yet," I say. "I am Sophie's godmother, remember?" Strange how the job description used to be limited to making the occasional phone call, putting her school photo on my refrigerator, and sending lots of gifts—at first, unbearably cute and tiny clothing, and, more recently, Ramona Quimby books and creepy American Girl dolls. Now the assignment is serious. A position above my pay grade.

"Of course I remember. I didn't mean . . . By the way, did you give Sophie that fake thumb I got her? Tell her there are a bunch of tricks for it in that *Magic for Beginners* book I sent a few months ago." Phillip, too, has relished his role as de facto godfather, especially because Sophie shares his childhood love of magic. He loves to send her surprise gifts for obscure holidays—Groundhog Day, Bastille Day, Canadian Thanksgiving, the Sox winning the World Series. Often, he'll send something for no reason at all, and I'll find out only later, when Lucy and Sophie call to say thank you.

"Yeah, I did. She liked it, I think. Phillip?"

"Yeah?"

"They need me here."

"I need you here," he says, but we both know he is pretending.

While I talk to Phillip on the Staffords' portable phone, I am lying on top of Lucy's guest duvet, the flowered Laura Ashley one that I used to tease her about. My evidence that Lucy is playing—was playing, was, was, was—posh London wife, in betrayal of our shared hippie roots in Cambridge, Massachusetts, where it was a point of pride to rescue and refurbish furniture from the sidewalk. The room is decorated with the delicate antiques she's picked up from Portobello Market through the years, giving the place a shabby-chic feel; everything looks both expensive and tattered, though more the former than the latter.

Phillip is sitting on our couch in our living room, in Sharon, a town that clings just to the edges of Boston, the perfect distance for suburban commuter glory and only thirty minutes from where Lucy and I grew up. Our couch is comfortable if not stylish, long enough that he can stretch his six feet of body out and not have to dangle over the arms, and wide enough that he can rest a drink on the cushion next to him. There is probably a stack of documents resting on his belly, a glass of red wine to his left, and the TV on mute.

I doubt he's mourning Lucy, because he never particularly liked her. Phillip thinks her murder is sad in a disturbing *20/20* special sort of way. Lucy was a bit too well packaged for his taste. He once told me she reminded him of a morning news anchor or even a late-night talk-show host—funny and charming and attractive, yes, a master manipulator of small talk, too, and yet still somehow not the real thing. The person you want at your cocktail parties, not in your foxhole. I am sure he is sad for me because he knows I loved her, but I imagine he thinks I will soon get over it. I don't think he understands that if Lucy had been a man, I might have married her first.

"We need to get an electric kettle," I tell Phillip now. "That's the one thing the Brits definitely do better. They boil water a full two minutes faster. Can you imagine if that caught on at home? We'd all have two more minutes in our days. It would change everything. I'll bring one back. We can use it for pasta."

"They sell them in Williams-Sonoma." My husband is the sort of man who knows what is available in Williams-Sonoma. He also knows a great restaurant you must try in Napa, how the dollar is doing against the yuan, and which fish are on the PETA do-not-eat list.

"That's good. Now all we need is a royal family."

"Ellie, are you okay?"

"You already asked me that."

"You're doing that thing you do."

"What thing?"

"You know, that thing. Where you make not-so-funny jokes because you don't know what else to do. I am worried about you. You're making me nervous."

"I'm making you nervous? Try being here. Try being in this house. Try looking Sophie in the eyes." I raise my voice for a moment and then bring it under control; my emotions are too close to the surface, jumbled and raw. I am angry at Phillip; that much is clear. But this is not really about Phillip, and that's one more thing that we both know.

"How is she?"

"Holding up. Not talking. She's a tough kid."

"Like her mom."

"Yeah."

"Maybe I should have come with you," Phillip says now, guilt creeping into his voice. I can tell he feels far away and helpless.

"Yeah, maybe you should have." I know I should throw him a bone, but I am too tired, too shattered, to be fair right about now. Phillip is not here because I told him he didn't *have* to come. Yes, it was a test, an accidental one, maybe, but a test nonetheless. (Phillip didn't pass.)

"You told me not to come," he says now. "You said that your brother would be there and that you'd be okay."

"I said you didn't *have* to come."

"It's the same thing, Ellie. Just semantics."

"No, it's not the same thing," I say, but my petty tone disgusts me, and I try to backpedal from silly marital warfare. I called Phillip for comfort tonight, to hear his voice and remember that I have a life across the Atlantic. Guilt creeps into my voice now, too, a result of this unnecessary volley that I don't know why I started. "I'm sorry. Never mind. It doesn't matter. I'm fine."

"If I realized . . . I mean, you know I would have come. You know that, right? Tell me that you at least know that," Phillip says, his voice almost as sad and tired as mine.

"I know that. Of course you would have." And the truth is, I do know that. If there is anything you can say about Phillip—beyond the fact that he has an unnatural affinity for kitchen gear—it is that he is a good person who always makes sure to do the right thing. Which is why I've trusted my life to him, why, on that crisp fall day when we got married five years ago, I wasn't nervous about saying *I do*.

I know if I had said come, if I had said it clearly, like, *I want you to come to London*, without letting him fall through the trapdoor of language, he would have come.

3

Lucy's funeral was held in an old stone church perched at the tip of a private garden in Notting Hill. We looked out of arched windows, a slivered view onto a beautiful bit of earth, green and blooming. While Lucy was eulogized, a little boy in overalls and miniature Wellington boots played outside with a red plastic shovel. He was too small to do any real damage; he just kept turning the same spoonful of dirt over and over, taking obvious delight each time, as if the smell of the ground and the deep brown of it was a continuous surprise.

Though the locale for the funeral couldn't have been more picturesque—thank God for that little boy, who even managed to make me smile once or twice, and for my brother, Mikey, too, who sat next to me and held my hand—the sermon itself was soulless. We were all taken too off guard, Lucy's loss too sudden, too indigestible, for us to rally to give her the glowing tribute she deserved and, knowing Lucy, would have relished. Only the vast quantities of food, hand-delivered to the house afterward by an overpriced local caterer, would have pleased her.

That was really the best you could do? Seriously? You know I wanted to go out with a bang, I imagine her saying about the ceremony, equal parts annoyed and amused, shaking her head at me, like she couldn't help being charmed by my inadequacy to the task. *I guess if you want something done right, you gotta do it yourself. But, yeah, A-plus on the lasagna.*

I think she would have enjoyed the elaborate hats the women wore—actual feathers and netting and brims a foot wide—and laughed at how they all brought us tarts and pies to pay their respects, the British food Lucy had always hated most; she despised anything buried under a thick layer of dough.

"You want to know the worst part?" she would say, during one of her typical culinary rants. "You know those mincemeat pies? The stuff inside? Not. Even. Meat. Only in this country could you get away with calling raisins and some other crap mixed together meat."

So when Greg comes downstairs this morning and finds me nursing a cup of coffee in his kitchen, the first thing I ask him is whether he wants to keep all the pies. I want to honor Lucy's memory in every way I can; throwing out baked goods is a start.

"Chuck them, I guess," Greg says, looking at the dining table, which is full of dishes covered in Saran Wrap. "But save anything with rhubarb. Sophie loves the stuff. It's because she thinks it's cool that it can be toxic."

Greg smiles a weak smile—*that Sophie*—and then clears his throat. Today he is suited up, jacketed-and-tied and even pocket-squared; posh and dignified, as always. I guess he's going to work at his law firm, the one guaranteed death-free zone.

Greg was married to my best friend for almost a decade, and so, in some ways, I know more about him than I should: that his father was an alcoholic and he has deeply ambivalent feelings about his mother, that he thinks he's a better tennis player than he is, that he makes a nasally whine during sex, that he can be bossy in and out of bed, that the Beatles' "Two of Us" makes him teary, that he's well endowed, that he owns this house outright and has enough money to retire tomorrow if he feels like it but that he will never feel like it, that he loved Lucy so much that when she went on business trips he would sleep with her bunched-up nightgown.

Standing in his kitchen now, inserting myself into his Monday morning, I realize that I've mostly known Greg as one of Lucy's supporting characters. I'm not sure I've ever been in a room with him alone until this week. Without Lucy, this man I've known for ten years suddenly feels like a stranger.

"Ellie, I can't thank you enough for all of your help these last few days. . . ." Greg says, his tone taking on that of a fellow general at war. Not cold but formal. He understands the social rules and he follows them. In other words, he's British.

"Seriously, don't thank me. I couldn't—I mean, of course—" I stop myself, because if I keep talking, I will start crying, and I don't want to cry in front of Greg again. I did enough of that at the funeral. If he can get out of bed, and take a shower, and put on a suit, if his eyes can remain puff-free, then I can stop my sniffling for the fifteen more minutes it takes for him to get out of the house.

"Right. So, I really appreciate you dropping off Sophie today. I've taken the liberty of drawing up some directions to the school. It's a different route than she normally takes, but all things considered, I assumed it was best not to, you know, bring up unpleasant memories." I don't know what I believe about Lucy—if she is still here with us somehow—but if she's watching right now, she's cracking up. *All things considered? Unpleasant memories?* She may have hated the food, but she loved the understatedness of the Brits. She would joke that if the house were burning down, Greg would say, *Love, I think it's getting a little toasty in here. Do you reckon we should call round to the fire brigade?*

"You think she's ready to go back? Have you noticed that she's stopped talking altogether?"

"I know, but the headmistress said she should get right back into the swing of things. Routine, structure, and all that. Good for kids. She said that breaking from that will shake Sophie up even more."

"Okay." I'm second-in-command here, and that's fine by me.

"Also, you needn't worry about being safe on the walk. What happened. To Luce. That doesn't actually happen here." If the media coverage is anything to go by—I can still hear that constant stirring outside, the news vans still lined up, the reporters waiting for a quote—it's clear that Notting Hill is not known for its murder rate. The sidewalks are filled with children going off to day schools, the girls in tartan kilts and straw hats, the boys in suits and ties. Seems impossible that what happened to Lucy happened to her here.

"I'm sure we'll be fine."

"So, the family liaison officer has cut us a deal with the reporters. They'll film and take pictures of you both just till the end of the block, and then they promise to leave you alone. They're supposed to block out Sophie's face, but you'll probably be in the paper. I'm sorry, Ellie. I know this is all a lot to ask."

"Not a problem."

The police have assigned us a "family liaison officer," a burly, slow-moving cop named Nigel, who seems nice if ineffectual. He's stopped by the house twice, mostly to make sure the reporters are behaving.

Call me FLO, he'd said in his East End accent the first time we met. *You get it? F-L-O.* And then he actually laughed, as if that were a funny joke. Nigel is our point person for all things *accident*-related, including dealing with the media and the police. When he gives us updates, he uses words like *perp* and, my least favorite, *murder.* He hasn't caught on to our euphemisms.

"And there's a big merger going on at work, so I'll probably be back a bit late tonight," Greg says now.

He points to a schedule on a small wipe-it board in the corner that I hadn't noticed before. Along the top, below the words *THE STAFFORD FAMILY,* the days of the week are printed in Lucy's neat handwriting, and down the left side is a list of nanny shifts and planned activities for Sophie. Lucy and I talked at least once a day, e-mailed maybe four times that—strange that she never once mentioned three different nannies.

Seeing Lucy's handwriting, though—the same scrawl that Mrs. Roberts used to yell at her for in elementary school, the same haphazard *L*s that used to decorate the letters she would write me when I went to Girl Scout camp in the summers—makes me feel dizzy, and I close my eyes against the rush. She always called me L—not Elle, like Phillip calls me, elongating the sounds, but L. Short and abrupt.

"Ellie? Umm, I just wanted to let you know, I'd love for you to stay as long as you can. I mean, as long as you like. I—*we,* Sophie and I—could use the help. As it happens, Lucy had recently hired some new people, nannies, but I have to sack them all. It looks like they've been selling information to the tabloids."

"Are you serious?"

"Yeah. My address book has suddenly gone missing, some of our wedding photos, too, and all my old Eton friends are getting phone calls from reporters. It's all just . . . bloody ridiculous."

"I'm so sorry—"

He waves away my sympathy, and even his hand gestures are mannered. He looks like he is conducting a symphony. "Anyhow, I'm not sure how we would have survived any of this without you. It feels good to have at least one person I can trust."

"I'm happy to stick around for as long as you need me," I say.

"Thanks. Yes, okay, well, I guess I'm off." Greg crosses through the dining room on his way to the front door. He stops, though, takes another long look at the table, wooden and sturdy, examining its vast array of covered treats, as if deciding what he wants to take for the road. But then his fist clenches, and my body prepares for the noise before my brain understands.

Greg smashes the pies, one by one, clean and careful. Punch, punch, punch. Like he's playing an artful game of Whac-a-Mole.

"Right, then," he says, just before walking out the door. He slaps his hands together to shake off the few crumbs that made it through the Saran Wrap. "Yeah. That's better."

After he's gone, I notice there is a single pie left sitting on the table, whole and untouched. I don't have to taste it to know it's the one with the rhubarb.

4

I wake Sophie by kissing her temple. She is warm with sleep and slow to move. I wish we could skip school and I could crawl into this mini-bed with her and let that warmness wash over me. I've been cold since I arrived in London. No, I've been cold since I heard about Lucy. After I got the call, Phillip wrapped me in a blanket to fight full body shakes. Somehow, I was on the floor, though I don't remember my legs giving way.

"Okay, let's get you ready for school," I say now, with this new chipper tone I've adopted when I talk to Sophie. I wonder at what age cheerfulness can be misinterpreted as condescension.

I open the closet and see a neat world of little girls' clothing. Each crisp item on a small hanger, grouped by category. T-shirts with other T-shirts, long-sleeved kept separate from short-sleeved. The colors are bright and childlike, a rainbow of soft pastels. When did Lucy get so organized? When we were roommates for those two requisite postcollegiate years in New York—two years of beery nights on Avenue C in Alphabet City—she never got off the couch without leaving something behind: a single sock, a crusty wineglass, sometimes even a pair of underwear. Maybe having kids really does change a person.

I remember Lucy saying after Sophie was born that all the clichés existed for a reason, that once you have a child *everything* is different.

"You'll understand one day, L. I think until you have one of your own, you won't really get it," she had said, doing that thing she did every once in a while that made me feel like she got a secret joy from being one step ahead.

I pick out a yellow hooded sweatshirt for Sophie, since I figure it is probably raining, and a pair of Levi's that are no longer than the distance from my wrists to my shoulders. Sophie, now bespectacled, reaches out for the clothes in my hands and hangs them back up in the closet, in the spots from which they came. I brace myself for a fit, remembering that picking out what to wear is notorious for setting children off. Today, of all days, Sophie can wear whatever she wants. I couldn't care less if she matches.

She opens a drawer in the dresser next to the closet and takes out a navy-blue wool V-neck sweater and tights. From the closet she takes a stiff-collared light-blue shirt, a plaid skirt, and Mary Janes.

"Shit! Your uniform—I forgot." Sophie looks at me, and for the first time since I have been here I see a small smile. A slight pursing of her lips, a brightening of her eyes. It's amazing how this kid can talk without saying a single word out loud: *Hee-hee, you just said shit.*

"You didn't hear that." And then I realize I have the power to make her smile. "Fuck, I really have to learn to stop cursing."

I get a full-out laugh this time. It sounds exactly like a normal kid's laugh, and it feels so good to hear that I don't care that I've resorted to bad jokes and cheap tactics. Sophie steps into her uniform and stays still while I brush her hair into reasonable submission and a tight ponytail.

"Dude, you look so cute in your uniform. I love this skirt. Do you think they make it in my size?" I realize I am pandering here—I don't think I've ever said *dude* before in my life, and I wouldn't be caught dead in plaid—but there it is. Sophie is engaging with me, and according to my mother that's the most important thing. She may not be using actual words; nonetheless, she is alert and cooperating.

"I'm not sure about the tights, though. They look itchy. Are they itchy?" Sophie doesn't shake her head yes or no, she just pulls them up under her skirt, redistributing the material systematically from her ankles to her nonexistent waist. I could learn a thing or two from this kid. When I wear tights, they always sag in the knees.

After I offer her breakfast four times—sugar cereal and oatmeal, even some rhubarb pie—and she still refuses to eat, we set off for school. I've already studied and memorized our route; still, Greg's map hides in my purse, just in case. Without stopping, we step around the garish memorial that has popped up outside the front door: carnations wrapped in plastic, candles, children's drawings, notes of condolence, all from people who have read about what happened. People who have never even met Lucy.

I handle the umbrella and angle it so it envelops both of us, while Sophie drags a pink backpack with wheels down the wet sidewalk. The bag is comically big for her and stuffed to capacity with books for recess. She keeps it from tipping with an inhuman amount of concentration. I've made her a bag lunch: peanut butter and jelly, an apple, and a granola bar. I also slip her a couple of pounds in case she wants to buy lunch instead, though I don't know if kids can do that at The Pembridge Place School. I couldn't even tell you what grade she is in, because they do things differently here. I don't even think it's called a grade, as a matter of fact. A *form*, maybe?

Lucy got such a kick out of the fact that she, she of Cambridge, Mass., who in high school wore a *Just Say No* T-shirt ironically and still listened to our old Grateful Dead bootlegs, made this little British child, who wears a fussy uniform and calls her Mummy.

I keep Sophie close as we pass the news vans lining the street, the metallic monsters a sharp contrast to the connected houses painted in elementary pastels, soft and bright. The Staffords' house is baby blue, its neighbors pale pink on the left, yellow on the right. All the color seems out of place here, naive in the face of the constant gloom, or the surrounding city, much of it constructed out of post-war ruins with brick and cement. Muted, practical materials, devoid of color. But this is Notting Hill, after all, money and charm and faux-bohemia all wrapped up together into a foggy package; a community defined, at least in part, by a Hollywood interpretation of it, rising to the occasion with skyrocketing real estate prices and pushing its soul, the real bohemia, out of its private gardens and into its shady edges.

The media is obsessed with our tragedy; Lucy was white, attractive, and wealthy. A journalist too. One of their own kind. The randomness of the crime, the subtext that *it could happen to anyone at any time*, the ability to play on the British obsession with class and money, make for cheap and easy copy. The reporters are respectful, for the most part, if you ignore the fact that they've turned the block into a street fair and ring the doorbell at regular intervals. I have not once turned on the television, as I have no interest in seeing Lucy's life reduced to a thirty-second segment or this new disheveled version of myself whispering a hoarse, "Please, no comment," as I pass the filming hit men.

Yesterday, when I ran around the block to pick up some orange juice—really just to get out of the house—one reporter kept asking, "But who are you?" as if he took personal offense at my part in this family drama in which I have no reportable role. He is outside again, trying to get my attention, despite the fact that I have Sophie as a shield. He's handsome in an artsy way, with a shiny flop of brown hair, a fitted sports coat, and a foreign accent. French, I think. His speech is overly polite, perhaps to make up for the fact that his presence is not. Unlike the others, he doesn't have a notebook or a pen or a cameraman backing him up.

"May I ask you a question? Please? Off the record, of course," he says to me, though he is looking at Sophie. Examining this portrait of grief. "Who are you? What is your relation?"

I don't answer him; suppress my desire to scream back, to rip into him, tear someone down. I pretend like I can't hear or see or speak. Borrow Sophie's tactics.

"Almost there," I whisper.

When we turn the corner, only about twenty yards from the front door, after less than a minute of flashing lights and a moving mob, we are freed from cameras and inquiring minds. In addition to our FLO, Greg's law firm has been doing some threatening for us; the newspapers know they will risk an invasion-of-privacy lawsuit if they follow us to Sophie's school.

To release the tension, I do what I do best: I vomit a constant stream of nervous babble onto Sophie.

"You see that mailbox? You see how it's red? At home, ours are all blue. And our money is called dollars, not pounds. I'll give you some dollars to keep if you want. So you can see what they look like. And where I live, the houses aren't attached to one another like they are here. But you already know all this. Remember when you came last year for the Fourth of July? That was fun. I swear you seem so much more grown-up now. And you came to visit the year before that, too, and the year before that, almost every year since you were born, come to think of it."

Just a few weeks ago, Lucy had canceled our annual tradition with vague excuses, something about work being too busy. I told her I understood, that it wasn't a big deal, that we'd do it some other time soon. Meaningless platitudes to cover up my tangible disappointment. I had been looking forward to the long weekend for months, an imagined reward at the end of a particularly tedious spring semester, painful enough that I was wondering if it was time to move on from teaching. None of my future MBAs would miss me and my glossy PowerPoint presentations about the hypothetical Acme company, its ridiculous widgets. The Fourth had almost already happened in my head, in the expectant part of my consciousness, where the script gets prewritten in anticipation: Lucy and I sitting on the back porch with a couple of glasses of wine, discussing how different adult life had turned out to be from how we had fantasized as kids, and watching Sophie and Phillip and maybe Greg, if he was able to get some time off from work, try to catch fireflies with tennis-ball cans on the lawn. We were supposed to laugh like we used to when we were in our twenties, free and loud and uninhibited. We were going to time-travel back to when our world was as large and as small as a stolen conversation over a couple of Bud Lights, when the big questions—love, work, who we were going to be one day—were still unanswered and theoretical. Back to before I started living this new life, this one where I know how to order a decent bottle of wine and lecture on topics that don't interest me, the one where I come home to a too-quiet house and the mocking plastic playground in the backyard that Phillip and I are too paralyzed to take down. Disassembling it is a statement neither of us has the courage to make.

Sophie isn't listening to my chatter. She is steadying her backpack and watching her feet, careful not to dip her Mary Janes into the growing number of puddles.

"Let's turn here," I say, as casual as my voice will allow. My map says turn, but Sophie keeps going straight. She stops and shakes her head. Points down the fated shortcut, down the mews, the quaint alleyway that she used to walk with her mother, every single day, until the meth-head stopped all that.

"I know, honey," I say, as if she actually said something out loud. "I know that's the way you usually go, but we're going to go a different way today. Okay? I think it's . . . it's probably better we go this way."

Sophie looks at me with Lucy's brown eyes. They are heavily lashed and borderline dopey behind her plastic glasses. Pleading and stubborn. I am not sure what to do. I can't take her this way, past the accident spot. Sophie is no longer walking, and when I try to tug her hand, I am surprised by her sudden weight. She has made her body heavy in that way that dogs do, so they can't be dragged in the wrong direction.

"Come on, Soph. Your dad wants you to go this way." I know I've said the wrong thing now, though, the exact wrong thing, because Sophie folds over, drops her pink backpack, and lets its plastic handle splash to the ground. Her head is eye level with her knees, and her arms wrap around her stomach.

And then she does something I have never seen a child do before, something a child should not know how to do, something I hope never to see or hear again.

Sophie keens.

* * *

She hits a clean note of grief, a wail, a soul-piercing eruption of sound. Whatever she may have witnessed, Sophie is only eight years old. There are limits to human endurance.

I want to scoop her up and run off until we are in a place where it might hurt a little less. But this is impossible, since she's crumbled into an angular form in her standing fetal position—elbows, shoulders, top of her head jut out, prickly and unyielding. I can only stand here and wrap my arms around her.

After a few moments, Sophie straightens up, reaches for the plastic handle of her backpack, wipes her eyes with her sleeves. She has squeezed herself dry. I swallow the tears I still have to spare.

A half nod tells me she is ready. Back to the task at hand. Let's make that left.

A couple of blocks later, we are in front of The Pembridge Place School and kids are spilling out of cars, and parents and nannies and volunteer traffic wardens in fluorescent vests are corralling them through the front doors. Lots of running, and yelling about not running, and a few *don't forget your backpack!*s are cried with urgency, as if any of this is important.

Sophie gives me a quick hug, which I return, my desperation apparent in the way I grasp her bony shoulders for too long and the way she wiggles out of my hands. Then she runs into the school, brave and stiff, pretending she's just like all the other kids. An act she will have to keep up until four o'clock.

5

Twenty seconds into the launch and fifty-three seconds before the explosion, Lucy passed me a note in our eighth-grade history class that said: *Ten bucks the shuttle goes down.* A typical Lucy comment, perverse and poking fun at everyone else's earnestness—the way the school had celebrated Christa McAuliffe, the "teacher-naut" from New Hampshire, with a full rah-rah lesson plan around the space program, and the way we were all watching now, clichés of patriotic wonder: slack jawed and glassy eyed. And of course the *Challenger* wasn't going down; it couldn't, because Christa was on board, the whole world already on a first-name basis with the woman with the perfect jumpsuit and the permed hair, who looked just like all of our friends' mothers.

Fifty seconds into the launch, and twenty-three seconds before the explosion, I wrote a note back that said: *Lu, just shut up and watch!*

When we couldn't see the shuttle anymore and it was just a plume of smoke, I thought: *Wow, Christa's in space.*

And then the explosion: a globe of fire erupting, loud like ammunition, right there on the television, right there in the Florida sky. A voice was still reciting coordinates—later we would find out that mission control was reading from its notes, not looking at the screen—and so for a moment there was a disconnect between what we were hearing and what we were seeing, and what we understood but were not yet ready to believe. We had just watched seven people die.

Lucy made the transition to reality the fastest, even before our teacher, and it was only when I saw the scared look in her eyes that I realized that Christa wasn't in space after all.

"Ellie, you know I didn't mean it, right? You know that," Lucy whispered, ashamed and horrified by how wrong she had gotten it, or how right. "I was just—I don't know—kidding around."

I didn't say anything back; I was still digesting. Of course she hadn't meant it. She was just trying to be outrageous, and she had, as usual, succeeded. No one could have believed it was possible; for weeks afterward our teachers would say that, over and over again, as we all wrote letters of condolence to President Reagan, just like Gorbachev did: *I can't believe it.*

Today, more than twenty-two years later, I am thrown back to that moment—those seventy-three seconds—as if I am still sitting at that wooden desk, watching the thirty-inch television screen brought in on a rolling cart, Lucy shaking next to me, both of us wearing side ponies tied up with hot-pink scrunchies. I feel the weight of her note in my pocket, and I remember that I kept it, later flattened out its creases and glued it into my journal. Though Lucy and I never discussed the *Challenger* disaster, never added weight to the memory with repetition like we did with so many others, it suddenly looms large, in that way that memories can do. In the clarity of hindsight, it now seems a foreshadowing of all that was to happen after.

Because standing here in Lucy's living room, trying to figure out how to pass Tuesday afternoon before I pick Sophie up from school, I am stricken with horror when I realize that at thirteen we had missed the whole point, hadn't even scraped off the first level of that tragedy. The worst part of all: While Lucy and I were watching liftoff, so were Christa's kids. They were watching too.

When you meet someone at the age of four, tumbling and doing the "downward doggie" in Mommy & Me yoga, and their house is just two blocks away and they make you laugh for over three decades, starting that first day when she stuck out her tongue and made stupid faces behind the yoga teacher's back, a friendship is inevitable. Maybe even fated.

"Ellie's on my team," Lucy would say whenever we had to partner up for anything, and her choosing me, fast and with confidence and without waiting to see how the rest of the pairings shook out, was flattering even after it became so routine she didn't need to say it out loud.

At the age of nine we became blood sisters, since we were already sisters in all ways but one.

"Ready?" Lucy asked.

"Ready," I said, and so we pricked our fingers with a safety pin and rubbed our blood together, a glorious red smear. We believed that this small ritual would change something between us, elevate us to the status of "real" relatives, and I secretly wondered whether a drop of Lucy's blood might make me more attractive. Maybe boys, and parents, and teachers would pay attention to me, too, the way they always did her. At twelve, when we each wore half of a broken "Best Friends Forever" heart necklace that we bought at the Copley mall with our lunch money, I felt superior to the other girls in school. I never noticed that these rites of passage had all been done before, were ingrained and banal, that other girls had their own best friends and blood sisters. I felt special and singular and lucky. And maybe that's what was most distinct about our friendship—that the lucky-to-have-found-each-other feeling never went away.

Only twice did we waver: two fights in three decades, both of which left behind the invisible fissures that remind people that they are two separate wholes, the scars from incidents that can never be mentioned again.

I forgave Lucy her indiscretion at sixteen—I found her kissing my first boyfriend, Stuart Tannenbaum, in plain sight, just a week after I'd confided in her that I thought I might be in love with him; and she forgave me mine at twenty-six—I told her, less than twenty minutes after she and Greg got engaged, that marrying him would be a mistake.

Today I dig up the memory of Stuart Tannenbaum and his blue eyes and heart-shaped lips, so I can hate her and stop the incessant missing, if only for a second. I relive the horrible moment I rounded the corner at that backyard high school party and saw them to-gether: a drunk Lucy, an arm looped around Stewie's neck, and his mouth on hers. Stewie was mine, I was supposed to be kissing him and maybe letting him get to another base, but she was right there, her new acquisition illuminated by the moon, and the entire junior class got to see that he wasn't mine after all.

And I remember the one time I hurt her too.

"You can't be serious," I said when she told me Greg had pro-posed. "You barely know him."

"What you're supposed to say is, 'Congratulations.'"

"But I don't understand." How could she be ready to settle down in London in this grand house, when she was still getting drunk three nights a week and sometimes kissing other men near the restroom in bars? When had Greg turned from one of many to The One? He was just some guy she had met at a cocktail party about a year before, the one who called every time he was in town for work, and the one who seemed nice enough if only because he took her to fabulous restaurants and had a charming accent and told her she was "lovely."

"Ellie, why can't you just be happy for me?" She was right. I wasn't happy for her. I was scared. "I'm getting married. Didn't you hear me? I'm getting married!"

"Congratulations . . . if this is what you want. It's just that—" I wanted to remind her that she had lost her father less than three months earlier, that this was all too sudden, a shortcut to an easier, more glamorous life when things didn't seem to be going her way in New York. But that seemed like too much truth, even for us. "I thought you weren't even sure if you liked Greg."

"I never said that."

"I thought you said—"

"I never said that. I said that he seemed more interested in me than I was in him. And that was months ago. That was before."

"Before what?"

"Nothing, Ellie. Never mind. I wish I hadn't called you." She hung up on me then, the first and only time she ever did that. When she finally came back to our apartment, she told me I was just jealous, which I was, and that I was afraid of losing her, which I was, and I told her I was sorry and that I didn't mean it, although I did. I spent twenty-four hours apologizing, a record for me, and it became like a mantra: *I'm sorry. I never should have said anything. What do I know about love? I'm sorry.* I became a bad '80s album on repeat.

Turns out I was wrong. Greg and Lucy got married nine months later at Hampton Court Palace, and she wore a beautiful princess gown made of raw white silk and said her vows with confidence. I was her maid of honor, and she let me pick my own dress, which I appreciated. I made a toast, and in the video, after everyone repeated, "To Lucy and Greg," you can just about hear the words she whispered to me when she made a show of coming over and giving me a hug: "You'll always be my favorite."

Last Thursday, when Lucy stopped breathing, there is no doubt that a part of me died too. The history of who I am—the accumulation of a million memories from a thirty-one-year friendship, the knowledge that at least one person in the world could see me, that at least one person in the world would always know me—has been washed empty. I picture her blood trickling between the cobblestones, and one of the most important voices in my head, certainly the most constant, goes with it.

6

Sophie's bookshelf looks just like mine at home. Overstuffed, and warped by weight, and without an organizing principle. All fifty-six of the original Nancy Drew series; a few American Girl doll books; *Magic for Beginners;* an out-of-print edition of *The World Is Round*—Gertrude Stein's only children's book, a masterpiece better left to adults, which I bought as a gift for Lucy a couple of years ago; *A Wrinkle in Time; The Phantom Tollbooth; The Lion, the Witch and the Wardrobe;* all of Shel Silverstein, including, in my opinion, his best, *A Light in the Attic.* They lean against one another, front to back, spines lined up like dominos. Many of my old favorites that Phillip and I have sent to her in care packages through the years, usually with a couple of Hershey bars thrown in for Lucy, now look old and battered and read, some crinkled by bathwater, just the way a good book should be. Exploring the shelf, seeing all the hours of entertainment right there to get lost in, a siren call to burrow our heads into another world, comforts me. I can tell, in that way that kindred spirits are able to recognize each other, that Sophie feels it too. She may be only eight, and yet I can tell she's already a real reader, a habit or an addiction or a crutch, depending on which way you look at it, that will carry her through the rest of her life.

When I picked her up at school today, Sophie was sitting on a short stone wall, reading an old Sherlock Holmes hardback. The other kids just played around her—jumping off the ledge, walking an imaginary tightrope, occasionally pushing by as if she were permeable. Sophie didn't even look up.

Lucy, unlike her daughter or me, was never a voracious reader. From time to time she'd recommend some nonfiction, usually something about the Iraq War, but generally books didn't grab her. Music did. That's how she'd remember things, by song, as if her life glided along to a soundtrack to which the rest of us weren't privy. Her memories were all cataloged by musical reference. Junior high was the rock power ballads: "Living on a Prayer" and "Sister Christian" and "Every Rose Has Its Thorn." High school was all about Nirvana, and, somewhat strangely, at a time when our attention spans were at their shortest, Lucy was interested in the long riff, too: the Grateful Dead, Phish.

Remember that time, I would say, and Lucy would always remember, her life built on the same big pile of shared experiences, and she'd be able to tell me what was playing on the radio or sometimes what she was humming in her head at the time. When we got our driver's licenses on the same day, since our birthdays were only a week apart ("We Didn't Start the Fire"); when we both wore matching off-the-shoulder dresses to the eighth-grade dance ("Kiss"). The first time we took the T alone to buy preripped jeans at Urban Outfitters ("Walk This Way").

For me, it has always been about books. I can tell you what I was reading when the Twin Towers fell (*White Teeth*), or when Lucy crashed her mother's Buick and broke her nose when she was seventeen (*The Prince of Tides*), or when Greg called to say that Sophie had been born, 6 lbs., 7 oz. (*The Accidental Tourist*). When in fourth grade, Eric Schwartz passed me a note saying *I like you* and then asked me to give it to Lucy for him (*Sweet Valley High, #3, Playing with Fire*), and in eighth, when Lucy got elected student-body president and I was picked to be a delegate (*Pet Sematary* and *Love Story*, alternating between the two). When my parents told me they were getting divorced (*The World According to Garp*), and when Phillip asked me to marry him (*Play It As It Lays*).

So this is no small decision, choosing what we are going to read today, what book both Sophie and I will forever associate with this moment, what we read *after.* And when the answer is right in front of me—of course, *The Secret Garden*—all I have to do is touch the mint-green cover and I am thrown back twenty years to my parents' bedroom in the old house in Cambridge. My mother and I are tucked into her queen-sized bed, though we usually read in mine, just hours after my grandmother's funeral.

"Have you read this one?" I ask Sophie now, trying to keep my tone neutral, though I can think of nothing better than dipping back into *The Secret Garden*. I have read it dozens of times over the years, and it has not yet lost its power. Little Mary Lennox and her locked garden—sweet, yes, but redemptive too.

Sophie shakes her head no.

"My room or yours?" I ask her, but then I realize the guest room is not *my* room and wish I could take it back. A disturbing presumptuousness considering the circumstances. Sophie doesn't seem to notice my slip and simply points toward the guest room, and then runs down the hall and jumps onto the bed, her feet kicking in the air. A moment of giggly childishness, and when she shows me these glimpses of the real Sophie, or maybe now the old Sophie, I melt. I dive onto the bed next to her and tickle her ribs. She laughs, rides the giddiness for a moment or two, before she remembers why I am here, and why she is hanging out with me and not her mother. So the suspension passes; new mute Sophie is back.

"Okay, I've got to tell you something before we start. This isn't like reading your Nancy Drew or even Ramona Quimby. You only get to read *The Secret Garden* for the first time once. This is my favorite book, and now I'm sharing it with you. But this is the thing. Are you ready for it, Soph? Because we just can't waste *The Secret Garden.*" Her eyes widen, and her nod is solemn. Excitement and challenge in the set of her jaw.

"Let's shake on it," I say, and so we do, and this adds some gravity to the moment. Then Sophie hands me the book and cuddles in closer.

I begin to read, and the story of miserable and ugly Mary Lennox unfolds before us with all its sweet release. We are transported far away from this house, and this moment, where it has only been one hundred and five hours since Lucy died. The clock rewinds a century, and Sophie and I are now in India under British colonial rule. We watch young Mary—pale and cross and yet somehow lovable to us—as she wakes up to find that she has been forgotten and orphaned by a cholera epidemic. Before long, she is taken to a creepy manor house in England to live with a distant, disinterested relative, alone and scared and far away from everything she knows.

Time and place fall away. We dip into the book, as if bathing. There will soon be a garden. A buried key. A hidden door. We keep reading, and we can almost forget everything that has been lost and taken.

7

I don't think I'm coming home," I say to Phillip over the telephone, and the six words hang there, across the Atlantic, suspended in the invisible line between us. Once I say them out loud, though, I feel something akin to déjà vu, finally hearing the sentence out loud that's been playing on repeat in my head.

"Come on, what are you talking about? Of course you're coming home." Phillip doesn't sound mad. He sounds like we are negotiating.

"I can't, Phillip. Not while Sophie's like this. She hasn't said a single word in days."

"So, what, you're planning on just picking up and moving there? Permanently?"

"I don't know. For a while, I guess. I need to be here for her."

"You can't make this decision unilaterally." When words fail him, Phillip turns to investment-bankerspeak. He says things like he'll *ring me*, and we can *circle back* and *reconvene later to discuss*. We should certainly *think outside the box* here. Maybe *decision-tree our options*. I've always found the habit endearing, if only because I spend my work-days teaching business-school students how to talk just like this.

"I don't have a choice. I made a promise to Lucy," I say, hoping the tone in my voice will tell him all he needs to know, that being here is the right thing to do.

"Give me a break."

"What's that supposed to mean?"

"You really believe when Lucy asked you to be Sophie's god-mother she thought it through? Like, *Hmm, if Ellie accepts here, then if I get murdered one random Thursday morning during the school run, now I know Ellie will move to London and take care of things. Phew, that's a load off my mind.* You really think that's what she thought? Need I remind you that Sophie has a father?" His voice has gotten louder and faster, tinged with the slightest edge of fear. He is not shouting—Phillip doesn't shout—but that doesn't mean his words don't erupt. This shouting without shouting is a powerful weapon. One that's not in my own arsenal of self-expression.

"Do you realize how callous you sound?"

"I'm not callous. It's a tragedy, what happened. No doubt about it. But though Lucy may have been selfish—there is no question about that either—even I think she wasn't selfish enough to expect you to give up your life if something happened to her. Come on, Ellie, be reasonable." Phillip's favorite expression, his fallback position: what is reasonable and rational, or, as he likes to say, "what makes sense." He sees everything with a clarity—a clarity wrung of all emotion—and then trusts in what he sees. It wouldn't occur to him that it's inappropriate to mention Lucy's selfishness right now, so soon after her passing. In his mind, her selfishness is a fact, and to state otherwise, regardless of the circumstances, would be akin to lying. And what could be wrong with speaking the truth out loud?

"Phillip, you be reasonable. You always talk about doing the right thing; well, there's clearly a right thing here."

"I think you're taking this godmother thing a little too literally."

How do I tell him that Sophie needs a glass of water before bed and that I leave it on her nightstand; that, still, despite all evidence that it will go untouched, the glass of water feels like the most important work I've ever done. That Greg is not even home from the office yet and won't see his daughter today. That the things that bound Lucy and Greg together—their cold, diffident mothers, their dead fathers—have left Sophie alone. That Greg's mother is at her home in the south of France, because that's where she "summers," though I think it should be illegal to turn seasons into verbs. That Lucy's mother lives in San Francisco now with her new multimillionaire husband, and though she flew in this weekend for the funeral, she left the next morning, giving Sophie a typed list of contact numbers and e-mail addresses and false-sounding promises that she'll visit again soon. That even Sophie's nannies have left, after having been fired by Greg for their petty theft and nasty indiscretion. That there is no one else but me to read her *The Secret Garden*.

"She needs me. Sophie needs me."

"I need you, El. How many times do I have to say it?"

"Phillip, please. I have to do this."

"Ellie? One question," he says.

I pause to take a breath, gather myself. I know where this is going, and I don't want to go there.

"Is this about Oliver?"

"No," I say, keeping my voice flat, devoid of emotion. "No, this is about Lucy, and this is about Sophie. This is about their family. Not ours."

I have had two big love affairs in my thirty-five years, and both were with Phillip. Sometimes, when I think back to those times, of being so infatuated I couldn't see anything else but him, I can almost distinguish between the first and the second time, between young PhillipandEllie and older PhillipandEllie, though the memories and our photographs from both eras contain the same patina of shamelessness: saying words you should never say aloud, like *forever* or *no, I love you more* or *to the moon and back, babe, to the moon and back*. We didn't hear when strangers shouted at us to get a room. Didn't notice as our coupled friends started calling less and less and our single friends stopped calling altogether. We were too busy finally realizing what all the *fuss*—the music, the art, the everything-*everything*—was all about.

The first time, in college, we were too young to know any better. To know that you can't spend a lifetime staring into each other's eyes. Ours was an unsustainable kind of love, and when Phillip graduated two years before I did, we combusted. I cried, he cried, both of us reveling in the delicious brutality of our first heartbreak. And eventually we both stopped crying and started sleeping with other people.

And that was that.

The second time, almost a decade later, we were old enough to know that you can't just discount those hormones. I like to tell people that when I saw him, all those years later, on the packed train home to Boston, I knew immediately I was going to marry him. But that's a lie. In reality, I knew I was going to kiss him again and that it was going to change me, though I couldn't have told you how. He likes to tell people that the very first time he spotted me, braiding my hair into neat rows as I studied in a carrel in the library, he knew that I was The One. But that's a lie too. I think he realized then that he might just spend the rest of his life, like we all do, chasing after that feeling of certainty.

Less than two years after remeeting, Phillip and I got married in my father's backyard, not too far from where we live now. We had a white tent, with white lights, and I carried calla lilies, like you see in the magazines. Afterward, we always described the wedding as beautiful. And it was beautiful, as all weddings are where two people who love each other get up there and make promises that they hope to keep.

After Oliver was born and lost, all at once, the two events one and the same, Lucy had said, "Don't worry, you'll have another," which was the exact wrong thing to say. My baby had died in the womb—had died inside me—with less than one month to our due date, and that's all she could come up with: "Don't worry, you'll have another."

Even amid the overdose of grief and numbness, I remember thinking I hadn't expected this from Lucy, for her to somehow utter the sentence I was least ready to hear. Not from Lucy, who had given birth to her perfect little Sophie, who even as an infant, fresh from Lucy's body, looked exactly like her mother, beautiful and so alive. Not from Lucy, who had given birth to a child whom I loved immediately, because loving her was the same as loving her mother. And so she said the exact wrong thing, and until this week I wasn't sure I would ever be able to forgive her.

Phillip, though, was the one who spoke the truth, and that hurt more than anything else. What he said was: "I think this may be harder for you than it is for me."

And then a year later: "It's time to put this behind us."

But it was harder for me and there's never been time. And I wish I had the nerve to tell him the truth: *You don't understand, and I don't think you ever will, and maybe that's unforgivable too.*

"This is about me wanting to, *needing* to, be here for Sophie," I say now, bringing us back to the real subject before we career even further off course.

"What about your job?" Phillip asks, back to the practicalities.

"I don't have to go back till after Labor Day, when the fall semester starts, and then maybe I'll take a sabbatical. I think the university will survive without me." Since I stepped off the tenure track last year, my work feels like more of a hobby than a career. Something that I do to fill time, not to fill me.

"And money? What are we going to do about that? Did you know that London is the number one most expensive city in the world?"

"I'll stay here at the house for a while, so no extra rent, and if that doesn't work, you know I have savings." My savings were supposed to be for Oliver's college tuition, or maybe private school, if we had decided to go that route. My comforting bank balance, the product of a short and lucky stint during the dot-com craze. These days, I teach a business-school class about entrepreneurship, though I'm not sure how long they'll let me capitalize on long-stale work experiences.

"So I guess you have it all figured out, then." A statement, not a question.

"Not really. I'm just going to take it day by day and see what happens. I may be home soon. I'm not sure."

"And I'm supposed to just wait here, not knowing when my wife is coming back?"

"I know I'm asking a lot, Phillip. I know that. But I need to be here. Can't you understand that?"

"No, I really can't."

"Can you at least try to understand?"

"Okay, I can do that. I'll try." And here's the thing about Phillip. Just when you think you may stop loving him, that you can give him up for good, that enough distance has grown between you that there is no climbing back into this thing, that he's become more stranger than husband, he goes and says something that makes you forget why you could have ever doubted him in the first place: "Of course, I can try for you."

8

I'm analyzing whether to vote for Kelly or Stephanie, who are both up for eviction on *Big Brother UK*—an important decision, since it will cost me two dollars to vote and both deserve to be kicked off the show—when my real-life brother, Mikey, calls.

"You need to get a cell phone. And I know it's safe in Notting Hill or wherever, but you make me nervous. Your senses have long been dulled by the suburbs. This is a big city. You need to protect yourself," Mikey says, as usual all sincerity. "Remind me to show you how to hold your bag on the tube, and I'll buy you a thing of Mace."

"I'm fine. Don't be ridiculous. Anyhow, I was going to borrow Lucy's cell phone, but that seemed . . . I don't know . . . weird. Tomorrow I'll get one of those pay-as-you-go thingamajigs."

"So is it really true? You're planning on staying? Phil asked me to talk some sense into you, but—and don't tell him I said this—I think it would be great if you stayed for a bit. I could use the company."

My little brother, who's thirty-two, is getting his PhD at the London School of Economics. He spent his twenties teaching tenth-grade history in Roxbury and then, after seeing one drug deal too many in the hallways, decided he really needed to understand why a fifteen-year-old girl would think she had no other option than to peddle crack. And so now he works with the world's leading expert on the intersection between poverty, addiction, and crime. He lives the life of the scholar, my brother, and has the social life of a monk.

"I don't know what I'm doing. But I'm not going home just yet."

"Can I take you to lunch tomorrow, then? I'll even come to you."

"You okay, Mikey? You *never* want to hang out with me."

"That's because you're usually three thousand two hundred eighty-three and a half miles away. Seems a long way to go for lunch." Typical that my brother knows it's exactly 3,283½ miles between 11 Lexington Road, Sharon, Massachusetts, and 349 Nottingham Court, Flat B, London. He's also read all six novels of the *Dune* series, can tell you the capital of Belarus, has traced our family tree back ten generations and made a poster-sized diagram for all of us for Hanukkah last year, collects antique stamps and baseball cards, and, at night, after he has finished his research for the day, plays his Sony PlayStation with a headset, so he can compete against his best friend from high school, who has six kids and lives on a farm in Georgia. He's had only one girlfriend that I've actually met, and she was both awkward and sweet and would have benefited from owning a pair of tweezers.

The irony is, after surviving the indignities and clichés of the high school dork—glasses and science fiction and acne—he has now surpassed us all to win the crown of the best-looking Lerner. I have always been attractive enough, not stunning like Lucy, who always captured the room, and not pockmarked like Mikey was either. I tend to fall right in the middle, that place where you are neither ridiculed nor noticed, in some ways, the safest place to be. Now I'm cursed with the fine lines around my mouth endemic to mid-thirty-somethings who are afraid of Botox, a deep crevice of blue under my eyes, and, let's face it, my breasts and ass aren't what they were, even five years ago. And Mikey has turned handsome and shaggy and has these blue eyes that lack any genetic sense, as he is fond of reminding my mother. Come to think of it, I am not sure why he hasn't had a girlfriend in a while.

"Lunch it is, then," I say.

"How's Soph? She seemed to be reasonably okay at the funeral."

"She's stopped talking altogether."

"Poor kid. I'm glad she has you. By the way, I spoke to Mom yesterday, and she had news."

"No, please say it ain't so. Not again. They can't be."

"Sorry, but it's true. Mom and Dad are dating again."

"Shit."

"Yup, that's exactly what I said."

9

The next morning, Sophie eats her Weetabix and then holds my hand as we walk to school. I have grown used to her being quiet by now, and I've found a way of talking for two; rhetorical and yes/no questions help, as does my incessant chatter.

"Still not talking, huh?"

Sophie shakes her head.

"Okay, I'll recap the book then. By the way, just so you know, you aren't allowed to read it without me. Once you start a book together, you have to finish it together. So we have Mary Lennox, who is, what? About nine, I think. A little older than you. And she's ugly. Not like you at all. But isn't it funny how the book just spells that out? She's an ugly, miserable pain in the ass . . ." Sophie giggles: *You said ass.*

"I love that, because in most kids' books, the writer always tells you how beautiful the main character is; I always picture a perfect little girl, with flowing hair and beautiful French dresses. And ribbons, for some reason. But this Mary Lennox is thin and sickly looking. And in real life, not everyone is clean and gorgeous or even nice, you know? Do you think Mary is going to stay ugly? Or do you think our friend is going to go all glam on us soon?"

Sophie considers my question and shakes her head. Our Mary will stay "true to herself," as they say on reality TV.

"You know, I never told you why I love this book so much. When my nan died—that's what I called my grandmother, my nan—afterward, I was a little freaked out, understandably. So that night, my mom took out *The Secret Garden* and started reading to me. And you know what happened? I forgot everything else and all I could think about was Mary Lennox and whether she was going to get fatter and whether she was going to find that lost key."

Sophie is enraptured by the book, as much as I was when I was her age, though when I decided to read it to her, I had forgotten all about the orphaning. I hope this is helping and not scarring her further. But it seems to be working, because Sophie has lost that disinterested expression that seems to parallel her muteness, and I can tell she wants to hear more.

"I wonder if it's good for Mary that until now she's gotten to do whatever she wants, whenever she wants. It doesn't seem to have made her very happy, does it?" Sophie shakes her head again, and I can tell she wants to say something out loud, because she raises her hand like we're in class, but then lowers it again when she remembers her no-talking rule.

"Tonight we'll read chapter two and maybe chapter three. I don't know, though. I'm not making any promises. Let's see how the day goes. Rumor has it you've been slipping out of class and reading in the bathroom. Don't do that. You'll get icky germs in there. Or the cooties." I turn my fingers into spiders and wiggle them in her face, and she half-smiles, and then we are past the alley and in front of the school, among the swarm of parents again. The atmosphere is like curbside check-in, each parent and child a tiny balanced ecosystem with procedures and checklists and routines. Each one moving faster, talking faster, making sure nothing is forgotten or left behind.

Sophie pecks me on the cheek, gives a wave over her shoulder as she runs into school, her backpack hiccuping behind her. A feeling of love rushes through me like vertigo, an overwhelming, sharp tilt, and then just as quickly a righting, slamming, shaming pain when I catch myself, for just a moment, pretending that Sophie is mine.

"So Mom was the one who told you they're back together?" I ask Mikey over lunch. We are in a tiny Indian restaurant called Panjabi Grill near Carnaby Street, and we watch a man with a hairnet make fresh chapatis on a flat iron pan. Three long pikes of meat—chicken, beef, lamb—spin behind him. The panoply of carcasses makes me hungry and nauseated at the same time.

"Yup."

"Damn it. Damn it. Damn it."

"Yup." My parents' four-decade-long love–hate relationship has been a source of constant drama. Certainly my mother prefers it that way, believing her children and ex-husband see her as unpredictable and challenging, like a 1940s movie heroine, but really, at least to my brother and me, she's fickle and domineering and exhausting. As the Brits would put it, in their enviable, spot-on fashion: a shit-stirrer.

Dr. Jane Lerner—we call her Jane to her face, as she has made us since I was the age of two—is one of those dangerous people who is satisfied only when there is excitement and novelty, and she bolts at the first sign of stasis, bolting being the only predictable thing about her. My parents were married for a tumultuous two decades of door-slamming and screaming and afternoons where Mikey and I were sent outside to play so they could have what they called "adult time," afternoons that were more confusing for us kids than the yelling, because they sounded awfully similar when we listened at the door.

They finally split up when I was sixteen, into two houses just three doors apart, and we became a somewhat broken, but by no means shattered, family. A good move on their part to ensure one didn't murder the other in their sleep. But now, in the last ten years or so, they've started this game of "getting back together" again and "breaking up," terms seemingly too childish and at the same time perfectly accurate to describe their reunions and partings, both the former and the latter almost always at my mother's instigation. Each time they go their separate ways, though, my mom feels liberated, my dad devastated, and then she ends up having to prescribe anti-depressants for him.

"When do they see each other?" I ask.

"Weekends. Apparently, Dad drives down on Fridays."

On the morning of September 11, while the rest of the family watched CNN from our safe academic perch in my father's Cambridge house, frozen in that bubble comfort of vicarious pain, the repetition of images making it feel no less real as we watched bodies fall and refall and a city covered in all that damn dust, my mother got into her Volvo and drove straight to Ground Zero to volunteer. Somehow, what was supposed to be a short stint turned into a permanent move, and, to everyone's surprise, she sold her house and opened up a therapy practice out of her new apartment in the West Village. In addition to her pro bono PTSD sessions, she caters to overworked, overanxious yuppies with too much disposable income, a comfy niche market that never bounces its checks. And, apparently, she's good at what she does; every few years or so, she gets a free chicken dinner and an award from the American Psychiatric Association.

"Did you speak to Dad?" I ask.

"Yup. He said not to worry about him. He'll be fine. That he's a grown-up."

"That's what he said the last time she left him."

"I know."

"And we almost had to hospitalize him."

"I know."

"Damn it. So we just let them keep making their own mistakes? Again."

"I guess so. Speaking of making your own mistakes, how are you and Phillip?"

"What does that mean?"

"It means, though I'd love to have you here, I'm worried about your, you know, your marriage."

"You're joking, right?" My earnest brother strikes again. A beautiful quality. In the abstract.

"Not really."

"I'm your big sister. It's supposed to be the other way around. I worry about you."

"Whatever. I know you're heartbroken about Lucy. Believe me, I am too. I had a crush on her, since, like, birth. And I know you want to help Sophie, but you can't just stay here forever."

"I know that."

"Okay, good. I'll tell Phillip. He'll be relieved."

"Since when are you and Phillip so buddy-buddy?"

"We've always e-mailed." I know my brother and my husband like each other, that they seek each other out at family holidays, like life vests, but I didn't know they kept in touch beyond the Thanksgiving turkey. I wonder what else I don't know about my husband's life.

"Sounds like you talk to him more than I do."

"Whose fault is that?"

"Shut up. Let's talk about you instead."

"Fine. So, I haven't gotten laid in six months. How sad is that?"

"Very. Want to hear something sadder?"

"Sure."

"Neither have I."

I don't remember when Phillip and I stopped having sex. It wasn't a conscious decision, at least on my end. We both just got busy with work, and somehow that activity fell out of our lives. Like how I stopped going to the gym last year after I got the stomach flu and never went back, even though I kept paying my membership dues. Phillip and I touch from time to time, a blot of a kiss on the lips, cheek, forehead, when running out the door, but not like we used to. We used to crawl under the covers just to be near each other, to whisper even though we were the only people in the room. We used to want to feel the other's breath on our shoulder blades, the other's fingertips on our bellies. We'd point to a spot—on our necks, our wrists, our temples—and we'd get kissed, right there, the exact right spot, as if by magic or secret language. We used to hold hands when we were sitting next to each other on the couch, for no reason at all.

Now I don't crave his touch, or anyone's touch, really. I no longer have dreams in which strange men take me home and ravish me. Or even about our frighteningly attractive FedEx guy. My sex drive had a slow leak, and now it's empty, and the idea of sex is about as enticing as heading back to the gym. Too much effort for the pay-back. Just like shaving my legs.

Phillip has never bothered me about our lack of sex this past year, nor has he mentioned the fact that my body has grown lumpy, my clothing less careful, my eyebrows unleashed. He seems not to have noticed that I am letting myself creep toward middle age without a fight. This letting myself go, which is what I suppose the women's magazines would call it, has little rational basis. If I was considering the D-word, which I do on occasion—*divorce, divorce, divorce*—surely I'd want to clean myself up and get ready for whoever else is out there?

The last time I went to New York, my mother wasn't shy in mentioning my new look.

"Honey, let's be honest. You've put on some emotional weight. Right there," she said, and grabbed a bit of flab cresting over the top of my jeans. "See, that's not real weight. Emotional fat. You let go of some of your pain—which is partially boredom, isn't it?—and that will all melt away. Let me write you a prescription for Effexor or Prozac." My mother's solution to most problems involves a prescription, which, I'll admit, comes in handy from time to time.

But why hasn't Phillip, brutally direct Phillip, said a thing? Doesn't he miss the old me? Could there be someone else? I don't know. I didn't even notice that my husband and my brother were friends.

And how would I feel if Phillip were seeing someone? Would it pierce my heart or would it be a relief, an answer? *You can walk away now, Ellie.* Or would that just be another cop-out?

I know how to play the victim. I've done that before, maybe have been doing it for almost two years, since Oliver. And after a while, playing the victim is a form of complicity too. Seems to me that marriage can spin a thousand species of betrayal. Adultery is only one of them.

"Can I give you a bit of advice?" Mikey asks, and brings me back to this restaurant, to its hard plastic chairs, and to its overpowering smell of turmeric and sautéed onions that I can feel seeping into my clothes.

"Sure."

"We came from the same womb, so I get it. You know, I still have a scar on my left ear from when Mom pierced it with that horrible peace-sign earring when I was a baby. Who pierces their baby boy's ear? Anyhow, I know how screwed up we probably both are—God knows I haven't had a relationship in, what, like forever—but you and Phillip . . . I don't know how to say this without sounding stupid, but you guys gave me hope. That maybe one day I would actually grow up and have a real live girlfriend that I could marry and, you know, build a life with. So, my point is, you guys might not be so good now, but your marriage is probably something worth fighting for, Ellie. And you owe that to Phillip."

"I am not sure what I owe to Phillip."

"Then to yourself."

"I am not so sure what I owe to myself either."

"You're impossible."

"Yeah, well, I am my mother's daughter, after all."

10

"Nope, not a peep. Sorry, Ellie." Claire, Sophie's teacher, tells me this when I come to pick Sophie up from school. "But she didn't hide in the loo. I reckon that's an improvement."

Sophie spends her days in a place that seems more like a house than a school. Situated on one of the white-mansion blocks of Notting Hill, it is distinguishable from its identical, freshly painted, Ionic-columned residential neighbors only by the discreet sign, the paved front with a bike rack for pedal scooters, and the slew of parents wandering over for the afternoon pickup. The place has a garden-party atmosphere, civilized and orderly. Everyone knows who belongs to whom. The adults are all women, well dressed enough that I presume they are mothers, not nannies, and, to my surprise, very few of them are British. Instead, I see sleek and scarved and perfumed French ladies who do-not-get-fat, their casual and slack-bottomed American sisters, and diamond-encrusted, red-lipsticked Russian oligarchs' wives. Somehow, all of these women seem to have given birth to well behaved—my mother would argue a little too well behaved—British children.

I'm getting to know Claire—Ms. Walters to Sophie—from this new world, where parent and child part and reunite for morning drop-off and afternoon pickup, and where she makes sure, depending on the time of day, everyone gets shuffled in or out in an organized fashion. She is a petite and pretty woman, what my father would call an "English rose," with straight, delicate brown hair and a Zen-like evenness to her voice. She's probably just shy of thirty, blessed with that milky skin of the British, the lucky by-product of a lifetime of never seeing the sun. Her warm smile, kind and soothing, is a welcome contrast to the exaggerated pity or social awkwardness that seems to have colored most of my interactions lately. She's different from the women who came to the funeral, Lucy's "friends," who sat coolly, watchful and appraising, as if they were in the front row of a fashion show, who had the nerve to say, over and over again, "It's such a pity she fought back," as if by assigning blame they could reassure themselves that their families were safe, that our tragedy was not, in fact, contagious. The proceedings merely an event to make them feel better about their own lives, not to honor one prematurely lost.

Claire and I look over at Sophie, who is sitting cross-legged on the stone wall, with Nancy Drew this time, and again ignoring the other children swirling around her. I am not sure why she loves the Girl Detective more than Harry Potter, but that seems appropriate for Sophie, to revel not in a fantasy world but in a preppy one.

"The good news is, I'm sure this not talking is a conscious choice. Today I purposely asked the class some questions that I knew she would know the answer to, and, each time, she would start to raise her hand and then remember herself. My guess is it's only a matter of time." Claire's eyes are filled with compassion. I suddenly have the urge to be one of her students. I want to be eight years old again, sit in a desk that wraps around on the right side even though I am a lefty, and I want to store my already made lunch and floppy schoolbooks in its belly. I want to laugh when my teacher gets chalk on her back and get called on to recite my multiplication tables. I want my responsibilities clearly laid out: to go to school, to do my homework, to go to bed at bedtime, and to brush my teeth twice a day. I want to surrender all of my decision-making power, the cruel weapon of too much freedom, and hand in my adulthood badge. I don't want to keep falling up.

"So, I'm not sure how you and Mr. Stafford will feel about this, but here's the number of a psychologist mate of mine for Sophie. He's an expert in this sort of thing. He spent a lot of time studying children in violent circumstances, mostly in Sudan. Really interesting guy. I think he and Sophie would be a perfect match."

The thought that Sophie, insulated and privileged Sophie, who claims her favorite food is sushi, would have anything in common with children in the midst of war—something that sounds like an oxymoron, children and war—makes me want to cry. I picture African babies with machine guns and bloated bellies, an image foreign and dehumanizing and heartbreaking. One that takes me as far away as I can get from that little girl in her uniform.

But Claire is right. Though she may not have lived through a genocide, Sophie has seen more violence by age eight than I have in my whole life.

"Thanks. I'll talk to Greg."

"No problem. The thing is, Sophie was having a tough time at school before all this happened. So, not that there ever could be good timing, but I reckon this wasn't it."

"I thought Sophie was a great student. Lucy always brags—bragged—about how advanced she is."

"She is definitely the most advanced student I've ever had, but she's eight going on forty, as they say. At her age, kids don't usually notice when they aren't that popular—that's a distinct pleasure reserved for adolescence—but Sophie can sense that she doesn't really fit in. The other kids don't like to play with her, and, bless her, she doesn't really like to play with them either. She can't be bothered, I guess."

I glance at Sophie. She has taken down her ponytail and is now sucking on the strands as she flips through the pages, embroiled in Nancy's mystery-solving shenanigans. She does not look up. Not once.

11

The *Secret Garden* is illuminated with the single bulb from Sophie's Winnie-the-Pooh lamp, the big bear and his jar of honey holding up the base. The walls are a soft yellow, made softer by the light, and I remember when Lucy had them painted, when she didn't know whether she was having a boy or a girl. A white rocker sits in the corner, where Lucy used to nurse and read bedtime stories and occasionally watch Sophie sleep. The mobiles of infancy have long been taken down, and the crib is packed away in the attic, but the yellow walls with their stenciled cartoon animals remain, like an artifact of a more hopeful time. I picture Sophie at age fourteen, with contact lenses and a nose piercing, perhaps a neck tattoo, demanding that her father repaint the room black.

I wonder now how many times Lucy sat in this exact spot, on Sophie's bed, with the weight of Sophie's head against her shoulder. If she, too, felt that sharing her favorite book was the purest way to express love, like telling your secrets or saying a prayer out loud.

"Hey, Soph, I bet you didn't know that in certain cultures you aren't supposed to put books on the floor or go near them with your feet. The idea is that they're special, almost like magic or something."

Sophie moves in a little closer, looks up at me, her expression impenetrable. I've dropped my kid tone, because I think I've been underselling her. I've noticed that she holds books with the same reverence as I do, taking a breath before she opens the cover, sitting still for a moment when she closes one. The way she gets lost in Nancy Drew, lets herself be carried off to one girl's adventures in Indiana, tells me she has a much richer inner life than I've been giving her credit for.

"And you know what else? Books are almost a religion for me. Probably the only guaranteed way to get out of my own head and escape for a little while. You know what I mean?"

She doesn't answer, and I don't mind. I know she knows what I mean. I see it every day when I find her at The Pembridge Place School, dipping into a world where no one else can reach her. And I see it every night, when I tuck her in and we read *The Secret Garden*, both of us equally absorbed, finding delight in the unlikeliest of places—a fictional locked-up piece of earth behind a fictional manor house in England.

"So, tell me, what's your favorite book?" I ask Sophie now.

She points to the book in my hands. *The Secret Garden*.

"Are you just saying that because you know it's my favorite?"

She shrugs. She gives me a small gift: a *maybe*.

As I read chapter two out loud, Sophie follows along the page, guiding my words with her finger. We learn more about Mary Lennox, and her disagreeable nature, and how the other kids tease her and call her Mistress Mary Quite Contrary.

"*Mary sat in her corner of the railway carriage and looked plain and fretful. She had nothing to read or to look at, and she had folded her thin little black-gloved hands in her lap. Her black dress made her look yellower than ever, and her limp light hair straggled from under her black crepe hat,*" I read, but I stop because Sophie is looking at me instead of the book.

"What is it? What's wrong?" Sophie points to the word *crepe* on the page. I act as if I don't understand.

"What? You can ask me. If you want, you can whisper your question in my ear."

She takes a deep breath. Her face betrays her, her decision almost written in the air. To talk or not to talk.

This time I decide to push. Gently.

"Yeah? You want to ask me something?" I put my hand around my ear and lean in.

"Her . . . hat," Sophie says, her voice soft, fragile, smaller than even she is. I try not to smile; I try to pretend that she has not just broken nearly a week of silence and that we are merely mid-conversation. "Don't laugh, okay?"

"Of course I won't laugh." I lower my voice, match her tone.

"How can her hat . . . be made of crepes?"

"Really great question, Soph."

"Really?"

"Yeah, the word *crepe* has two meanings. It's what you call a homonym, I think. I bet you're thinking of the food, right? But here they mean the material. You know that dress I was wearing a couple of days ago? That's made of crepe. That would be cool, though: a hat made out of a crepe. What would you put in yours? Chocolate? Strawberries? Spaghetti?"

"You don't put spaghetti in crepes," she says now, her voice back to its normal volume. "That's just silly. Mummy says they have great crepes in Paris, that you can buy them from carts there."

Hearing her voice is like an old song that transports me to a different time and place. It is two and a half years ago, and Lucy, Sophie, and I are having afternoon tea at the Ritz. I remember feeling vulnerable sitting under the grand chandeliers, pregnant and tired, and I whispered that thirty-seven pounds seemed like a lot to pay for some tea and minuscule sandwiches. My voice kept low so as not to be outed as a crude American unable to understand the satiety principles behind thinly sliced cucumber. And Sophie, at the age of six, turned to me and said, "Auntie Ellie, I think what we're paying for here is the room." It's the look that I remember the most, almost visceral, the look Lucy gave me over Sophie's head that said, *You believe I made her?*, that makes me burn with nostalgia.

"Can I tell you a secret?" Sophie asks me now, and her voice is still a thrill. *She's talking, she's actually talking.*

"Of course."

"When I'm bored, I sometimes sneak into Mummy's office and read her Encyclopedia Britannica. I am at the ALs right now. I know all about alopecia, that disease where you lose your hair—girls can get it, too—and aluminum, which has an atomic number of thirteen. I'm excited to get to AT to find out what an atomic number is. I made a rule that I can't cheat and look ahead." I am about to tell her about Wikipedia but then realize she probably already knows. Sophie, like me, just prefers the sturdy knowledge found in real books.

"That's amazing. You're going to have to teach me everything you know, because I'm a little rusty on my encyclopedic knowledge these days." I can't believe Lucy still has those books and that she bothered to have them shipped across the Atlantic. I remember when her dad first brought the set home—he had found them at a garage sale in the neighborhood—and the first thing Lucy and I did was look up the word *penis*. I still can see the pictures—an anatomical drawing, and a photograph, too, the pubic hair a full-on '70s-style bush. Thank God, Sophie is a long way from the P's.

"Hey, you want to show me how well you can read?"

Sophie takes the book out of my lap and puts it into hers. And so I answer Lucy's rhetorical question—*You believe I made her?*—two and a half years later, while I sit on Sophie's bed, listening to her read all of chapter three without stumbling once, watching the spitting image of my childhood friend reincarnated. *Yes, I can believe it, Luce. You're the only person in the world who could have.*

Greg gets home about five hours later, and as soon as I hear his key in the lock, I run to the door, excited to be the bearer of good news.

"Sophie's talking! She's actually talking," I say, before he even has a chance to drop his umbrella in the jug and take off his coat.

"What?" Greg stumbles through the door and steadies himself on the staircase banister. One look at him and I can tell he is more than a few drinks, maybe a whole bottle, past drunk. His blondish, uneven, and overgrown hair usually gives him a rakish charm, but tonight it's unkempt, and his eyes are bloodshot and red-rimmed. The top two buttons of his striped Thomas Pink shirt splay open, his purple tie is turned backward, loosened and thrown over his shoulder as if trying to escape. He is carrying his Savile Row jacket in a ball under his arm, like it's a football.

He looks at me, surprised, as if he didn't expect me to be in his house, and certainly not at two a.m. in my heart-themed pajama pants and matching long-sleeved top that Phillip bought me last year for Valentine's Day from the Gap. The confusion crosses his face and transforms into pain when he remembers. He spent the night drinking to forget, and one look at me erases hours of his hard work.

"Right, then. So she's, um, she's talking. Yeah?"

"Are you okay? Would you like a drink of water or something?"

"Nah, I'm fine."

"I thought you were at work."

"Yeah, but went to the pub with a few mates after." His accent deepens and he sounds even posher than usual. His syllables are drawn out, rounding over the tops of his teeth. If these were happier times, I would imitate him later for Phillip. *Went round to the pub with a few mates. I felt like getting pissed.*

"But Sophie—"

"I heard you the first time. She's talking. Great. Really great." He doesn't make it sound great. He makes it sound like he's sad there is this person Sophie to discuss in the first place.

"I know this is hard for you, Greg."

"Not now, for fuck's sake." He makes his way over to the couch and sits down, but far away from me, which I appreciate. Based on how he smells, I am pretty sure he threw up on the way home. His head falls, cheeks to hands, and his body folds into itself, like a convertible sofa. "Please, not now."

Within seconds he ends his day, passes out cold, without warning or sound. I take off his shoes before they stain the white cushions, tuck a blanket over his shoulders, and leave a wastebasket next to him, just in case.

Three in the morning London time, ten in the evening in Boston, and I'm in the guest bedroom, just down the hall from Sophie, unable to slip into sleep. While still riding the wave from the high of hearing her voice to the low of seeing Greg's face, in that draining cycle of restless energy, I decide to call Phillip.

"Sophie's talking," I say. "Can you believe it? She's actually talking."

"That's fantastic. I knew she'd come around. So when are you coming home?"

"I really don't know."

"But Sophie's talking now, right? So she'll be fine."

"Her father is passed out drunk on the couch. Her nannies have all been fired. And it wasn't so long ago she saw her mother murdered in broad daylight. I really don't think it's as simple as *she's going to be fine*. She's just a little girl." I start to get choked up when I think of all the suffering that is to come, when Sophie understands the permanence of her loss. I think I would give my life to make Sophie better. Maybe that's what I am doing right now. Maybe not my life, but very possibly my marriage. "It's too much."

"Please don't cry."

"I'm sorry, I just . . . I miss Lucy, and I don't know what to do here. I don't know what to do. Tell me what to do, Phillip. Please tell me what to do."

"You know what I think you should do."

"You can't really think I should just come home and leave her behind. You can't think that."

"Ellie, honestly, that's what I think. This isn't your job. Sophie has a father. And he'll rally; you know he will. Greg's a good guy, and I want my wife back."

"So you're making this about you." We do this—a stupid finger-pointing trick—from time to time, a reflexive bending of a competing request into the other's selfishness. I don't know when our marriage started making caricatures of us both.

"No. Ellie, I just, I don't know, you're really far away. Too far away. The last thing we needed right now was for you to be a million miles—"

"Three thousand two hundred eighty-three and a half miles, actually. Mikey figured it out."

"That sounds about right. You and me? We are three thousand two hundred eighty-three miles apart."

12

High-pitched screeching. My dream turns Amazonian and be- comes cannibalistic, savage and violent. Human heads spin on large pikes in a circle around me in a humid jungle. The smell of death and blood and dinner. I am a mere witness, the center of a horror-show carousel of fire and flesh, and I am rigid with fear in the middle. My mission instinctual: I look for Lucy and Oliver among the skulls.

"Mummy! Mummy! Help. Please. Mummy!"

Sophie.

I am ripped out of my dream and wake up running across the hall. I must have heard her before I heard her, because I am already outside her door, out of breath, by the time I realize what is hap- pening.

"Sophie, it's okay. It's okay." I squat by her bed and try to wake her up. I stroke her hair, her cheek, like my mom used to do to me when I was little. She doesn't feel it. Sophie's too busy thrashing about, dodging an invisible foe with her eyes closed. Her forehead glistens with moisture, her covers knotted up and kicked to the foot of the bed. She looks likes she's in the throes of an epileptic fit. "Sophie, everything's going to be okay."

I sit down next to her and scoop her into a full-body hug to still the convulsions. She's light, even lighter than I would have imagined, and it seems impossible that this amount of weight adds up to a whole person. I rock her back and forth, patting her back, and finally she opens her eyes and looks at me with the same surprise and disappointment her father wore when he walked in the door just a couple of hours ago.

"Mummy. Where's Mummy?" She looks around the room, hoping to find her in the dark shadows by the closet. There is no possessive, not "my mummy." Just "Mummy." "I need Mummy."

"Soph, it's me, Auntie Ellie. I'm here, I'm here. You just had a nightmare, that's all. It was just a nightmare."

Sophie's gaze meets mine again, and reality seeps slowly back into her. The nightmare was less nightmare, more nightmarish memory. She's not crying now, but her body goes stiff, like a corpse, when it dawns on her that Mummy isn't coming to help make the fear go away. She will not bring a glass of warm milk, and rub her back, and stay with her until she falls back asleep. Her eyes are big and frozen with horror.

"But . . . but . . . I want Mummy."

Her lower lip begins to tremble, but she's trying to be strong. Sophie is that strange sort of kid who values manners. Throwing a fit and its consequential tears and mucus are shameful; fits are for children less self-controlled. I think she's inherited this stoicism from her father. When I was here last time, and Sophie fell off her bicycle, Greg said, "We Staffords don't cry. It's not in our blood."

And Sophie, already forgetting her clotting knee, didn't miss a beat: "You mean like in our DNA and stuff? That's so cool. What else don't we do?"

I am dealing with something much larger than a bloody knee now, and there are no distractions. Mummy will not be making an appearance, no matter how badly we both want her here. Substitutions are unacceptable.

"I know, sweetheart. I know you want your mummy. But I'm here, and I promise nothing is going to happen to you. You had a scary dream, huh?"

"He was here. And he was coming . . ." She hides her face against my neck and her breathing gets labored now; I feel her tears before I can see them. The shaking too. "I couldn't do anything. I couldn't stop him."

"No one is here. No one is coming to get you, I promise. No one is going to hurt you." I rock her to the beat of my words, trying to loosen her body out of its pulsing.

"Not me. Mummy! He was after Mummy! And I didn't help. I just, I just . . . I was naughty."

"Oh, Sophie, you're not naughty. You're perfect. You're just a little girl. And you were—you are—so brave."

"But I . . . I . . . I need Mummy. Where's Mummy?"

"Sophie."

"Where's Mummy!" She screams the question, her composure broken. She needs an answer, and I don't have a good one.

"Remember you and your daddy talked about this? She's in heaven."

"Then I want to go to heaven. Now."

"Sweetheart, you can't go to heaven. Not yet. Not for a very, very long time. I'm sorry, heaven doesn't work like that." I say it like I know how heaven works, like I'm a believer. My performance is convincing.

"But what if he's in heaven too?"

"He's not in heaven. He's in jail, and he's never coming out." There is clearly no need to specify who "he" is.

"But Mummy's there all alone." I am trying to hold back the tears, deep breaths through the nose, out the mouth, a hardening in my soul—I am the adult here—but these five words unravel me. Wherever Lucy is, Sophie is right; she's all alone.

"Don't worry. Your mummy's not all alone. She's with both of your grandfathers, and I promise they'll take care of her, just like your daddy is going to take care of you."

I lied to Sophie. Twice, maybe three times in the last thirty seconds. The man who killed Lucy has confessed and is locked up, though who knows for how long. His capture and immediate confession may have spared us a mystery—he was caught with Lucy's blood all over his shirt, less than two blocks away—but it may buy him sentencing leniency. I saw his face on the cover of the *Daily Mail* yesterday, when I was walking by a newsstand. I saw his face, cold and blank, like the London rain. I saw his face, and I ran.

At the moment, I don't know if Greg is even capable of taking care of himself, not to mention Sophie, and if there is such a place as heaven, if it's reserved for believers, Lucy isn't there. She was an aggressive atheist. But Sophie is a child and should believe in something, and if she loses that front tooth she's been teasing, I hope she'll think that the money under her pillow comes from the tooth fairy. And maybe she'll grow up to be one of those people who believes in things like heaven and hell, and right and wrong, all clear-cut and distinguishable, so different from her mother and me. To be honest, I am not sure that would be such a bad thing. Maybe we overvalue nuance. Maybe it's easier to see the world cleaved into two clunky categories, like caped characters in a comic book: good and evil.

"Does it rain in heaven?"

"Nope, it's always sunny. Why?"

"Because Mummy left her brolly. What if it rains?"

"Oh, Soph. I promise she'll stay dry. And happy too. That's what heaven is all about. No cold. No rain." I don't know what Greg and Lucy have taught Sophie about religion, if anything. There is no one to ask right now, and I do my best. I kind of like the idea of Lucy in a warm, dry heaven, protected by her father, who always smelled like cigarettes when we were kids, back during the time when that smell was still comforting, and who would surprise us with Carvel chocolate crunchy ice cream cake on a summer evening. Lucy's dad was gentle and funny, a professor of linguistics renowned for his scholarship as much as for his attention to his female students. Lucy adored him.

"Promise. You promise?"

"I promise. Cross my heart."

"Auntie Ellie? Can you get me some other pajamas?" Her voice is so quiet, barely a voice, that I am worried she'll slip into the crevice of silence once more. "I, uh . . ."

Her crying starts again, revving up fast like an engine. Sophie doesn't want to have to say it out loud, and she shouldn't have to.

"Don't worry. I know, sweetheart. Not a big deal at all. I'll get you some fresh pjs and some new sheets, and we'll get you fixed up in no time. Okay?"

"Okay."

"And after we get you changed, I'll stay here with you until you fall asleep. I'll be right here. Okay?"

"Okay."

We change the sheets together and leave the wet ones behind in a pile outside the door to be dealt with tomorrow. I help Sophie into a clean pair of pajamas, a kid-sized version of the Gap ones I am wearing. Phillip got her the same pair for Valentine's Day.

Once she's under the covers again, I rub her back and stay with her long after she has drifted off to sleep, watching the rise and fall of her rib cage, how the red hearts expand and contract with each breath. I say a silent prayer that she's dreaming of a happy place, one with unicorns, and rainbows, and Lucy. And as I see the sun starting to rise, blotted light behind her yellow curtains, I close my eyes and hope that my dreams might take me away to that place too.

I wake up to Sophie's chin digging into my back and a sharp pain in my neck. This mini-bed is way too small for the both of us. I tiptoe out of the room and pad down to the kitchen, hoping to catch Greg before he sneaks off to work. Other than last night's brief encounter, I haven't had a chance to talk to him since Monday morning. He's been leaving for work long before Sophie and I wake up for school, and when I call him in his office in the City—what the Brits call the center square mile of London—his secretary gives me a repeat performance: "He's not in at the moment, but I'll leave word that you rang." The casual dismissal is exactly the same every time.

He never calls back.

I wait in the kitchen booth, Greg's kitchen booth, alert for the sound of him stirring upstairs but exhausted too. My head hurts from lack of sleep; my eyes burn. Today feels like something I'm not sure I can handle. Facing Greg, walking Sophie the long way around, getting through another day in this proxy life, suddenly seems to require a Herculean effort, a tireless stamina that is failing me this morning.

The smell of coffee brewing soothes my nerves; a promising smell, a hopeful reminder that this feeling could be temporary and that my stores of grit might soon be renewed. I try to remember the victories of yesterday, pre-drunk Greg, pre-talking-to-Phillip, pre-nightmares; try to recapture the sound of Sophie's voice, its lilts and uncertainty, her soft words breaking through the barrier of silence. Sophie's talking is a big deal, more than a baby step, and I should appreciate that, despite the regression back to wetting the bed. We have a long road, I know; contrary to what Phillip may think, an eight-year-old doesn't bounce back from witnessing her mother's murder in a matter of days.

He had the same issue after we lost Oliver. Phillip was sad, and then he wasn't, and he couldn't understand what I was still doing, all those months, even more than a year later, retaining the shape of a broken Ellie. He was ready to move on, ready to start trying again, so fast, fast, fast. If he could have, if it wouldn't have been horrible of him, I think he would have said, *Come on, time to get over it already.*

Five years ago, I said vows. And I believe in vows. I meant them, and not just when I said them out loud for an audience to hear but as a motto and a life choice. *For as long as we both shall live.* I hadn't anticipated the sandy flow of feeling, the yin-yang of love and dread, or the residual buildup of grievances and the slow draining of the benefit of doubt. *In good times and in bad.* Yes, sure, but in my naïveté, I interpreted this as external; we would support each other when the world imposed and intruded. No one tells you that it's the internal that's the real challenge: those moments of decisiveness equal to taking a vow, when you feel the clawing grip of your promises.

And now there are two vows in direct conflict. There was the ceremony eight years ago, when I became Sophie's godmother. One that was less makeshift than our wedding, come to think of it, with catered platters of caviar and salmon on toast and crystal flutes of champagne. I flew to London for the event, even though I had been here only a few months before, immediately after Lucy gave birth.

When I got to this house, the day after Sophie was born—she was sleeping upstairs and I hadn't even met her yet—Lucy was on the white couch, looking tired and desperate, dark hair fanned around her head like a halo or Medusa, depending on the angle. The baby monitor spurted occasional gurgles into the air, the dull punctuation the sound of thunder in the distance, far enough away to be safely ignored.

"I know, I know. I look like a fat mental patient in this robe," Lucy said, and closed a ratty white fleece robe around her still-enlarged middle.

"You do not. You look like someone who just gave birth."

"Thank God you're here. L, I'm scared fucking shitless," she had said, her eyes turning almost savage.

"I know."

"Tell me I can do this. I'm not sure why I thought I could do this. This was insane. Huge mistake. I can't do this." And then Lucy started to cry, the first time I had seen tears since we were sixteen. She looked young and fragile with her porcelain tears and silly robe, too young to be responsible for anything but herself.

"You can do this. Of course you can do this. You're just exhausted, that's all. And scared. This—" I swept my hands around the room to take in the baby gifts, and the baby stroller, and the baby changing table, to include them in my verdict, as if announcing the fear was akin to its disappearing. "This, Luce, is scary and exhausting. If anyone can do this, though, it's you."

"I realized today that I just did the only irreversible thing in life. I'm an idiot that it took me this long to realize it. You know, I could always divorce Greg. Or move away. If you screw up, you can apologize. But the baby isn't going anywhere. She's only going to get bigger, and bigger, and I'm always going to be her mother. What have I done?"

I had no reply. She was right: Sophie wasn't going back up the birth canal. It seemed to me Lucy had just played her part in one of only two irreversible things—birth and death—and she had chosen wisely. So I told her to rest, and I helped out with the baby—I thought of her as *the baby* then, too wrinkly and squinty and slithery to own a name like Sophie yet, and tried my best to make it all seem less overwhelming. Lucy's fear eventually was overpowered by love, and she stepped up to motherhood, embracing it with the same hearty zeal with which she'd approached graduate school.

Later, at the ceremony in which I became a godmother, she laughed about her initial freak-out and spoke in unequivocal cliché, which was the only way she spoke when it came to her daughter: "Sophie is the best thing that has ever happened to me."

And then, to me privately: "You should have one, L. Not yet, I guess. *Soon*, though. Trust me, it'll be the best thing that has ever happened to you too." Though I tried to tamp it down, I couldn't help feeling a bit put out. I hadn't the slightest stirrings of baby lust, nothing like the pangs I have now, and still it felt like a rebuke. Lucy couldn't help but remind me that once again she had gotten to a finish line first.

I am not proud of those moments of jealousy that used to hit unannounced and sometimes unprovoked. Now I would give anything to have Lucy sitting in this kitchen booth waiting for her family to rise. I would stand in that alley in her place, feel the tip of a sharp blade, if that would mean Lucy could be here and Sophie wouldn't wet the bed, if that would mean Sophie would sleep through the night.

If it could have been me, I would have done it. I would have given my irreversible life. But that's easy for me to say now, in the cruel early hours of a morning like this, considering I know it's the one vow I'll never have to keep.

13

Greg comes down to breakfast smelling clean and sober, like baby shampoo, and heads straight for the coffeepot. I now know more things about my best friend's husband that I shouldn't. How he breaks his Weetabix into little pieces before taking a bite. Briefs not boxers. The threadbare, randomly snagged sweaters and faded sweatpants he wears around the house on weekends to keep warm against the damp chill of summer. At night, he snores, foghornlike and arrhythmic. What he smells like during the occasional bender, and how different he smells the next morning.

"Sorry about last night. Got a little carried away, apparently," he says, while I wait in the kitchen, feet tucked under me, hands wrapped around a mug. His voice is sheepish, and he avoids my eyes. I used to think Sophie looked and acted exactly like her mother; now I notice her mannerisms are all Greg. This look on his face—cherubic and ashamed—is identical to Sophie's last night.

"No problem, but—"

"Right, then. I'm off." He drops his mug in the sink, even though he has barely had his first hit, the move so abrupt that coffee splashes his sleeve. He heads through the dining room, toward the front door.

"Greg? Wait. We need to talk about a few things. About Sophie."

"Not now, Ellie. Please, I'm late."

"She's talking."

"Good. I knew she'd come around. I told you she's a tough kid."

"Yeah, but last night she woke up screaming and wet the bed."

"I didn't hear her."

"No, you didn't. You were passed out." I don't mean to be as rude as I sound, but I need him to remember Sophie's existence. I understand that he just lost his wife, but there is a little girl upstairs who, as far as I can tell, hasn't seen her father in three days. I wish I could change my tone, sound less petty-wife, more understanding, but it has seeped in already—maybe I've had too much practice—and it feels too late to change things.

"Leave the sheets for the cleaning service." His tone now matches mine, dulled and cooled by frustration. "Is that all?"

"Well, no, not really. I got the name of a psychiatrist. For Sophie."

"A psychiatrist? But she's talking."

"Greg—"

"Can you please just back off? It's too early to have this conversation. Later, okay? Please, let's just do this later." I don't know if he means that it's too soon since Lucy died, or too early in the morning, or both.

His desperation makes me lighten my voice and my expectations of him, since I have no right to expect anything from him at all. I am not the person here to whom he owes something.

"Have a good day at work, Greg."

"Thanks. You too. I'm sorry, I don't know how—"

"Forget it. It's okay. You're right. Not now. Go, you're going to be late."

Greg nods, one of those businesslike male nods you'd give to an employee, the one that says, *Well then, I must be going; there is money to be made elsewhere, and I should get there first*, and heads toward the refuge of the front door.

I watch his departing back and feel the full weight of my intrusion. I have burrowed my way into his home, penetrated the deepest intimacy of his life at its most vulnerable moment, even tucked his daughter into bed, and still, without Lucy, we wear the awkwardness of strangers.

Three hours later I am shepherding a gaggle of kids through the Gorilla Kingdom in the stinging rain wearing the inappropriate pair of black alligator peep-toe sling-backs I wore to the funeral. The exposed skin is frozen and throbbing. My first time at the London Zoo—which, truth be known, is like any other zoo, if a little bit more compact and scaled down to urban limitations—and I am one of six chaperones for thirty kids, a job that mostly involves corralling. Not how I originally planned on spending the day—I am supposed to be in the Stafford living room, watching reality television on the gigantic flat screen—but when Claire asked me to fill in after a last-minute parent dropout, I couldn't say no.

The other chaperones, all mothers except for Claire, intimidate me with their posh chatter and perfect bodies—alienlike flat bellies and pert breasts, the sort of body only retouched celebrities return to postchildbirth, when they schedule simultaneous tummy tucks with their C-sections. They're decked out in skinny jeans, knee-high brown leather stiletto boots, form-fitting cashmere sweaters (mostly navy), and a double string of pearls: as much a uniform as the kids are wearing, and their behavior as cliquey. They don't seem interested in talking to me, perhaps because they worry about the contagion of our tragedy or because they notice their children aren't friends with Sophie. Or maybe because I am not tall and thin and effortlessly glamorous, like they are. Either way, I ignore the feelings that were a constant staple of high school—not quite being cool enough, not special enough to sustain anyone's attention, the feeling that all my tangential friends tolerated me because of Lucy.

It doesn't matter, because I have found my friend for the day, and you really need only one. That's maybe the grand lesson of my lifelong friendship with Lucy. Most of the time she—one—was enough. So Claire, when she is not yelling in her mannered way at the kids, chats with me, happy to have an excuse not to interact with the hands-on mothers. She is unmoved by their desire to have soy milk served in the cafeteria and their pleas that the school teach Chinese in addition to the already mandatory French in year one. It's evident that parents are her least favorite part of the job.

"Look at her," Claire says to me in a whisper and points over to Sophie, who is making eye contact with a gorilla ten times her size, fifteen feet away. She stands apart from the rest of the class, not noticing the commotion of the other kids, who are screaming and giggling, running in circles closer to and then away from the exhibit. Sophie walks right up to the fence, unafraid to court the gorilla's attention. She befriends one in particular; he's huge and hairy and named Bobby, Jr., a name better suited to an American trailer park than the London Zoo.

"Hello, Mr. Gorilla. I am Sophie Stafford. I wish I could lend you my brolly, because it seems you're getting quite wet."

"She has no fear," I say.

"I know, it's amazing, isn't it?"

A boy joins Sophie in front of the cage. He has dark, thick hair tied up in a black cloth bun in the center of his head and long legs that seem to still be unfurling. There are a couple of Indians in the class, but he seems to be the only identifiable Sikh. He's quiet, like Sophie, and hasn't imitated the gorillas, like the other children have done. Instead, he's stopped our tour guide a few times and whispered questions in his ear, which the guide then answered for the whole group. Because of him, I now know that Bobby, Jr., was wild born, originally captured for the circus, and weighs in at about thirty stone.

"Who's that?" I ask Claire.

"Inderpal. Sophie's reading partner. Great kid, though he has some of the same problems in class that Sophie does. The other kids tend to treat him like an outcast because of his topknot. I paired them together because they're both so ahead of the rest of the kids academically."

"He's adorable. All the kids are."

Sophie and Inderpal are standing next to each other now, and I notice I am examining their behavior much the way they're examining the gorillas': with complete awe and curiosity. They are so beautiful and so foreign. I have no understanding of their capabilities.

"I wish we were at a dinosaur zoo," Inderpal says to Sophie. "How cool would that be? Like a real-life *Jurassic Park*? The cages would have to be gigantic, especially for the T. rex. They're carnivores, and I'm an herbivore. So they could eat me, but I couldn't eat them."

"Have you ever eaten astronaut ice cream? That's probably okay for herbivores. My dad bought me some when he took me to the science museum, and it was so weird. Like ice cream, because it melts in your mouth, but it's not cold or anything. It's freeze-dried." I picture Sophie and Greg together in a museum, following the map on the brochure through the exhibits, room leading to room, learning about space and weather and the human body, finally ending in the gift shop, buying trinkets to remember the day by. The image soothes me.

"Nah. Hey, do you watch cricket? I have seven Monty Panesar posters in my room. You'll have to come over and see them one day."

"Who is Monty Pane-whatever?"

"Panesar! You must know Monty Panesar. He's only the best cricketer in the world. My cousins from Luton actually got to meet him and everything. Mum says I look just like him, or I will do when I have a beard too. They call him 'the Turbanator' because he plays wearing a *patka*."

"Seriously? They call him 'the Turbanator'?"

"Yup. Mum thinks it's rude, calling him that, but—don't tell—I think it's funny."

"I won't tell." They turn their attention back toward Bobby, Jr., now eating a banana. The gorilla's gigantic brow is furrowed, and he's sitting with his legs crossed on the ground. He peels and then chomps his fruit, quick bites in succession without pause; when he finishes, he immediately picks up another and throws what's left over his shoulder.

"Wow, he's going bananas," Sophie says, a corny joke, a Lucy joke, but her delivery is shy, almost whispered, like she is practicing before committing to saying it out loud. *Please, Inderpal, please laugh*, I think, as I watch him take stock of her, examine this previously uninteresting species: girl.

"That's a good one, Sophie," he says, and my heart swells when he giggles.

* * *

At the next exhibit, a red-faced black spider monkey is walking the ground on all fours with her baby clinging on—a mini-monkey along for the ride, upside down, belly to belly with its mother.

"Cute," Claire says. There is a longing in her voice that I recognize as my own. I adjust her age up a few years. A thirties' tone, that longing.

"Yeah."

"You have any? Kids, I mean. Not monkeys."

"No." Is this technically a lie? I don't know, I don't know, I never know. "You?"

"Nope, not unless you count these guys."

We enter Butterfly Paradise, a hot and humid tube shaped like a gigantic caterpillar and set to mimic Caribbean weather conditions. Though Sophie was unafraid of the gorillas, she is disturbed by this exhibit and stands closer to my leg, practically hugging my thigh. I see why she's scared. The butterflies, with their large stained-glass wings, are free to mingle with us here, flying just by our ears, sometimes landing on our shirts. The flapping of their wings looks frantic, like they are desperate to hurl themselves forward through time, their efforts inefficient and spastic and not up to the task.

The other children sense Sophie's fear, and, strangely, this brings them closer to her. They stop their imitations—arms thrown up and down, bodies jerking—to talk to us.

"So are you Sophie's mum?" a cocker spaniel of a boy, with a bowl cut and an overbite, asks as a couple of the other children look on.

"No," I say.

"Yes," Sophie says.

Our answers overlap each other, and he looks at us, confused.

"I'm her godmother," I say, and feel both sadness and pride that Sophie has claimed me as her own. Is she worried that this is one more thing—the lack of a mother—that will divide her from the other kids?

"Are you from America? You have a funny accent," he says.

"She's from Boston, that's why," Sophie says. "Which is in the state of Massachusetts, which is in America."

"Well, you sound like one of the Transformers. I'd like to have a godmother who is a Transformer and can become like a car or something. That would be awesome," he says, his whole body shaking with excitement at the prospect. He turns *awesome* into two words: *awe some*. "And then my godmother would go *RRRRRRRRRrrrrrrrroar.*"

"That's enough, Stephen," one of the mothers—presumably his—says, and leads him away by the arm. A few minutes later, it dawns on me that he's allowed to continue making his Transformer noises; she meant that's enough of talking to the two of us.

"Ellie, thanks for coming along. You made the day lovely." Claire and I are back at school, at the pickup and drop-off point where I seem to be spending an inordinate amount of time.

"My pleasure. Though those other mothers are scary. You notice how they're all going for coffee now and they didn't invite Soph and me?"

Claire looks down at her feet, embarrassed that I would come right out and say it. Apparently, I've made a social faux pas: my American reflex to say more than is necessary.

"Yeah, they're not the warmest group of people. Sorry, Ellie. I hope you don't get the wrong impression about this place. All the parents aren't like that."

"I know. Listen, I may be way off base here, but may I ask you a personal question?"

"Sure."

"Are you seeing anybody? I ask because my brother lives in London, and, well, you seem perfect for him."

"Really?" I can't tell if the surprise in her voice comes from my breaking another cultural taboo—maybe Brits don't set up friends they barely know—but then her face breaks into a grin. "Thanks! I'm actually terribly single at the moment. Just barely survived a horrible breakup not too long ago and haven't quite made it back out there. You think these mums are scary? You should try dating in London."

"So you'd be interested? He's a great catch. And I'm not just saying that because he's my brother."

"Yeah, sure. What's the worst that can happen?" I have a few answers for her: that she and Mikey could turn into my parents, or into Phillip and me, or that they could have an awkward dinner where the lack of conversation seems like code for your own inadequacy.

I keep my mouth shut. I know a rhetorical question when I hear one.

14

It's nine o'clock, past Sophie's bedtime, and she's begging me to let her read one more chapter of *The Secret Garden*. Though I'm tempted—I love lying here, smushed up against the wall, feeling her warm back against my shoulder—it's getting late. I'm no longer the old Auntie Ellie who used to annoy Lucy by serving Sophie fast food for lunch and running around with her before bed.

"Nope. Bedtime, missy." I slip into sitcom parenthood again. "We gotta get you brushed up."

"Let her read another chapter," Greg says, startling us. He leans against the doorway and watches Sophie and me with a faux-bemused expression. We didn't hear him come in, or up the stairs, and I wonder how long he's been listening to our negotiations.

"Soph, I have an idea. Why don't you read chapter six with your dad? Bring him up to date on our book. I'm getting tired."

"But you said we have to read this together. You said it was a rule. Daddy, Auntie Ellie said it was a rule."

"Did she?" Greg says. "Making rules already?"

His tone is jokey, not hard, and I wonder if he's been drinking again. He's probably just playing nice after our heated discussion this morning.

"I can make an exception this one time, right, Soph? I know your dad really wants to hear you read."

"No, Auntie Ellie. You said it was a rule. Why can't I read to the both of you?"

I look at Greg, waiting for my cue to stay or to go. The last thing I want to do is take away their time together. I already feel like enough of an intruder.

"Seriously, stay," Greg says, and we make eye contact for perhaps the first time since I've been here. His look says, *I'm here and I'm trying, but I could use some backup.* "I'm sure you want to hear what happens next, don't you?"

I'm stuck in this family scene, my presence a dissonant place-holder. Greg sits on the other side of Sophie, so he can read along with her. I push my body flat against the wall, trying to take up as little space in the mini-bed as possible.

"Daddy, guess what? We went to the zoo today, and Auntie Ellie came, and we saw gorillas and everything."

"The zoo?"

"Class trip," I say, just in case he thinks I took his child out of school.

"Guess what I said when I saw the alligators? Guess. I said, 'See you later, alligator.' And then Auntie Ellie said, 'Not for a while, crocodile.' It was so funny." Sophie laughs, but it is fake laughter, like her father's bemused expression: laughter intended for enter-tainment purposes only. She is performing for her dad, desperate for his attention. I hope he notices it; she needs him to notice her.

I have no right to do this on my own.

"Really? Lions and tigers and bears, oh, my!" Greg singsongs, playing his own part, the three of us all terrible and earnest actors.

"How'd you know? Lions, tigers, bears, giraffes too. I really liked the giraffes. And zebras. Which look like painted horses."

"Sounds like fun. I wish I could have been there. By the way, sweetheart, it's really nice to hear your voice."

"Thanks. It's nice to hear yours, too, Daddy," Sophie says, and then picks up her book again. "Okay, can I read now?"

After we put Sophie to sleep, we sit in the living room, very adult-like and civilized, drinking merlot and resting our wineglasses on lime-green tiled coasters. We have survived a whole week without Lucy, the worst of it, and now we are sitting here, ready to discuss Sophie. Rationally. As if this is normal—Greg and I alone in his living room at ten o'clock on a Thursday night. This time we play our roles well: affected relaxation, swallowing our grief whole, so it's locked away somewhere, far enough in the distance so it can't sneak into our conversation. This is a part I've played before.

"So Claire gave me the name of a child psychiatrist for Sophie. He apparently specializes in this sort of thing." I try again, leaving out the Darfur thing for now. No need to freak him out.

"You really think this is necessary? A psychiatrist? She's eight."

"I know. But what happened is as traumatic as it gets. I mean, not only did she lose Lucy, but, you know, she saw it."

"Things are different here. One doesn't just run to a psychiatrist when there is a problem. I mean no offense to your mum." Greg's accent is at once charming and too posh. The use of the third person, which seems to be a habit of the upper-crust British, annoys the hell out of me.

"This isn't some little problem. She's having trouble at school, which apparently started long before the accident. Last night she wet the bed. We need a professional."

"I don't outsource my parenting."

"Come on, I've seen the wipe-it board." Greg gives me a sharp look, which I do and do not deserve. Part of me wants to remind him that this is the first bedtime he's made it to since I've been here. "Anyhow, this isn't outsourcing. This is making sure your daughter gets the help she needs. And if she doesn't like it, or you don't think it's helping, then she can stop. But it can't hurt to go a couple of times. To see how it goes."

"I don't know."

"It's what Lucy would have wanted." I know it's manipulative, playing the Lucy card, but it's true. It's what Lucy would have done, had the situation been reversed. Sophie always came first.

A shadow crosses Greg's face, almost rage, a surge at his temple, a flushing of his cheeks, but it's temporary and it passes. I am not sure at whom his anger is directed—me, Lucy, the guy who did this to us, maybe God.

"Okay, she'll go once and then we'll reassess and strategize." Greg delivers his verdict and, like Phillip, can't help but slip into nonsensical business jargon when he feels powerless. "What else is on the agenda?"

He gives a half smile. An agenda, typed out with boxes for checkmarks, would make us both feel better.

"Well, we need to talk about me."

"Therapy is probably not a bad idea for you either."

"What?"

"I'm kidding." I laugh a real laugh, not my actor laugh that I've been using for Sophie. He's probably not wrong. The only problem is that, in my family, refusing to get therapy is one of the few ways left to rebel.

"What do you need to talk about?"

"Well, I'm thinking about staying here, in London, for a while. To be around Sophie. To help out. And I wanted to make sure that was okay. I don't want to step on your toes or be in the way. Like this morning—"

"You can stay as long as you like. I meant what I said the other day. Seriously, we'd love to have you. I'm not so oblivious that I don't realize Sophie and I need all the help we can get."

"Thanks. I mean, okay. I don't really know how long I'll be around; I need to talk some more to Phillip and to work. But that kid . . . she's just . . ."

"Amazing."

"Yeah. She really is."

We stop talking for a minute and sit in comfortable, contemplative silence. The mere recognition that we both care about Sophie, that we are on the same team here, takes the pressure off. We just want to make sure we say what needs to be said while we have the chance.

"Ellie, since you've already started making rules around here, may I make one of my own?"

"Of course."

"While you're here, staying in my home, please don't judge me." Greg's voice is now free of anger. He is asking like it's a favor—like taking Sophie to school or tying up the garbage.

"I'm not judging you. I would never—"

"No, you were. This morning. And I don't blame you. I judge me too. But if I am going to survive this . . . I don't know." He drops his head into his hands. Greg—despite the suit and tie and neat cuff links—looks like exactly what he is, a grieving widower. "What I am trying to say is, I'm doing the best that I can here."

"I'm sorry. I didn't mean to—"

"Yeah, you did. And you were right. One shouldn't be passed out drunk on the sofa when one's beautiful daughter is having nightmares upstairs. I just don't know . . . I'm not sure I can do this." He's talking to the floor, his head still resting in the pillow he has made with his palms. Greg looks like he is about to cry, and I don't know what I'll do if he does. He rocks his body forward and back. A ritualistic calming motion. A man at prayer.

"I'm so sorry. I didn't mean to judge. I was just trying to, I don't know. I'm sorry."

Greg doesn't hear me. He's too far lost in his own thoughts and doesn't need my apologies. That wasn't what he was asking for, anyway.

"I can barely even look at her. It physically hurts to see what she's going through, and this is just the beginning. Sophie's going to have to live an entire life without her mother, and I can't fix it. I spent half an hour on the stairs today just psyching myself up to go into her room," he says. "What does that say about me, that I can barely look at my own daughter?"

"It's going to be okay." If Greg wasn't a grown man, almost forty, with a few speckles of gray in his hair, I would rub his back, like I do Sophie's. He is not a child; he doesn't have the luxury of other people's indulgence or of abdicating responsibility. This house, the girl upstairs, this tragedy, all belong to him. His face is creased at his mouth, his eyes, the tips of his nostrils, all new lines that I don't remember being there the last time I was in London. "I don't know how just yet. But we're going to figure this out. You can do this, Greg. I know you can."

A pep talk almost identical to the one I gave Lucy eight years ago. That time I was more hopeful about life, about what we were capable of. That was back when I assumed we could do anything we wanted. This time, I believe my own words only because I don't have any other choice.

15

For the next couple of weeks we pretend that we are an ordinary family, that a human-sized hole has not been blown into the fabric of this household, and that I am not an imposter mother and wife trying to fill it. That all of us, through sheer will and a new routine, can make things okay. Sophie wakes up every morning at four a.m., like a standing date, and Greg and I take turns comforting her and getting a fresh set of sheets and pajamas. I am on the Monday, Wednesday, and Friday shift.

The news vans have packed up and left, even the relentless Parisian who stayed a few days longer and peppered me with questions whenever I left the house. This makes the school run easier. So does Claire, who finds time to chat every time I drop Sophie off and pick her up. Her first date with Mikey, who has made me introduce him as Michael, is next week, and I'm more excited for them than I should be. A vicarious indulgence, considering I won't be the one having drinks and possibly enjoying a delicious first kiss. I'll be "at home," reading more of *The Secret Garden* and tucking Sophie in.

Now that the nightmares and bed-wetting have become a constant battle, now that Greg has seen firsthand the look on Sophie's face when she wakes up in horror—a knowing look that shows the spillover between dream and waking—Greg is fully on board with Operation Get Sophie Therapy. The earliest appointment we could get—even with Greg offering to double the guy's normal charge—was next Thursday. We are praying the doctor can work miracles. During daylight hours, Sophie never mentions her sleep issue, and neither do we. And at night, when she wakes up screaming for Lucy, we tell Sophie she is safe, that her mummy is in heaven, that everything is okay.

Each evening, after Sophie gets tucked in and before her terror begins, I call my husband, and for half an hour I return to the life I used to live. We talk about what Phillip will eat for dinner—will he take in Chinese or Thai?—and Phillip's work, and some of our friends, and does he know our car insurance bill is due soon. He asks about me—how I'm doing, have I been to the Tate Modern yet, did I read that *New York Times* travel article he sent about London literary haunts—but we skirt the real issues. He never asks what my role as pinch hitter is really like, and I don't tell. We are mostly polite, and accommodating, and try not to let too much of our expectations and disappointments creep over our long-distance line. We have become masters of garden-variety small talk.

I feel like a double agent or a polygamist. I no longer consider catching the next Virgin Atlantic flight home, popping an Ambien and wrapping my feet in those warm red socks. I no longer wonder what I am doing here. My mission has been clarified. Sophie needs me. Greg needs me. And, though I hate to admit it, right now, with Lucy gone, I need them too. They are the closest things I have to a purpose. They understand, they appreciate, what has been lost.

"When are you coming home?" Phillip asks me tonight, and

suddenly I decide to change the script. No more "I don't know" and "we'll see" and "I'm taking this one day at a time."

"I don't think I am." My heart is beating fast, and my hands are shaking. I am not sure what I'm doing—this was not premeditated—and I am trembling with this new clarity that has rolled over and flattened me: *I don't want to go home.*

"Fine," Phillip says, his voice as angry as I have ever heard it.

"Fine." Flat resignation.

"So that's it, then? You're leaving me."

"I don't know. I didn't mean that."

"So now we are back to the 'I don't know's?"

"Phillip, I'm just trying to be honest here. I'm so confused." I am not sure what I expect from him: to convince me to come home? To give me a yearlong marital reprieve so I can be here for Sophie? To understand that I love the school run, and tucking into my favorite book, and getting lost in my new neighborhood, where no one knows me and no one remembers that I had a beautiful, promising belly that deflated? To allow me this feeling that my days, even if they are difficult and drenched in grief, have some sense of meaning?

"Confused? Give me a fucking break."

"Please—" Again, I don't even know what I am asking. *Please what?* I feel muzzled and slow. I have stepped up to the abyss, and now it seems I can't jump after all.

Of course he is angry. He has every right to be.

"Please what? You want honest? Here's honest: Fuck you, Ellie."

"Please stop," I say. Suddenly I want to move us away from the edge.

But I am too late. Phillip has already hung up.

* * *

Kensington Gardens, a must-see in any London guidebook, is less than ten minutes up the road from the house. I lead Sophie through its majestic gates—black and pointed with tips of gold—and down one of the gravel paths lined by flower beds that divide the expansive green lawn and give the place its sense of scale. We are shielded from the summer sun by leafy trees.

"You okay, Auntie Ellie?" Sophie asks me, when she sees me staring a little too long at a square box of pink flowers that I can't identify. Sophie doesn't want to be here; she'd rather be inside reading or maybe watching cartoons, now that I've gotten her addicted to the world of Disney. Certainly not my finest parenting act, exposing Sophie to princess culture—*Cinderella; Beauty and the Beast; The Little Mermaid*—but I couldn't help it. I'm a little hooked myself, especially now that I feel like I could use a little rescuing, and sometimes it is so much easier to plop her—plop both of us—in front of the television than to do anything else.

The world is awake and outside and stripped down to appreciate the rare rays drying up this moist piece of land on this glorious summer day. Women in bikinis and men shirtless and in shorts are scattered on hilly lawns or on public wooden lounge chairs. They dot the landscape like happy sheep. Both Sophie and I could use the fresh air and a bit of sun, seeing as we are both too pale these days, and so I've forced her on this walk, which will end at the "Diana, Princess of Wales, Memorial Playground," about half a mile away. I am not sure Sophie, when we get there, will know how to use the equipment. I picture her going all posh on me and slipping into the third person: *What's this thing called 'playing'? How does one* do *that, exactly?*

We've left her backpack behind, an unburdening that makes us both feel naked, since we have not a single book between us.

"What?" I ask her now. Did I forget to respond to something she said?

"I asked if you're okay, Auntie Ellie. You haven't been listening at all."

Right now, surrounded by couples with linked hands, my brain is saturated with Phillip. Not with the recent Phillip. I can't get a hold on the recent Phillip—who has become something like an acquaintance, someone I wouldn't presume to know or understand—the one who said, "Fuck you" a couple of days ago and meant it. No, the old Phillip, the one who has somehow blocked out everything else, pulls me away from the here and now. The one who used to bite my butt whenever I stepped out of the shower, and the one who asked me to marry him on a day just like this one, right by the Charles River, surprising me with a ring in our picnic basket.

The recent Phillip, who spends days and nights in the office, who rarely asks what I'm thinking in a way that says he needs to know, stays out of the picture. That Phillip has no place in a hopeful day like this one, when it seems at least possible that the good weather could stick. I know how those people are feeling, relaxing in the reprieve of the sunshine; it's exactly how Lucy and I used to feel on the first day of summer vacation more than twenty years ago, when we would take out our beach towels and walk down to the river to sunbathe until our oiled skin had turned brown. Now both Sophie and I are covered head to toe in SPF 45.

"We're here, Auntie Ellie. What do we do?" Sophie says, as expected, when the hulking playground creeps up on us.

I survey the elaborate playground equipment and look for the usual suspects—slide, swings, sandbox. Instead, I see a giant pirate ship, a bunch of canvas teepees, wooden sheep—none of which looks capable of giving us the exercise we could use.

"Well, we need a bit of fresh air, that's all. Something that gets us moving. Like Mary Lennox running on the moors."

"But I don't see any moors. I don't even know what a moor looks like," Sophie says.

"Me neither. But I have a better idea. Monkey bars." I point to a set, just off to the left.

"You're kidding, aren't you?"

"Nope," I say, like the disciplinarian I have become.

"But I'll hurt myself. I don't know if you noticed, but I'm really small. I can't even reach."

"You worry too much, Soph. I'll spot you."

So I boost her up and Sophie hangs there, on the first bar, unable or unwilling to move.

"Come on. Go to the next one, and then keep moving. It's good for you." Sophie starts swinging, and it turns out she is a natural. If monkey bars were an Olympic sport, my Sophie would win gold. She wouldn't even need to train at some Russian camp, where she would miss her prom and be verbally abused by a coach named Boris.

"Look at that. You're doing it. You're amazing."

"One arm, Auntie Ellie! One arm!" And there she is, managing to support her body weight with one of her thin wrists.

"Soph-E. Soph-E," I start to chant, and she starts to giggle and finally lets go. "Sophie-bear, that was awe some."

I split the word into two syllables, like that kid from her class, and we high-five like frat boys. For a moment I feel like I am eight also, capable of getting lost in the joys of the monkey bars.

"Your turn, Auntie Ellie. But I can't spot you."

I place my hands on the bars, which it turns out are about a foot shorter than I am. In order to use them, I need to bend my knees, to cut my height in half.

My first thought is, *Damn, I'm heavy.*

My second thought is, *I need to get my ass to the gym.*

My third thought, as I fall to the ground and hear something of mine crack, is, *Oh. Shit.*

Sophie is already next to me, and her tears are immediate, as if they have just been waiting all this time to be unleashed. I try to catch my breath, to say something to make her feel better, but I can't focus.

"Auntie Ellie, are you okay? Please don't be dead. Oh, God, please don't be dead."

"Stop, sweetheart. I'm fine. I'm fine. Just fell. That's all." I try to make my voice sound calm, though I hurt everywhere. Somehow, my hands must have slipped, and I didn't put my feet down fast enough.

I am still lying on the ground. My head smacked the pavement—at least that's what I assume, because I feel gravel in my face and my brain aches—but I need to get up, and fast, for Sophie's sake. People are starting to look over; I am making a spectacle of myself in the Diana, Princess of Wales, Memorial Playground.

My left arm is at an unnatural angle. That's what cracked. The pain, sharp and demanding, echoes through my body, and I blink back reflexive tears. *Shit, shit, shit.*

"Oh, this is all my fault. I'm sorry, Auntie Ellie. I'm so sorry. Please be okay."

"I'm fine, Soph, seriously. I'm just a klutz. This isn't your fault. You didn't do anything."

"I'm so sorry." Her tears are still falling, and her posture has turned fetal, her arms wrapped around her belly, bent forward and rocking. Seeing her reaction hurts even more than my arm.

"I'm fine, sweetheart. Please stop apologizing." I start to get up, slow and steady, wipe the gravel from my face, and feel relief that there's no blood. Sophie should not have to look at my blood. "See, I'm fine. I'm good as new."

I do a little good-as-new dance—only a mini-shuffle, because moving hurts—and Sophie stands up straight, wipes her tears with her shirtsleeve, and nods, not at me but at herself, as if accepting the proof that nothing has happened. We give up on the playground for the day, walk over to the nearby café, and I order us both ice cream sundaes to prove my good cheer. A perfect opportunity to sneak five Advil from my purse while Sophie isn't looking. We even stop to see the famous Peter Pan statue: Peter standing on a tree trunk, playing his flute to an audience of squirrels and fairies and tourists. And when the pain shoots through my left arm—fast and splitting—and I hear the steady knock of my headache, I refuse to wince, use it as a reminder instead to smile wider, pretend bigger, that no part of me hurts.

Of course, I am not good as new. I find out five hours later, after Sophie is home and tucked in, and I make my first solo trip to the emergency room, that my left arm is broken.

16

Phillip's secretary patches me through to his office. Even though it is eight o'clock Boston time, they are both still there, perched at the top of the Prudential Center, amid marble and glass and sitting on ergonomically designed chairs, immune to the glorious view of Boston Harbor. I bet Phillip is finalizing a pitch, surrounded by a harem of young analysts eager to stay up all night at his whim and "run the numbers." Before, when we were deciding whether to get pregnant, we ran the numbers for that, too, and Phillip created a multicolored, expense pie chart that took residence under a magnet on our refrigerator; it lasted for far longer than Oliver's sonogram.

"Ellie," he says, a sarcastic edge to his voice, all the more cutting because he's calm. "How nice of you to call."

"You hung up on me."

"Three. Days. Ago."

"I was waiting to cool down."

"Bullshit. It took you three days to call back. Over seventy-two hours. Did you just forget to call? I bet you forgot. Too busy with your new life?"

"You told me to go fuck myself, Phillip. That's not something I'd forget." Our conversation is like a flat tennis rally, purposeful re-strained hitting before the game.

"No, since you like to be the semantics police, allow me to cor-rect you. I said, 'Fuck you.' There's a difference."

"Phillip, please."

"Why do you keep saying that? Please. Please what?"

"Please stop."

"Stop what? I'm not supposed to be angry? You go to London, and all of a sudden I get a call that says you're not coming home. Ever."

"It wasn't all of a sudden," I say.

"This is a marriage, Ellie. That should mean something."

"It does mean something."

"Then you can't just do this. Who does something like this? It makes no sense."

"Lucy died, Phillip. She died! And they need me here. You don't need me the way they do."

My voice cracks, and I hate myself for it. I want to stay calm like Phillip, I want that piercing anger and targeted rage.

"So, we're getting a divorce because your best friend died."

"Who said anything about a divorce?"

"Are you kidding me? Are we just playing games here? Is that what's going on?"

"I'm not playing games." My chest—no, my heart, my literal heart—clenches. We have never before said the word *divorce* out loud to each other. We have said *separate*. And I hate to admit it, but *fuck you* or variations thereof have been in the arsenal long before this week. But never *divorce*. I understand I am on my way, that I have started the long walk to D-land, but using the word now seems premature all of a sudden. "I just . . . Phillip. I'm not talking about divorce. I'm talking about a separation, or maybe not even that. I'm not sure what I'm talking about. I just know I need to be here right now."

"Well, why don't you think about what it is *you* want and get back to me? What, in say, I dunno, three fucking days?"

"Phillip, stop being so angry."

"Yeah, right."

"I broke my arm, by the way. It hurts a lot. That's what I called to tell you."

"You broke my heart. I have a feeling that this hurts a hell of a lot more."

The following evening, after we have tucked Sophie in and Greg and I are settling into the final empty space at the end of the day, we watch *Big Brother UK* on television, both of us fascinated by its soapy appeal. Today there is a burgeoning couple and another splitting, and it looks like they may switch partners, though I hope not. I don't care that their wrong decisions will make for better television; they seem like real people, with real loves, and to screw them up for the sake of plot will be sacrificing too much.

"So there's an English tradition that when you break a bone, you have to go out and get pissed," Greg says, clicking his finger against his drink. "And we have approximately four hours before the pub closes and, what do you think, at least six before Sophie wakes up?"

"We can't leave Soph alone."

"I'll call the girl next door to babysit. She's always up for making some extra pounds."

"I'm pretty sure I'm not supposed to drink with my pain medication."

"Ah, but, see, there's another English tradition you're forgetting about. When one's friend suddenly becomes a widower, and before the age of forty, you're required to pass along any and all narcotics prescribed by one's physician. In fact, I believe it's a law."

"Really."

"Okay, not really. But, come on, I fancy getting pissed. That's what we English do when we are upset. Everyone knows that. That was definitely made law during the Thatcher years."

Two hours later we are in the King's Head pub, and I am watching Greg drink his eighth pint. One after the other, without pause. As soon as Greg's drink reaches the quarter-empty mark, a fresh pint appears, just in time for him to gulp down the rest of the last one. I don't try to keep up, not that I could even if I wanted to. Instead, I've been sipping the same glass of warm water; I need to stay sober. I am the one on call for Sophie duty tonight.

The pub has wooden chairs with green seats and a hideous Persian carpet, which stinks of beer and maybe urine, a unique combination I haven't had the pleasure of smelling since my last frat party, the week before I graduated from college. The place is surprisingly full for a Thursday night, mostly middle-aged men drinking frothy pints, and the atmosphere is not dark and charming, the way it is in some pubs. The posters on the wall announce that the place serves a Sunday afternoon roast, with a picture of a slab of beef to prove it. I can't think of a less appealing place to eat a meal. This pub is for one thing and one thing only: drinking.

"Another, mate," a sweaty, snaggle-toothed slab of a man tells the bartender, as he sways on his stool; "Me, too, keep 'em coming," says his equally unsteady twin or cousin or drinking buddy. And that's how it goes, on and on, *another, me, too, keep 'em coming*, a never-ending cycle of wrist to mouth, including the occasional trip outside for a "fag." I don't know why Greg chose this place, which seems a little rough around the edges for him, and not the cleaner, cuter one down the street, with the Old English sign and the dry heat of a fireplace.

With each progressive pint, Greg's demeanor changes. He starts as faux-cheerful—we are just a couple of friends having a drink, after all. We are playing the game that we have mastered over the last few weeks, a pleasant game that allows us to forget how weird our circumstances are.

As the night has worn on, he has become borderline hostile. The alcohol is unleashing his anger, loosening his tongue. But he doesn't sound angry with me. He's angry with Lucy. I guess we both are for her making us take part in this charade.

"Know what pisses me off the most?" he asks me now, his finger pointed in the air and then forgotten. "You know what drives me crazy? That I couldn't talk her out of it."

"What are you talking about? You can't talk a person out of death. This wasn't her choice." Maybe mortality is something that we can wrap our minds around only when we are sober. Because even then, even when we have access to the cruel sharpness of intellect, the whole life–death divide still seems insurmountable. There are degrees of absence. I realize that now. Lucy's takes us to one end of the spectrum, to the realm of absolute.

"I felt like if she only listened to me—"

"Greg, you're being ridiculous. You can't even talk God out of death. Believe me, I've tried. Many times. And I'm not even sure I believe in God."

"I just thought, you know, it would all blow over. But it didn't. It got worse and worse. And, bam, now it's done. Just like that. I wasn't even given a shot. And Sophie—"

"Yeah." I have no idea what he is talking about. I'm humoring my drunk friend.

"I want to kill the guy. I would have no problem cutting his heart out. I fantasize about it. You don't destroy a family like that."

"We all want to kill him. But please let's not talk about—" I see his face again, the man who has done this, and for a moment I worry that he is sitting in this pub, too, or is in wait outside, like he is less a person, more a deadly gas, somehow infused in the British mist, slowly poisoning all of us. He penetrates my consciousness, and sometimes, when he pops up in my thoughts, unwelcome, I turn around just to make sure he is not behind me.

I wish I could believe he is mere boogeyman, an apparition, Sophie's nightmare sparring partner, not someone who exists in my world. People like that shouldn't exist in my world.

"You'll stay with Sophie, right, when I go to Paris and strangle the living daylights out of the fucking . . . fucking . . . fucker?"

"Paris? What does Paris have to do with anything?"

"Everything. The city of love. Screw love. What does he look like, Ellie? Is he better-looking than me?"

"Who? Greg, I think it's time to go home."

"Please tell me. Is he better-looking?" Greg looks like he is about to cry. His hair is mussed again, and he's spilled some beer onto his polo sweater. He's messy, but I guess I would be, too, if I had drunk even half of what he has consumed tonight.

"I don't know what you're talking about. Come on, let's go." I start to usher him out of the pub into the chill night air. "I promise, things will look better in the morning."

Greg weaves as he makes his way out the door, but no one takes notice of us; he looks just like every other guy here who's had one too many. Once we are back on the street, he stops me with his arm, turns in my direction. For the moment, his eyes are clear and he seems sober.

"No, Ellie. That's where you are wrong. Tomorrow I'll still be alive. And Lucy? Lucy will still be dead. No, things will *not* look better in the morning."

What can I say to this, other than, *You are absolutely right*? I link arms with him, my right through his left, and attempt to keep him from falling down. My skin is itchy under my cast, and I feel a shooting pain straight to my fingertips, right from the center of the break point.

We pass a few of Notting Hill's private gardens, hulking and off-limits and silent, fairy lit on their borders with old-fashioned lamps. Neither of us says another word until we are finally outside the Stafford front door, the walk home somehow much longer than the walk to the pub. I crave the refuge of my bed.

"Ellie, how did you let her do it?" Greg asks, peering down at me from the top step. Since he has made no effort to find his keys, I search through my purse for the spare set with my one good arm.

"I don't know what you're talking about."

"She must have talked to you. You could have talked some sense into her."

"Greg. This isn't funny. Let's just get inside, and you can pass out. You've had too much to drink."

But Greg doesn't want to go inside, and he grabs the house keys out of my hand.

"She didn't tell you, did she?"

"What?"

"She didn't tell you. Not even you. Wow."

"Tell me what?"

"Nothing. Sorry, I know . . . I know I'm talking nonsense. Come on, let's get inside. I'm shattered." He easily opens the door, another flash of sobriety that is more alarming than his drunkenness.

In the hallway, just before we part to go into our separate bedrooms, just down the hall from each other, Greg looks at me with clear eyes once more.

"Good night, Ellie. And thanks. You actually made me feel a hell of a lot better."

17

M y new pay-as-you-go cell phone wakes me up at six a.m. with
its shrill cry.

"What? Hello?"

"Eleanor, it's Jane." My mother is the only person in the world
who calls me Eleanor.

"What the hell? It's, like, the crack of dawn."

"Don't say 'like.' You're thirty-five, not thirteen."

"What do you want? What time is it there?"

"One in the morning. Anyhow, listen, darling, your father and I
are coming for a visit."

"What? You and Dad? Together?"

"Come on, Eleanor. Don't pretend with me. I know your brother
already told you about us."

"I was hoping it was a joke." I picture my mother calling from her
tiny apartment in the West Village, with its walls covered with
woven tapestries and framed posters of modern art. No doubt she is
wearing a silk kimono and smoking a clove cigarette. It's a week-
night, so I assume my father is still in his old house in Cambridge,

reading a paperback on his cracked leather recliner and wondering how to hold on to my mother this time.

"We're landing at five o'clock next Friday. And we'll see you and Michael for dinner. Your father has already taken care of the reservations. He's recently become something of a foodie."

"Mikey has a date on Friday night."

"Really? With a man or a woman?"

"Mom."

"What? Just asking. I can't remember the last time he brought someone home."

"November 2004. Remember? You told him you thought she was so boring that you'd rather spend the afternoon memorizing pi than talk to her?"

"Oh, right. Homely girl. Good teeth. Childbearing hips. So he'll meet us for drinks after his date."

"This is very last-minute."

"What can I say? Your father and I live on the edge."

"He certainly does." My mother ignores me, per usual. She sounds happy, though. I'll give her that. Maybe there's a chance that this time my parents will stick.

"Whatever. You're available, right? What could you possibly have to do?"

"Thanks a lot. Yeah, I'm available. I'll make sure Greg can be here. Or I guess I could find a sitter."

"Wow, we've slipped into this new mommy role rather quickly, haven't we?"

"I hate when you resort to the first person plural. It's rude. Is that how you talk to your patients?"

"Most of them aren't as difficult as you."

"How long are you staying?"

"We'll be there for only about a day, and then we're off to Paris." She says it the French way: *Par-E*. "We haven't been since we back-packed through Europe when you were a baby. We're hoping to make love under the Eiffel Tower again."

"Please. Stop."

"Oh, Eleanor. Prudish as always. So, how are things going over there? Phillip tells me you're not coming home."

"He told you that?"

"The better question is why haven't you told me?"

"Since when do you talk to Phillip?"

"What are you talking about, sweetheart? Phillip and I talk all the time."

"Yup, I heard," Mikey says by way of answering the phone when I call him a couple of hours later. "Both of them. In London. Together."

"Yeah. Did she tell you about their plans for the Eiffel Tower?"

"Are you trying to kill me? Of course she did. She always does."

"Maybe that's why we never get to have sex. Our parents are getting it on enough for the both of us."

"Ellie, stop. I'm still feeling sick."

"And we do nothing, right? About Mom and Dad? We just trust that she won't destroy Dad? Again?"

"We do nothing. Ellie?"

"Yeah."

"Can you do me a favor?"

"Anything."

"Please call your husband."

* * *

So I call my husband, and he screens my call. Fair enough, I think. I would be angry, too, if he left me behind. But whatever he says, I'll still need to be here. Whatever he says, I'm not going home. Whatever he says, I don't want to hurt him—either of us—more.

> To: phillip.klein@excesscapital.com
> From: ellie.lerner@yahoo.com
> Subject: Arms race
> Are you okay over there?

> To: ellie.lerner@yahoo.com
> From: phillip.klein@excesscapital.com
> Subject: Re: Arms race
> Did you really break your arm?

> To: phillip.klein@excesscapital.com
> From: ellie.lerner@yahoo.com
> Subject: Re: Arms race
> Yes. Did I really break your heart?

> To: ellie.lerner@yahoo.com
> From: phillip.klein@excesscapital.com
> Subject: Re: Arms race
> I don't know, but let's finally be honest. It ain't looking good, kid.

18

I am snooping—there is no other way to spin it—when Claire calls on the following Wednesday, and at first I am too distracted to hear the warning in her tone. What started with me looking for a power adapter for my laptop—to turn DC to AC, or AC to DC, or whatever it is—has ended with me rifling through Lucy's office. An all-consuming exercise of looking over and under and next to for evidence of the person I used to know. I don't mean to do it, to violate her privacy—though to be honest, I am not sure what privacy means in relation to the dead—but there is a pile of papers on her desk, and a couple of photographs I have never seen before, and how can I not look?

And being in this room, which is one hundred percent Lucy, down to the small first-edition collection on her bookshelf, the black-and-white picture of her rubbing noses with a two-year-old Sophie, and a *French 101* CD makes me feel like she is currently away on a short vacation. She has to come home to us. There is French to be learned and books to be read, and a daughter to parent, after all.

Certainly she can't be lost if there is still the matted diploma from the Columbia School of Journalism on her wall, a pair of her favorite flip-flops, solid pink, soles worn thin, still on the floor, a pile of research for an article still unwritten. Too many *stills*—an identity frozen by things—for the object they represent to be gone.

"Ellie, can you come round the school? I'm sorry to do this to you. I tried Mr. Stafford first, but his secretary said he'd be out for the afternoon," Claire says, and now I'm listening. I've turned away from Lucy's desk, have closed my eyes to concentrate on Claire's words, and it is then, and only then, that I hear that her voice sounds like defeat. Claire is an elementary-school teacher; her voice never sounds like defeat.

"Is Sophie all right?"

"She's fine—"

"What's going on?"

"Please, just come pick her up. There's been a bit of a row, but I'll explain when you get here. And, Ellie?"

"Yeah?"

"Please hurry. Sophie needs you."

Headmistress Calthorp reminds me of one of those rubber-band balls you find in an office cubicle, obsessively compact and tightly bound and the useless product of time wasted. I hate her on sight. The way she is dressed like her students: plaid skirt, navy sweater, collared shirt underneath, and blond hair kept in place with a matching plaid band. The way she refuses to get to the point, leaning back in her leather chair, which is brown and antique and has studs that look like they leave marks on her back. The way she crosses her legs and sensible navy pumps, in a proper and unnatural way, calf to calf, ankle to ankle, and parallel. I bet her wool tights are control-top and she feels virtuous about the fact that they hurt.

"What happened? Where's Sophie?" I say, bypassing the usual pleasantries, hoping she'll unsteeple her gnarled fingertips and tell me what the hell is going on here. I ran here in Lucy's flip-flops, a size too small, and I'm out of breath and shaking with fear.

"Sophie is waiting in the front office. What happened to your arm?" she asks me, staring at my cast and its childish doodles—Sophie's doodles—with distaste. Her tone is curt, judgmental, and wooden like her office. The desk she presides over is an obviously expensive antique, just like her chair, which has thick legs, just like her own.

"Fell off the monkey bars. So Sophie's okay?"

"Excuse me? You fell off what?"

"The monkey bars. Is Sophie—"

"You mean a climbing frame." She says it like I've made a mistake and it is her civic duty to correct me. "What were you doing on a climbing frame? Those are for children." *So are plaid skirts*, I think but don't say.

"Is Sophie okay?"

"If you define *okay* as being in a lot of trouble. She is suspended for two days."

"Suspended? But she's only eight."

"We take violence very seriously at this school."

"Violence? Are you kidding me? Have you met Sophie?"

"She attacked another student. I know in America children take guns in their lunch boxes, but that's not how we operate here at The Pembridge Place School." She pats a brochure on her desk, filled with kilted girls and bow-tied boys, for emphasis.

I want to hurt her.

"What was the fight about?"

"We don't know yet, but one might say it's irrelevant. Don't you agree?"

"No, I think *one* might say not."

"Well, as I said, Ms. . . . what was it, Lerner?"

"Call me Ellie."

"Oh, we don't refer to adults by their first names here. We believe it breeds disrespect. As I was saying, Ms. Lerner, we have a strict no-violence policy."

"You do realize Sophie just lost her mother, right?"

"Yes, I do. A tragedy." She sniffs. "But regardless of the circumstances, we can't accept such behavior. If Sophie doesn't apologize, she will be expelled."

"Let me get this straight. You know that Sophie's mother was murdered—only a few blocks away from this school, in fact—and your concern at this moment isn't, *Let's see how we can help Sophie?* But instead, *if she doesn't apologize we're going to expel her?* An eight-year-old? One of the smartest kids in your fucking school?"

"Please, we do not use language like that here, Ms. Lerner." She waves her hands in the air and then sits back with crossed arms. She is not afraid of me. "One must understand—"

"Where is Claire? I'd like to speak with her."

"I am not sure whom you mean. We don't have a student named Claire." She says it primly and in all seriousness. She won't let her act drop, not even when speaking to a fellow adult.

"Sophie's teacher. *Claire.*"

"Oh, I see. You mean *Ms. Walters.*"

* * *

I follow Headmistress Calthorp out of her office and watch as she hoofs down the hallways with the Queen's gait. Flatfooted and stiff. The students cower in doorways as she passes, and I don't blame them.

"Soph?" Sophie is sitting next to Claire on a chair outside the front office. She has folded into herself, all parts of her bent to take up as little space as possible. What I have come to think of as the *mute look*, that deadness in her eyes she had when I first got to London, is back. "Come here, sweet pea."

Sophie runs across the hall to me. She buries her face in my stomach and hugs me with her whole body. She is shivering, like a dog.

"It's okay, Soph. Whatever it is, it will be okay." I bend down and pick her up, so I am holding all forty-five pounds of her with my one good arm. She wraps her thin legs around my back, turns her head so it is resting on my shoulder. And that's when I see it. My little Sophie, sweet little Sophie, has a black eye.

I look at Claire, who is still sitting down, just behind the headmistress. She looks beaten and sad. We make eye contact, and she quickly makes the *I'll call you* hand motion behind her boss's back.

"Sophie is not welcome back to school until Friday."

"All right."

"And it goes without saying that you and her father need to have a long talk with her. She doesn't seem to understand that she has no choice but to apologize."

"All right." Sophie is crying on my shoulder. I'll agree to anything to get us out of here. Now.

"Thanks, Headmistress Calthorp." On the way out, I curtsy—with Sophie still clinging on—I actually fucking curtsy, as if the headmistress is, in fact, Her Royal Majesty. I don't know what comes over me.

Sophie and I take the long route, weaving through the streets, past the fancy shops of Ledbury Road and the newsagent where we sometimes stop for chocolate, and along the white-mansion blocks with their comforting fresh paint and hearty columns. Past the private gardens, where children with special keys get to play.

Though my broken bone is throbbing under the plaster pushed up against her back, I carry her the whole way home.

I don't ask what happened right away. First we go inside, huddle in the kitchen booth, and I make her a cup of tea and give her some of her favorite chocolate biscuits. They call them biscuits here, but they're cookies. Sophie has had another shitty day, one more in a recent outbreak of them, and no matter what happened at school, she needs a little comforting.

"Does it hurt?" I ask, and hand her a frozen bag of broccoli from the freezer to put on her eye.

"No," she says, the first word she has spoken since we left the school. "Not really."

"It looks pretty bad."

"Yeah."

"You sure you're okay?"

She shrugs her shoulders and stares into her tea. I eat one of her biscuits.

"Wanna talk about it?" Sophie doesn't say anything in response, so I keep talking. "The headmistress said that you attacked a kid."

"So."

"So? Come on, Soph. You can do better than that. What happened?"

"Nothing."

"You have a black eye, sweetheart. Something obviously happened."

"Stephen Devereaux is a big fat jerk." Stephen is the kid from the zoo who asked if I was Sophie's mum, the one whose own mother treated me like a leper. "He said . . . Anyhow, he deserved it, Auntie Ellie. And I didn't even hurt him that badly. He just has a couple of scratches and stuff."

"How'd you get the black eye?"

"That was an accident. His elbow hit me when I, um, when I bit his leg."

"Sophie!"

"He deserved it. I swear. You would have bit him too. He's an idiot and a jerk and he thinks he's a Transformer, but he's just a stupid little nasty kid."

"What did he say?"

"I don't want to tell you."

"Why not?"

"Because."

"Because why?"

"Because."

"I can do this all night, Soph. I have nowhere to be. Because why?"

"He said . . . he said a lot of things. First he called Inderpal a knob-head, because of his knot, and was making fun of him. Like, his skin is brown 'cause he's dirty and he should take more baths and get a haircut. And I told him to stop and was like, Inderpal is from the Punjab region in Northern India. He's not dirty. But big, fat, stupid Stephen wouldn't stop."

"You should have told on him to Ms. Walters. Not bit him."

"But that's not it. Then . . . then he said things about Mummy. Bad things. Really horrible stuff." She starts to cry again, and I am doing my best to hold it together. I can't cry, too, not now. Definitely not now. She is the child, and I am the adult here. "He said that she . . . she deserved it, to be killed, and that she was a slut, and other stuff."

"Oh, Soph." I can barely breathe. The air is stuck in my lungs, and my stomach burns. "I'm going to fucking kill Stephen and his fucking mother too."

She looks at me, shocked and scared. She can tell that I'm not just using bad language to make her laugh.

"Sorry, forget I ever said that. I'm angry, that's all. You should never, ever have to listen to stuff like that, Soph. You're right. Stephen is a big jerk. Come here."

Sophie puts her head on my lap and stretches her legs along the booth. I stroke her hair and rub her back.

"It's going to be okay. I promise, sweetie. It's going to be okay," I say, though less for her benefit and more for my own. Her tears have stopped and she looks close to falling asleep. Her eye is now eggplant purple. "We'll fix this."

"Auntie Ellie? Can I ask you a question?"

"Of course, Soph."

"What's a slut?"

19

How bad is it? Single or a double?" Greg says, hands waiting on the bottle of scotch. He has already been upstairs to check on a sleeping Sophie, to see, at least from a distance, the blue shadow of her black eye, the way it looks incongruous and ridiculous on her kid face.

"Triple. And I think you'll need one too."

Greg sits next to me on the couch, pours our drinks, and hands mine over.

"To us finally hitting bottom," I say, and clink his glass.

"That bad?"

"I think so. But you'll have to tell me. I don't really understand what's going on here. The kid who Sophie had a fight with? His name is Stephen Devereaux." Greg stares at me, and I can see him take the force of the news in the way his face opens and shuts. He puts down his drink, and the coffee table vibrates.

"Okay. Okay," he says, and folds over, resting his forehead on the tip of his glass. He is making himself smaller, just like Sophie.

"I'll be honest, I don't understand, Greg. Not really."

"I assumed you knew. I thought you were just being polite. Not saying anything."

"Knew what?" My arm aches, and I suddenly wish I were home with Phillip, sipping wine with him after a joint effort at a stir-fry dinner. Far from this dramatic shit storm. I want to walk away and start over. That's what I was trying to do by staying here, after all. Right? Hit the restart button on my life.

Well, I need another try. This is too much for me.

Lucy, what the hell did you get me into?

"It doesn't matter now, does it? It's all over. One way or the other."

"Yeah," I say, and consider letting that be enough. Maybe I don't need to know. None of this is my business. Then I remember Lucy at the age of twelve, flaunting our BFF necklaces, one of two people I thought I would always know and understand in this world. I thought we'd jumped the invisible line, and I remember I used to feel that way about Phillip, too, that I didn't know where one of us ended and the other began. I've now been wrong twice.

"It apparently still matters," I say, and point to Sophie's abandoned Mary Janes at the door.

"What did that little bastard say to her?" I was hoping Greg wouldn't ask, so I wouldn't have to say the words out loud. Stupid of me.

"He called Lucy a slut and said she deserved it." My delivery is flat and without emotion. If I do it any other way, I'll break, clean in two.

Greg sips his drink. Eyes on the floor. Hands on his knees. Deep breaths, in and out.

"What did Sophie do?"

"She bit him."

Greg chokes on his drink.

"Really?"

"Really."

"That's my girl."

"It's not funny."

"No, I guess not." He rubs his hand over the stubble on his face. "One can't help but feel sorry for the kid, though. He's just parroting his mum's rubbish. And the craziest thing is I don't blame her either. I'd have said the same thing about her husband. I *have* said worse things about him."

And then, of course, it all falls together, all of the parts I did not want to see.

"So, just to be clear: Lucy had an affair? With Stephen's dad?" I think back to the zoo and how Stephen's mother ushered him away from Sophie and me, like we had cooties.

"She was going to leave me for him."

"What?" I had pictured a one-night stand, a stupid, drunken mistake. The sort of slipup that could be, might be, forgivable.

He shrugs a what-are-you-going-to-do shrug. Too casual and practiced. Betrays that the wound is still fresh and deep. He has lost Lucy twice now, and the second time has not made the first any less painful.

"Who is he?"

"I don't know. I've never met the guy, but he sounds like this cocky French asshole. Apparently they worked together at the paper. She was moving to Paris to be with him."

A French reporter. I think back to the week after the funeral, to the floppy-haired man who kept asking me questions: *Who are you? Who are you?*

And then I return to the question I keep asking myself, which has been humming throughout the conversation: *Why didn't she tell me?*

"How'd you find out?" I ask.

"She told me. A few days before the accident. I mean, I knew something was weird—we hadn't been all that happy for a while— but I never thought she'd leave us."

"Paris?"

"Yup, Paris."

"My parents are coming—did I tell you that? They're coming here, and then they're taking the Chunnel. They want to have sex under the Eiffel Tower. Again." I am not sure why I volunteer this information, but I don't know what else to say. I still can't believe Lucy was having an affair.

No, that's not true. I can believe Lucy was having an affair. Her moral code was different from mine, which wasn't a problem as long as I wasn't her victim. What I can't believe is that she didn't tell me about it.

"How lovely for them," Greg says, and gives me a weak smile.

"Wait, what do you mean you never thought she'd 'leave us'?" I ask. My body feels the betrayal first, before my brain does. And when it does, it's obvious why she didn't want to tell me. I'd never have allowed her to do it.

"She was leaving both of us behind. Not just me, but Sophie too."

I decide to forgo my painkillers tonight, and, instead, Greg and I proceed to get very drunk. The throbbing in my arm recedes, my head thickens, and things start to seem a bit more manageable. I am a happy drunk—never maudlin, maybe because I am too maudlin in real life—and I enjoy my surrender to the scotch and the ice in my glass. A pleasing numbness takes hold.

"A clean slate. A fresh start. That's what she said she wanted," Greg says now. His voice is a touch slurred, but it could be from exhaustion as much as the alcohol. "Like Sophie and I were some burden she couldn't bear to keep carrying. That's what she made me feel like, in the end. Heavy baggage. No fun to feel like heavy baggage."

"No, it's not." I wonder if Phillip feels like that, that I am one more thing he has to contend with in the already challenging enough game of Life. And then I think back to when I was sure that being together was the simplest part. Back when we made each other feel lighter.

"She said Sophie and I would be better off without her. Can you believe that? She said we deserved to have someone in our lives who actually wanted to be there. Such bullshit. Selfish, self-serving bullshit."

"It's weird that she didn't tell me. She told me everything."

"Maybe she didn't want you telling her not to do it."

"Probably."

"Maybe she thought you'd judge her."

"Probably."

"I gave up trying to understand her a long time ago."

"I thought I *did* understand her."

"Can you believe she's gone? For good? I mean gone, gone." He closes his eyes when he says it, as if he can capture her fleeting image if he tries hard enough. A shadow slipping under a door.

"No, I really can't."

We sit quietly for a while, stare into our drinks, wonder how to unravel the confusion that Lucy has left in her wake. Does it matter anymore that she was going to leave? I think of how Greg looks at Sophie, with love and loss and longing, and more than a little pain; though he could stand to get home a few hours earlier, I am not sure he could love his child more.

"How are you and Phillip?" he asks, apropos of nothing.

"You know, we're hanging in there." Neither Greg nor I is naive enough to think that Lucy hasn't passed along each of our secrets. As I know things about him that I shouldn't, he knows just as much about me. One of these days, we should compare notes. I'd be curious to hear how Lucy transposed me to her husband and who I became in the recounting.

"Marriage is hard. Why don't people tell you that?"

"They do. I think we all just expect to be the exception."

"Yeah, I guess. Listen, thanks for being here." He says it slowly, almost too slowly. Like he wants his words to convey more than their meaning. I feel his hand on my cheek before I see it. My stomach drops out, my organs are somewhere on the floor, tight and twitchy and frightened and uncomfortable.

He wants to turn my face.

He wants to kiss me.

I do not want him to turn my face.

I do not want him to kiss me.

"Greg." I shake my head back and forth, as if to shake his hand away. I keep my eyes staring forward. If I don't look at him, this won't be happening. At the very least, it will keep it from happening more. "Not a good idea."

"Yeah, you're right." He takes back his hand, puts both of them in the air, in a you-caught-me gesture, moving the moment along to whatever we are going to feel next in one quick motion. "I'm sorry. Totally inappropriate."

"It's okay."

We sit in silence for a few moments, trying to erase our embarrassment and to bounce back from bottoming out.

"You think I should get my own flat?" I ask. My mind is spinning the possibilities: going home to Sharon, staying here in this house, or starting a whole new life in London.

I am thirty-five years old and have no idea where I belong.

"Because of my moment of weakness and drunken desperation and possibly, yes, I'll admit it, revenge? No, of course not."

"But the way we're living is bizarre."

"I'm an idiot, Ellie. Please don't leave because I'm daft."

"Not because of that. Because this situation is unsustainable."

"Funny, that's exactly what Lucy said about our marriage."

Hours later, when I'm alone in the guest room, no longer drunk and unable to sleep, I feel the sting of Lucy's betrayal. What kind of person *chooses* to walk away from her own kid? My best friend has posthumously morphed into a stranger.

The fury sweeps over me in waves, gaining ground on the replay of tonight's events. Lucy's not here to defend herself, but it doesn't matter. There is no defense. Only one brutal fact: Whether Lucy had lived or died, Sophie was getting left behind.

20

We approach Headmistress Calthorp as a united front. Greg and I stand before her, shoulder to shoulder, hiding our thick hangovers. Though we may not feel like it, we are adults, and we will not let this woman turn us into schoolchildren with her icy condescension. Greg and I may be an awkward team in this coparenting thing, but we are a team nonetheless, and no one messes with our Sophie.

"I was surprised to find that you threatened to expel my daughter," Greg says, and leans into her desk. He is wearing a black pin-striped suit—the white striping a bit thick for my American tastes—a matte gray tie over a crisp shirt, and his hair is combed to the side today, at once boyish and responsible father. I get a glimpse of what he must look like during daylight hours, in that gaping hole of time he spends in the heart of London, drafting multimillion-pound merger agreements. Commanding and authoritative. A man unbroken by loss and betrayal. He still wears his wedding ring, another badge that tips him over the edge from boy into serious man. He is someone to be reckoned with.

"How much have I donated in the past three years to this school? I seem to recall that my checks have been in the five figures. No, excuse me, make that six," he says.

"Mr. Stafford, Ms. Lerner, please sit down. Would you like some water?" Headmistress Calthorp nods at her assistant to fetch us our drinks. She smiles up at Greg and plays with the pearls around her neck. The effect would be coquettish, if it wasn't tempered by her cold eyes.

"I don't have time to stay and chat," Greg says, his tone brisk. "The student that Sophie was involved in an altercation with said some unforgivable things about my late wife. Not to mention made racist comments about another student. If anything, I believe I would be well within my rights to insist that *he* be expelled."

"Now, no one is talking about expelling anyone."

"Really?" I ask. "Maybe I was confused yesterday, then, when you suspended Sophie for two days and insisted on an apology. Oh, yeah, and then threatened to expel her."

I feel hatred for Headmistress Calthorp—not anger, even, but pure hatred for her lack of imagination, her oversize ego, her desperate need to draw lines. I hate her with such intensity that for a moment I blame her for Lucy's death. I know she was probably right here in this office when it happened, drawing up a detention or demerit list. But she, this woman stuck in a headband and kilt at the age of sixty, represents why rebellion exists in the first place. Makes sense that Lucy and a woman like this couldn't coexist on the same planet. Rules never applied to Lucy.

"You see, Mr. Stafford"—Headmistress Calthorp ignores me, as if we are not in the same room. She looks only at Greg—"we have a zero-tolerance policy to violence here, and, as you probably understand, one has a school board to answer to. I was simply following protocol. But of course this can be worked out."

"Yes, it will be worked out. Immediately."

"I see," she says, and grips her pearls a little tighter. I wouldn't be surprised if she had this exact same conversation yesterday, with Stephen's mom. Maybe she came in flashing checkbooks and threatening lawsuits, armed with Polaroids of Sophie's teeth marks in Stephen's spindly leg.

"I will not force my daughter to apologize, when she doesn't even understand the circumstances. She was defending her mother—who I needn't remind you passed away less than a month ago—and her best friend from profanity and racial slurs."

"I'm not defending the other student's actions, Mr. Stafford. Clearly, they were very wrong, but surely you can understand that we cannot allow our students to, well, to bite each other."

"And surely you understand that this is a one-off occasion born out of a messy personal situation and an eight-year-old's bereavement."

"But an apology—"

"Enough," Greg says, his voice harsh, suggesting that any negotiation up until this point has been a mock discussion for Headmistress Calthorp's benefit, to preserve some modicum of her dignity. But now he's fed up and can't believe his dead wife's adulterous affair has led him here—defending his innocent Sophie in this horrible woman's office. He should be at work negotiating an indemnity provision, and Sophie should be in class right now memorizing an acronym for KingdomPhylumClassOrderFamilyGenusSpecies. And Lucy should be—he doesn't know where she should be but certainly no more than a tube stop away. "Here's what's going to happen. Sophie will be back in school tomorrow. There will be no formal apologies. I have talked to my daughter, and I can assure you there will be no more incidents either. But if Stephen Devereaux goes as far as to breathe on Sophie, if he says anything to her even slightly resembling the verbal abuse she had to endure yesterday, God help me, there will be hell to pay."

His eyes flash with the rage I have seen on and off over the last couple of weeks—a high tide of anger and then shallow shame, cyclic and jagged.

"I will immediately withdraw Sophie from school and personally ensure that every one of my colleagues does exactly the same thing with their children. No, I will go one step further. I will single-handedly destroy your endowment. I don't often have to remind people that I am a very powerful man. Do I make myself clear?"

Greg takes a deep breath and uncurls his hands, so they are no longer fists. He catches my eye, a blink of embarrassment, but I nod at him in encouragement.

I like watching him kick some headmistress ass.

"Absolutely, Mr. Stafford."

"I realize there are only a few weeks left in the school year. But I very much hope that next year Sophie and Stephen will not be placed in the same classroom. Putting aside the personal differences I have with the Devereaux family, I find it abhorrent that my daughter was exposed to any sort of racist rhetoric. I have not yet spoken to Inderpal's parents, but I intend to, and I'm sure we can all agree he deserves a personal apology."

"That's quite right, Mr. Stafford."

"Oh, and, Bernadette, I think we've known each other long enough." The demon version of him has retreated, tucked back into the recesses of his gut, and he is once again a charming man–boy. He smiles and then winks. "Please call me Greg."

21

Dr. Boyd's office is located at the bottom of Portobello Road, near the end where most tourists don't bother to venture. They tend to become enthralled with the first few blocks of market stalls, the clothing and fruit and antique chests, and turn away when the air fills with the rich fatty smells from shops twirling kebabs or kielbasa. On Saturdays, when Portobello Market is in full swing, the streets are filled with the pedestrians who flow from the Notting Hill Gate tube stop. During the week, though, without the traders loading and unloading and the heady tension of buying and selling, the place seems almost sleepy. Today, the multicolored stores that often get blocked by the stall umbrellas look almost Caribbean with their bright, alternating pastels. Shop doors are propped open to allow customers to wander in and out. Sometimes, after the school pickup, Sophie and I explore Portobello's secondhand bookshops, flip through the dusty treasures in the children's sections, and then stop for a soy hot chocolate at Gail's bakery on the way home.

Today there is no time for lingering. I am on a mission to get this child to her first therapy session. Surprisingly, she hasn't asked too many questions about why she is going to a "feelings doctor," which is the way we've described Dr. Boyd to Sophie. As a safe place to go to discuss what's going on in her head. I guess she's too young to worry about the silly adult stigmas attached to seeking therapy.

"So I have to go back to school tomorrow?" Sophie asks as we walk up the three flights to the office, which is above a Moroccan restaurant that advertises its daily belly dancers and a five-pound tajine. There's a coffee shop next door, where I intend to eat a chocolate croissant and read *Hello!* magazine while I wait.

For her big therapy day, Sophie is wearing jeans and her "favorite" T-shirt—long-sleeved, pink, and with a picture of the organs of the human body, all clearly labeled. It is supposed to correspond to the figure underneath, and Sophie proudly shows me where her liver resides. We have decided to Google the liver tonight, since I didn't know what to tell her when she asked what the thing does. All I know is that I did my own organ significant damage last night with that scotch.

Funny how often she asks me questions to which I don't know the answers. Who knew there was all this information that parents are supposed to know or, at the very least, pretend to? I feel like I should start reading the encyclopedia, too, just to keep pace.

"Yup. Back to the real world tomorrow. Why? You don't want to go?" I ask.

"I like hanging out with you all day. You're more fun than the other kids. All they do is talk about stupid stuff, like their pets. They're so boring."

"Come on, Soph, it's good for you to play with the other kids."

"I wish I were really old. Like you."

"Thanks a lot. Guess what?"

"What?"

"I wish I were really young, like you. Eight is, like, the best age."

"Really?"

"I don't know. To be honest, I don't remember being eight."

"That's good."

"Why?"

"I don't want to remember being eight either."

Dr. Boyd's office is a kid's mecca, but Sophie is not a normal kid. She is unswayed by the five-hundred-piece puzzle spread around the floor, the airplane-model kit waiting to be glued together with small hands, the crayons and white sheets of paper spread over short tables with long surfaces, and the pile of stuffed animals in the corner, which looks like it would be fun to dive into, headfirst. Even the bookshelf in the corner—an impressive children's library—doesn't move her.

"Hello, Sophie, I'm Dr. Boyd, but you can call me Simon." He crouches down to eye level to shake her hand in an official job-interview way.

"Hello," she says in a quiet voice, taking the measure of this Dr. Boyd, whose head is bald and whose hand is more than twice the size of hers. My guess is he's at least six-six, tall enough that I bet he gets asked at least once a day how tall he is. He's surprisingly graceful and spry despite all the footage, standing up to meet me after squatting to meet Sophie. The fold and unfold of his body, fluid. A six-six, two-hundred-twenty-pound yogi.

"And you must be Ellie. Nice to meet you," he says, enveloping my hand with his and then using his other to pat the top, a gesture full of good humor and warmth. "Cool cast. Can I sign?"

"Sure," I say, and he whisks a Sharpie from his pocket—he's the kind of guy who walks around with a Sharpie, and probably a Swiss Army knife, too—and puts a SIMON, all in caps, near my elbow. There is something seductive about this man and his big, unringed hands and bonhomie, the creases on his forehead and the crown of his head, but I remind myself that I am married, that he is Sophie's therapist, and a crush at this juncture—on anyone—would be wholly inappropriate.

He looks like he's about forty-five and still reads comic books and wears holiday-themed boxer shorts—green four-leaf clovers for Saint Patrick's Day, reindeer for Christmas. *Stop thinking about this man's underwear, Ellie.*

"So your dad tells me you're a big reader, Soph. So am I," Simon says, casually walking us back toward the bookshelf, trying to engage her interest. Dropping Greg is a smart move; it reminds Sophie of Simon's legitimacy. She is here only because her father wants her to be. "What are some of your favorites? I hear you like mysteries. Am I right?"

"Yes, but only the ones that aren't easy to figure out," she says. "And I kind of like science books too. I have that one at home." She points to a book on the human body. "I've read that a bunch of times, but now I mostly use it for reference. Oh, Auntie Ellie, we should look up the liver before we forget."

Simon pulls the book off the shelf, tosses it on the table, and pulls out a kid-sized red plastic chair for Sophie.

"Let's see what we can learn about the liver, but only if we can look up the intestines afterward, because I think they're really interesting. Did you know your small intestine is seven meters long? So if we stretched yours out, it would probably be about four times the length of this table," he says.

"Really?"

"Yeah, I'll show you." He starts flipping through the book, looking up *I* for *intestine*, and nods at me over her head. I take this as my cue to leave.

"I'll be back in an hour, Soph. I'll just be downstairs if you need me," I say, but she doesn't even look up. She's too busy looking at pictures of innards.

When I come back to pick Sophie up, the entire white sheet on the table is filled with drawings. It looks like they each worked from one end to meet in the middle, the left half of the canvas doodled by an adult pretending to be a child—planets, and superheroes, and turkey traces of his hand; the right by a not particularly artistic child—the now usual walled gardens and flowers and stick figures that populate my crowded cast. I wonder what they talked about over crayons and, based on the crumbs dotting the table, cookies too. Did Simon just come out and say it: *So let's have a chat about your mum being stabbed*? Or did he earn her trust first with play and sweets?

"Hello!" they both say in unison when I walk in, the two of them immediate teammates in Operation Doodle Therapy, relaxed and cheery, as close to playground demeanor as Sophie gets. I feel like I'm intruding and want to leave Sophie behind in his yellow-walled room, let her spend another hour with this man who somehow managed to transform her back into something closely resembling a child.

"Hey, guys," I say, my expectations raised irrationally by the doodle-filled paper. Is it too much to ask that Simon throw his arms up in the air and pronounce Sophie cured, silly to hope that tonight she'll sleep straight until morning, without the bad man visiting her dreams, without her drenching the sheets in sweat and urine?

I look at Simon—with his arms like a diorama of the Rockies, a tiny space between his two front teeth, a scar on his left ear, no doubt left behind from a ridiculous earring, and hairless, without even a wisp of an eyebrow—and I can see an entire integrated being, complicated and simple. This guy could save Sophie.

"So we're on for next week," he says, his thumb and forefinger poised like guns.

"Okay," I say.

"Bye, Simon," Sophie says, smiles at him, and gives her mother's wave. One hand, one finger at a time. If I didn't know better, I'd swear she's flirting.

22

My parents arrive with fanfare. A riotous mixture of cell-phone calls, e-mails, and texts; the blow by blow, in a flurry of technological innovation, as they check off each of their travel steps. When we're all home, dotting the East Coast with theoretical push-pins, whole weeks will go by when I won't hear from either one of my parents, both too busy and interested in their own lives to bother with my and my brother's quibbles.

My father, a professor, occupies himself with his inexhaustible research on the Civil War, the aftermath of which he has devoted his entire adult professional life to analyzing. He never bores of Abe Lincoln and Jefferson Davis, the Free-Soilers and the Know-Nothings, the abolitionists, and his particular parcel of the puzzle, Reconstruction, a topic on which he has written five very large books printed by very small academic presses. I plan to read at least one all the way through before I die. My mother spends her days consumed by her patients and her nights fulfilling the romantic vision she has of her own life: She sits in a French bistro—she has managed to find one that covertly allows smoking in today's smoke-free Manhattan—with a clove cigarette, of which she takes only an occasional drag, its purpose more for the billowing effect, a glass of red wine, a three-quarters-empty bottle on the table, and a yellow pad for her longhand notes on the Freudian novel she has been writing since I was a kid. It's called *Oedipal, Shmedipal.*

Now that we are all together on this country-island, my parents liberated from the library and the couch, they suddenly change course and become communication junkies. The first call comes while they are still on the plane. They sound anxious and jittery, desperate to escape the indignity of modern airline travel. My phone rings when they clear customs, again when they flag a black cab. Check-in to the hotel goes without a hitch, another reason to call me, since they "thought I might be worried." Not sure why I'd worry, seeing as both my parents are extensive travelers and surprisingly competent people.

My mother calls a fifth time, less than fifteen minutes before we are meeting for dinner, while I'm busy putting on mascara for the first time in months.

"Who are you and what have you done to my mother? You're starting to freak me out," I answer, when I see the caller ID.

"What do you mean, Eleanor?"

"In real life I hear from you, what, maybe every few weeks, and you've called a hundred times today. What's up?"

"You do realize this is real life, right?" my mother asks. "Just because you're far from home doesn't mean this is not real life."

"You've been here less than two hours and you're already starting with the shrink talk? Amazing."

"I am just saying that—"

"How about this? I am going to hang up and finish getting dressed and I'll see you in fifteen minutes."

"Wonderful. I like when you take control and say what you want. You used to be more passive–aggressive, like your father. Maybe England is doing you good."

"Love you, Jane. Hanging up now."

"Love you, too, sweetheart. Oh, and make sure to put on some lipstick. Studies show it's one of the quickest ways to boost self-esteem."

My dad has chosen the restaurant well, one of London's new hat-tips to the idea of a culinary renaissance, a shameless citywide attempt to repair the crushing and well-earned reputation of British cuisine. Here, fish and chips and wet, mayonnaisey sandwiches have been upgraded to delicious panko-crusted ahi and spit-fire-roasted guinea fowl with sea salt. The restaurant hums and flickers, and we sit around a low dark-wood table in a high-backed brown leather booth; the effect is a familial cave. The high ceiling, with elaborate moldings skirting the edges, is the only reminder that we are eating in a converted house.

My parents sit next to each other and make an attractive pair. My mother's muted graying hair hangs long and loose and wavy, probably too long for her age. Still, there is something girlish about her figure that makes it work. My father keeps his bright silver hair cropped short, and he wears his usual uniform—an old hunter-green corduroy sports coat and khaki pants.

"You look different," Jane says, once we are seated and she has a wineglass in hand, giving me that critical mother stare known the world over. The one that calculates the addition of wrinkles and extra weight, as if any gains in either department count as demerits to them in some grand cosmic score. I wonder how many points she'd lose if I got divorced.

Lucy used to give me the same look when we hadn't seen each other in a while. A literal sizing up.

"You look beautiful," my dad says. "As always."

"No, Christopher, she looks tired. And undergroomed. Is that dirt under your fingernails?"

"Please. Just stop," I say. I'm exhausted from Sophie's nightmares, from battling cold and fog and rain to walk a block despite the fact that it is almost July, and from the damn tube, which is cramped and muggy, regardless of the temperature outside. I'm exhausted from living in a place I don't know or understand and from feeling incompetent because I have to ask an eight-year-old whether I'm supposed to tip the Chinese delivery guy and where to buy some new underwear. I'm exhausted from grief, from the uncertainty of my marriage, from having to get through another day without Lucy, a person I am wondering now if I've ever even met. I'm exhausted and don't have the energy to defend myself against my mother, who happens to have this scary ability to always be right.

And I'm not being fair; my mother is not judging me for the cosmic tally. She's never cared about what other people think of us. She gave that up years ago, when she embraced what she calls, in uncharacteristically un-PC terms, "native wear"—my mother, for some reason only understood by her, loves to wear kimonos, saris, grass skirts, the occasional kilt. She says the outfits are part of her quest to find her "authentic self" and untether herself from cultural expectations. Needless to say, as teenagers, Mikey and I found her style infinitely embarrassing. Now we are just amazed by her stubborn ability to keep it up.

Tonight my mother is mentioning my appearance not to be critical. She knows me. Knows that when I'm not looking all that great, chances are I'm not feeling all that great either. I do look tired. I do have dirt under my fingernails. And my eyebrows are long enough to braid or, if I were an edgier sort or really my mother's daughter, twirl into dreadlocks.

"That cast. I get the whole 'please-sign-my-cast'-so-you-feel-like-you-have-more-friends-than-you-do thing—in fact, I may recommend it to some patients—but, sweetheart, it's a little . . . mangy."

"I think it's adorable. Look at that. Who drew all the flowers? Sophie?" my dad asks, pointing to a signature near my wrist.

"Yeah, all of these are from her."

"How lovely! Isn't that what the Brits say, *lovely*? And *cheers*."

"Yes, dear," Jane says, and pats my father's arm. The gesture is warm and loving. She has started humoring him. She never used to do that. "How are they, by the way? Sophie and Greg."

"You know, not bad. They're okay. I mean, I guess they're hanging in there."

"Listen, I didn't mean to make you feel bad before about the way you look, love. See, that's British, *love*. I'm just worried about you, Eleanor. This moving-to-London thing doesn't seem very well thought out," my mother says.

"That's because it's not. But maybe that's not a bad thing. Who says everything has to be thought out? Haven't you two ever done anything that wasn't well thought out but you couldn't help yourselves?"

My parents look at each other, a blush starting on my mother's cheeks and making its way over to my father's, like the wave at a baseball game.

From the guilty look on their faces, I'm pretty sure that sometime in the last ten hours, my parents joined the mile-high club.

* * *

We retire to the pub next door for a nightcap. My father is still recovering from the bill he offered to pay long before we sat down to eat. "How often do I get to take my two favorite girls out?" he had said; "it will be my pleasure," he had said, an extravagance he now clearly regrets.

"I don't understand it," he says, holding up a dollar bill to the minimal light—a votive candle in a glass holder—to get a better look. "How can something that once was worth something be worth nothing? And they can track it. Isn't that amazing? Every single day, every single minute, this dollar I have in my hand changes value relative to the pound." My dad is a lot like Sophie, I realize now. He's never outgrown his curiosity about the world. Because of Google, tomorrow my mother will be forced to endure a two-hour lecture on currency fluctuation, a subject he will become an expert on overnight and take to with the conviction of a Scientologist.

"Everything in life is like that. Nothing is constant," Jane says, with a small smile, an acknowledgment of her own fickleness.

"Yeah, you never know what's going to happen. You can be alive today and then dead tomorrow. Just like that." I'm thinking back to that Thursday, when I taught a class, picked up the dry cleaning, and then learned that I had lost my best friend. Alive. Dead. Nothing to Google there. Wikipedia has no explanations for what is simultaneously clear and unfathomable.

"Actually, not a great example, Ellie. Because you can't be dead today, alive tomorrow," my father says, unmoved by my foray into the morbid and, unlike most men his age, comfortable approaching the subject of the inevitability of death. He finds his colleagues' shameless bids for immortality through scholarship embarrassing. Instead, my father is a process man and harbors no delusions about the lasting impact of his work or his life. He is here for this one circle ride, not even turning to Mikey and me as a form of legacy; for him, this go-around—his go-around—is sufficient.

"Yup, you're right. Alive. Then dead. No going back. It's a fucking one-way ticket."

"Eleanor," Jane says.

"What?" I snap.

"Nothing." She shoots a look at my father, the same one she used to give him years ago at the every-other-weekend handoff, when I was sixteen and as difficult as any other teenager. An *oy vey* look, which I know right now I fully deserve. After playing parent to Sophie, it somehow feels a little too natural to regress around my own.

The waitress brings over our drinks, three honey-colored pints, whatever was on tap, since my parents were excited to use that word: *pint*. No doubt we'll be eating bangers and mash tomorrow, just for the novelty of the words.

I am not sure why I'm suddenly sullen and uncooperative. I want to claw at my parents for comfort, turn to them the way Sophie and I have been turning to *The Secret Garden*, for soothing and for refuge. Of course, my parents would be horrified; for my family, or at least for my mother, independence is sacrosanct. I am thirty-five, almost midlife, and for some reason I want my parents to tell me what to do and then complain about them being overbearing. I want to be tucked in, the way Phillip used to do it, locking the blanket over my shoulders, like a swaddle, a kiss first on my forehead, then my lips.

Even more, I want someone to promise me that there is no evil in the world, that people we love do not get murdered on the daily school run. And I want the daily aftershocks to stop, that horrible way my back stiffens and my stomach drops every time I think about the face of the man on the cover of the *Daily Mail*. When I think of Lucy *choosing* to leave Sophie behind.

Mikey arrives a few minutes later, saving us from the awkwardness I have unnecessarily created. I want to apologize, give them a *don't mind me, just having a rough go of things*. I will be lightness and accommodation from here on out. This trip is a vacation for them, after all.

"Michael!" my mother says.

"Mikey!" my father and I say in unison.

"Hey, guys," my brother says, and circles around the table, giving us each a kiss on the cheek, a bemused expression on his face when he notices our parents are holding hands under the table.

"So, how was the date?" my mother asks, saving me from having to pry. I'm dying to know if he and Claire hit it off.

"Um, great, actually. I mean . . ." He pauses, as if he is looking for the exact right thing to say. "Okay, I hope I'm not jinxing anything here, but I think I just had the best date of my life. She's amazing. And smart. Beautiful. And she's a closet sci-fi nerd, can you believe it? She has all the *Next Generation* DVDs. We're going out again tomorrow."

"When can we meet her?"

"Don't rush him," I say, remembering the first time my mother met Phillip. She called him "a bland foot soldier on the wrong side of the war against materialism." All because he was wearing a Tag Heuer watch that his father had given him as a college graduation present. It took me months—long after she had grown to appreciate his intellect and charm and, better yet, the way he treated me—to confess that he wasn't a director of a nonprofit, as I had originally told her, but an investment banker.

She wasn't surprised. Apparently the fact that he wore cuff links had already given him away.

"So you're in love with a capitalist," she'd said, and shrugged it off. "I knew you were bound to rebel at some point." And when my rebellion turned into a marriage, she'd shrugged again. "I never said bland was a bad thing in a partner."

"Yeah, not so sure I'm ready to spring my parents on her after one date. But she's already been thoroughly vetted by Ellie, so don't worry."

"We're not worried, honey," my mother says, and my brother and I exchange glances at the fact that my parents are once again united as a we. "Just excited."

"I can't remember the last time it was just the four of us sitting at a table together," my father says.

"It's almost never been just the four of us. Even when you guys were little. Lucy was always around, or one of Michael's friends."

Everyone goes silent for a moment, in honor of Lucy, and I start half choking, half sobbing, which is ridiculous, given that the mention of her name is nothing new: I live in her house and look at her things and Sophie talks about her fifteen times a day. I should be habituated by now. *Lucy, Lucy, Lucy.*

"Sorry," I say. "I'm fine."

"How's the arm?" Mikey asks, changing the subject with such ease that I want to kiss him.

"Unbelievably itchy. I've done everything I can to scratch it, even stuck a letter opener up the cast, but it doesn't work. No relief whatsoever."

"Well, we have news," my mother says, unconcerned and uninterested in the state of my arm. My mother does not believe in the art of indulgence.

"You're pregnant," Mikey says.

"Twins!" I say, feeling like we are kids again, in cahoots.

"You're not funny."

"It's kind of funny, Jane," my dad says, and smirks. "A sixty-seven-year-old woman gave birth to twins last year. Granted, she used fertility treatments, but who knows what you get up to in your free time? You're only sixty."

"And you are looking a little heavy, Mom," Mikey says.

"And that glow," I say.

"I am looking quite svelte, thank you very much. And that glow is because your father and I . . . well . . . we're getting married again."

"Are you serious? I mean seriously? You're serious," I say, once I regain a limited capacity for speech. "You really think this is a good idea?"

"Of course we're serious. We couldn't be happier." My mother turns to my father, and a look of such naked longing passes between them that I find I'm the one blushing.

"But . . . but, Dad," Mikey says. "What about what happened last time?"

"You don't get it. We're getting married. You guys should be happy for us."

"What if she changes her mind? It will kill you," I say.

"Don't be ridiculous. I'm not changing my mind. And, if I do, he's in the hands of a qualified mental-health professional."

"That's exactly what we're afraid of," Mikey says.

"My beautiful Jane, I don't get it." My dad shakes his head sadly at my mother, his ex-wife, now his fiancée. "Why are our children so damn cynical about love?"

The next morning, before my parents head to Paris on an early-evening train, my mother and I set off to explore the city on our own. Mikey and my father are at the new British Library, where they have secured their reading-room passes long in advance, so they can happily geek out together among the fourteen million books and archival collections. My mother and I have what we consider a more ambitious agenda. Tate Modern, Borough Market, London Bridge—perhaps the ideal summer morning on a holiday in London. At the Tate, the artwork becomes an afterthought. We are taken with the sheer bulk of the place, with the cool, grim steel-and-warehouse feel of the entrance, Turbine Hall, where you have no choice but to look six flights up at the ceiling. Your neck stretches back, the same way little kids examine the stars.

Afterward, we walk along the Embankment until we reach Borough Market, where the immediate smells, which hit hard and rich, ignite our appetites. We cobble together brunch from the vast array of indoor stands—stinky cheeses, and dried meats, and a soufflé. Some of the finest food and produce in all of Europe under one slanted glass roof; a strange combination of the sophisticated and the primal—gourmands shop for the perfect slab or slice or pick from stuff freshly dug up or recently slaughtered.

"I forgot what a great traveler you are," I tell my mother, as we sip fresh organic apple cider because, though it's summer, the air still has that crisp British bite. "You should be a professional vacationer."

"The pursuit of pleasure is a skill like any other," my mother says, and then laughs at her own haughtiness. "Kidding aside, it's nice to just revel every once in a while, isn't it? I do this in New York all the time. Just play tourist."

After we stuff ourselves silly and even pick up a few things to take along with us—I buy an eggplant, which in all likelihood will never get cooked but is still something small and beautiful that I want to be mine—we continue on to London Bridge, to cross back over to the north side of the Thames.

"I love that bridge. I think it's the most beautiful bridge in all of London, maybe the whole world," my mother says, stopping to point down the river at the elaborate Tower Bridge, which is parallel to the one we are standing on. It's glorious in the sunlight, almost Disneyesque, with its golden spires, blue ropes, and Victorian towers shooting up from the water.

"Let's walk across it, if you like that one better," I say, eager to please after having been so ill-behaved last night. The morning feels stolen and luxurious and a balm for my raw feelings, a rare gift from my mother, whose presence, more often than not, has the tendency to chafe.

"Nah, you can't see how beautiful it is while you're on it. It's one of those things that you can only appreciate from far away."

We take a few pictures with my mother's digital camera, first my mother posing, then me, and then us together, taken with my own outstretched hand.

"Hey, Jane, did you used to love *The Secret Garden* when you were growing up too?"

"No, not at all. Frankly, I've always thought that book was overrated. I never understood why you and your father liked it so much. All that garden stuff seemed a bit hokey to me."

"But you read it to me when Nan died, to help me, you know, deal with it."

"I didn't read it to help you. I read it to help your dad."

"What?"

"He was absolutely distraught when his mother died. And I knew it was his favorite book when he was a kid, even though his sisters used to tease him that it was 'girlie.' Poor guy had to hide it under his mattress like it was a *Playboy* or something. Anyhow, I thought seeing me read it to you would make him feel better. Remind him of the circle of life and all that."

"So I was a stage prop?"

"That's one way to put it."

"Did it work? Dad seeing you read it to me?"

"I don't think he even noticed, to be honest. He was too out of it."

"I assumed it was a great book for children dealing with grief. I've been reading it with Sophie because I thought that's why you read it to me."

My mother looks at her bridge for a while, taking in its gleam from afar.

"Who knows? Maybe it is."

Part
Two

Oh! The things which happened in that garden!
If you have never had a garden, you cannot understand,
and if you have had a garden, you will know that it
would take a whole book to describe all that
came to pass there.

—THE SECRET GARDEN

23

Phillip left me once, about ten months after we lost Oliver. He left me—walked out, said, *sayonara; adios, amiga*—via magnetic poetry on our refrigerator door, no less. Even worse, it was a Wednesday, an average, midweek Wednesday.

I was given one line, ten words, if you count the ampersand, as a consolation prize, after well more than a thousand days of matrimony—of sharing a home, kissing each other good night, comparing workdays, cuddling up, body to body, to face the long, dark stretch of night. Of saying I love you—making sure to say it just once in case it was the last—before boarding a plane.

Phillip's message in its entirety: *U Don't C Me So I Go Now & Leave.*

I would have been angry, then, if I knew how long he'd been gone. At the time, I didn't know, I really didn't. Two days, maybe three? So I couldn't blame him, could I? Maybe he had left me on a Monday, after all. Instead, I felt sorry and sad and distant, like I was watching someone else get left on television.

Phillip was right to walk out at that point. I had stopped paying attention to him for a while, so much so that I didn't notice fewer shirts hanging in the closet, his keys not left on the counter, the toilet seat down. I noticed that his body didn't take up half the bed, I did notice that, but I figured he told me he was going on a business trip and I'd forgotten. Or I hadn't listened in the first place.

For that year after Oliver, I admit, I stopped listening. Phillip tried to be there for me, tried everything, and nothing stuck.

"Why didn't you tell me Scott's wife has cancer?" I asked, not two weeks before the Magnetic Incident, as we came to call it and eventually, at least once, to laugh about it. "I never would have told her she looked like she lost weight."

"I did tell you, Ellie," he said. "You just never listen."

"I would have heard cancer, Phillip. I mean, I know I don't know her that well, but I would have heard cancer."

"You would have," he said. "But you didn't."

Now, a year later, after we reunited with surprising ease just twenty-four hours after I saw the writing on the fridge—one session of marital counseling, and promises by both of us to make the other feel visible and important—I still wonder about what I missed. A year's worth of his words, maybe, piled high into a heap somewhere when they went unabsorbed by me.

And now it's Phillip turn to block. For four full weeks, he has screened the voice mails, the e-mails, the faxes I have zipped home, never answering, likely never even listening to or reading them. My thoughts treated as spam. Phillip has said that I will break his heart, and now he's doing it for me. This is heartbreak checkmate.

Maybe his radio silence begs me for a grand gesture, but I need to be here for Sophie. I still need to tuck her in, each and every night, to soothe her with images of secret gardens and refuge among thick rose-covered walls. And there is the glass of water I have to leave by her bedside, every night.

Perhaps these are the most frightening moments of married life: when you turn to your partner and realize you have promised to spend the rest of your life with someone you no longer recognize. Someone you can no longer even see.

I think about the Magnetic Incident while I snoop in Lucy's office again, this time looking for evidence of her marital unraveling. If I had bothered to ask Lucy to pinpoint her home spot while she was alive, I wonder if this would have been it: this chair, this view, a scrappy oasis.

My alibi is established. If Greg or Sophie asks why I'm up here, I am preparing a lecture on microcredit. No matter that I've already made my calls to the dean and taken a sabbatical; I have bought six months to figure my life out, to make my grand continental choices.

I power up Lucy's laptop and crack her e-mail password in two attempts. She would have picked something more challenging, I figure, had she really not wanted me to peek. Password attempt number one: *Sophie*. Number two gets me through: *Lulu*, her father's nickname for her when she was little.

I scroll through her in-box, which, except for the e-mails to and from René Devereaux interspersed, looks exactly like mine. Stuffed with the thousands of back and forths between us. I open one at random from about three weeks before she died.

To: Ellie Lerner, ellie.lerner@yahoo.com
From: Lucy Stafford, anamericangirlinlondon@yahoo.com
Subject: Feeling tight, tight, tight
Hey, do you do Kegel exercises? Please advise.

To: Lucy Stafford, anamericangirlinlondon@yahoo.com
From: Ellie Lerner, ellie.lerner@yahoo.com
Subject: Re: Feeling tight, tight, tight
Nope. Being loose has never been my problem. Why?

From: Lucy Stafford, anamericangirlinlondon@yahoo.com
To: Ellie Lerner, ellie.lerner@yahoo.com
Subject: Re: Feeling tight, tight, tight
Just read a magazine article that says that we should. Instead, I think we should go find this Dr. Kegel and kick his ass. We women already have enough to deal with.
By the way, did I tell you I'm getting laser hair removal? It hurts like hell, but can you imagine for the rest of your life never having to shave again? Absolute heaven.

My heart starts to beat fast, too much blood pumping at once, and I begin to sweat right through the chill in the room. Lucy is alive, she must be, there are all these e-mails here. She can't be dead, not when I look around this room. Dead people don't have e-mail drafts. But there it is, Lucy is gone, and her words are left behind, a pile of them right here on the screen, some of them unfinished, reluctantly speaking for her.

I pick a René e-mail at random from her in-box.

From: René Devereaux, renedever@gmail.com

To: Lucy Stafford, anamericangirlinlondon@yahoo.com

Subject: ILU

I miss you, I miss you, I miss you.

From: Lucy Stafford, anamericangirlinlondon@yahoo.com

To: René Devereaux, renedever@gmail.com

Subject: Re: ILU

Me too, baby. See you after work? Same place as usual?

From: René Devereaux, renedever@gmail.com

To: Lucy Stafford, anamericangirlinlondon@yahoo.com

Subject: Re: ILU

Oui. Oui.

From: Lucy Stafford, anamericangirlinlondon@yahoo.com

To: René Devereaux, renedever@gmail.com

Subject: Re: ILU

I love your oui-oui.

From: René Devereaux, renedever@gmail.com

To: Lucy Stafford, anamericangirlinlondon@yahoo.com

Subject: Re: ILU

Enfant terrible. What am I going to do with you?

From: Lucy Stafford, anamericangirlinlondon@yahoo.com

To: René Devereaux, renedever@gmail.com

Subject: Re: ILU

You're going to marry me.

From: René Devereaux, renedever@gmail.com

To: Lucy Stafford, anamericangirlinlondon@yahoo.com

Subject: Re: ILU

Name time and place.

From: Lucy Stafford, anamericangirlinlondon@yahoo.com

To: Greg Stafford, gregericstafford@gmail.com

Subject: Dinner

Hey. Won't be home for dinner. It's going to be a late one at work.

Kiss Sophie for me, will you? xx, Lu

I feel the shame of the voyeur. I should not be here, sitting in Lucy's chair, reading her most private e-mails with her lover, her false excuses to her husband. Still, I can't seem to stop. There are hundreds of love letters, and each one gives me a new angle, a toe dip into her other life.

From the early hours of the morning, just three days before Lucy died:

From: Lucy Stafford, anamericangirlinlondon@yahoo.com

To: René Devereaux, renedever@gmail.com

Subject: what are we doing?

Are we doing the right thing? I've always believed we are each entitled to grab up as much happiness as we can in this world, but do you think we're going too far? Taking more than we deserve?

Xoxo, Lu

PS—I am so happy with you sometimes it actually hurts.

From: René Devereaux, renedever@gmail.com

To: Lucy Stafford, anamericangirlinlondon@yahoo.com

Subject: Re: what are we doing?

Yes, we're doing the right thing. Anyway, I don't think we have any other choice. Can you imagine ever going back now? I can't.

Je t'aime.

Now go practice your French.

Xoxo, R

PS—Have you told Ellie yet? I bet you'll feel better when you do.

From: Lucy Stafford, anamericangirlinlondon@yahoo.com

To: René Devereaux, renedever@gmail.com

Subject: Re: what are we doing?

No. But I will. Soon. Promise. I just know she's going to hate me forever.

Here is where I finally stop; the mention of my name, probably what I was hunting for all along, now feels like a line I shouldn't cross. Lucy was still figuring out how to tell me when the man stepped out on the mews and ended things, once and for all. The man who I saw today in Pret A Manger, when Sophie and I were there to pick up lunch now that school has finally broken for summer; the man who followed us up Portobello Road when we went to see Simon; the man who stands behind me right now; I feel his heavy, coated breath on my neck. The man who my rational mind knows is in jail, who will likely stay there forever if the family liaison officer is right, and yet I feel him here, too, I feel him everywhere, following and infiltrating Lucy's office, her home spot. Robbing us of this moment even—Lucy wanted to tell me, she was going to tell me, and of course I wouldn't have hated her forever.

I think back seven months to the last time I saw Lucy, New Year's in Boston, and she accused me of having an early midlife crisis.

"L, stop your whining," Lucy had said. "What's wrong with you? I feel like one of these days you're going to just walk out on Phillip, buy yourself a Porsche, and sleep with that sexy kid in your class, you know, that kid John or Jack or whatever that you had the dream about. Be happy with what you've got. You have the real thing, you know? You are married to the man you love. What more can you ask for?"

"I'm just saying I'm itchy, that's all. This can't be it, can it? Is this my adult life? Because if this is it, if this is what it's going to be from now on, then that's just depressing."

"Come on, maybe you guys should start trying again."

"You don't understand, Luce. You don't understand what it's like to want something and not get it. You've always had everything." I was thinking about Sophie and her brown plastic glasses and soft, snaggled hair. I was thinking about shopping for little-people clothing and the indentation of a round head against my collarbone. After Oliver, we did make some halfhearted attempts to "try again," and then we didn't, and the whole time I was vibrating naked fear. Wanting may be the worst feeling of all, next to hope. But hope is the worst. Hope is the moment before peeing on the negative stick. Hope is the moment before they tell you they can't find a heartbeat. Hope is a setup, a bait and switch, an illusion.

Lucy didn't say anything back, and I realize now, from this bizarre time-travel perch, that she knew exactly what I meant. She knew what it meant to want, to feel stuck and lost, all at once. One of those inhumane mousetraps: Your feet are glued down, and yet you can still look around, horrified to find that you can't break free. That it's not as simple as just taking a couple of steps away.

24

Last night, Sophie refused to eat our healthy dinner of fish sticks and ketchup—two food groups covered: protein and vegetable—because the items were touching on the plate. When I insisted she eat it anyway, she used the line I had been waiting to hear since I arrived in London:

You are not my mother.

The moment was less painful than I had imagined. She looked so fussy and cute, rejecting dinner in a reenactment of every childhood cliché, furious over something as silly as the meeting of ketchup and fish, that all I could do was indulge her fit. I switched her plate with mine and tried not to laugh.

Poor Greg is awaiting an even more hurtful statement, one he confessed he's sure she'll let slip at some point, the one he's scared is true: *I wish it were you who died instead of Mummy.*

"I'm sorry for what I said last night," Sophie says now, during our short break between *The Princess Diaries* and *The Princess Diaries II*. The rain, hard and blurring, drums hypnotically and lulls Sophie and me into spending this wonderful, miserable day on the couch.

Our bodies melt into the leather, our limbs useless. We have accomplished nothing, comforted by the knowledge that this is nature's way of saying we should, in fact, waste this Friday eating prawn-cocktail kettle crisps and watching G-rated movies, occasionally discussing the ingenious and brave person—a Brit, no doubt—who first took that great leap for mankind and united potato chips with shrimp flavoring.

"Don't worry about it."

"I. Just. Yeah." She cups her elbows in frustration, a tic I've noticed happens whenever she bumps up against her limited vocabulary. She knows what she wants to say, only she's not yet armed with the words.

"Seriously, Soph, not a big deal. You were right. I'm not your mother. But so you know, just because I'm not your mom doesn't mean I can't tell you what to do."

"I know."

"Like in our book, right? Mary's better off when she isn't doing what she wants when she wants."

"Yeah, I guess."

"You're still little."

"I'm not *that* little. I am forty-two inches tall. That's the twentieth percentile for height. Daddy measured me and then looked it up."

"I meant you're still young," I say now.

"But you said little."

"I meant young."

"So why didn't you say young?"

I hate when Sophie reminds me of why she has so few friends.

* * *

The doorbell rings at five o'clock. Sophie, antsy from being inside all day, jumps at the distraction, tail wagging.

"Can I get it?" she asks, already at the door, hand on the knob to swing it open. I am too lazy to join her, opting instead to move to the warm spot she just vacated.

"Check the peephole."

"Can't reach."

"Stand on your tippie tippie toes. Who is it? The mailman?"

"Oh, my God! Oh, my God! Oh, my God!" Sophie screams and jumps up and down, clapping her hands. For more than a childish moment, I think it's Lucy through the hole in the door, that there's been some gross misunderstanding and she's home now, for good. She'll sit us down and tell us a riveting story, something heartbreaking and funny and impossible, just like Lucy.

"Who is it?" I am standing now, moving toward the front hallway.

"Uncle Phillip!"

Of course, Uncle Phillip.

Sophie swings the door open, and there is my husband, without a coat, arms full of bags, his sweater splotched by the rain. No, my dead friend is not standing next to him, and if I wasn't so overcome with relief at seeing Phillip, I would slap myself for my ridiculous optimism. It's like the start of a bad joke: *How many people does it take for Ellie to believe she will never see Lucy again?*

Phillip—his familiar slope of shoulder, his woodsy smell, the way his hair curls in the rain—makes my heart hurt, and I'm overcome with homesickness and nostalgia and, yes, love too. I want to stick my nose in his neck, right under his ear, where there's a gentle slope, where I've always fit. I want to kiss his perfect mouth, the mouth I've always thought of as mine.

"Soph-a-loaf," Phillip says, dropping his luggage inside and scooping her up in a hug in one impressive move. He shakes his hair onto her, wet-dog style, and she giggles that old Sophie giggle. Right now she is eight again. "How did you get so big? Seriously, you are, like, a foot taller since the last time I saw you. And what's that behind your ear?"

Phillip distracts Sophie and manages to pull a bouquet of fake flowers from his sleeve. He has just stepped off a seven-hour flight, and he's already her one-man show. He used to entertain me like this too. When I was pregnant, he would croon to my belly in a spot-on Frank Sinatra imitation of "Fly Me to the Moon."

"How'd you do that?" Sophie asks.

"A magician never tells his secrets," he says, and finally catches my eye above her head.

"Hey," I say, and move toward him.

I want to touch my husband's face.

"Hey," he says, flinching when I reach my hands to wipe a drop of water falling down his forehead. He eyes my pajamas and bare feet. I look a little too comfortable here, in this house that doesn't belong to me. Hopefully, there aren't crumbs on my top from the biscuits Sophie and I ate post-crisps. Once upon a time, Phillip used to feed me cookies after sex, so for a while there, the sweet tastes of chocolate and Phillip were one and the same.

I ignore his flinch, his concentrated focus on Sophie, and try to pretend like he hasn't ignored my telephone calls and e-mails for the past month. I miss my husband more than I realized. I see that now, as I stare at him, at his wet head and at his goofy magic tricks. I see that now, when I look at his platinum wedding ring on his long, slim man finger and remember how much that sliver of metal signifies.

Pull a coin out of my ear, I want to say.

Turn water into wine.
Make the sun come out.
Take me home.
What I say instead: "It's, um, good to see you."

The restaurant in the lobby of Phillip's hotel, the Royal Lancaster, is brightly lit and unforgiving. We can see too much of each other here, in our stiff-backed, wooden facing chairs. Through the windows, we can see Hyde Park, and its grassy vastness is menacing at night, its greens turned to black.

"Thank you for coming all the way here." I smooth the napkin in my lap, line up my silverware, set my chopsticks on their porcelain holder, move my wineglass from the table's edge. "It means a lot."

I direct my gratitude to the invisible speck on my fork that I flick away with my nail. I have trouble looking at Phillip. The familiarity of his face gives me vertigo. How many times have I looked at his eyes, his mouth, his lips, the angles of his cheeks, studied his terrain, like memorizing the states on a map? The tiny line on the left side of his nose, a scar from a long-ago scratch from our neighbor's cat. The beauty mark high on his forehead, just under his hairline. The faintest trace of a dimple, more a shadow than an indentation, that flashes when he smiles. I can't imagine ever loving another man's face the way I love Phillip's. I remember, when we were newlyweds, I would look at it with awe, the gaze of a mother at her newborn.

"We needed to talk in person, and . . . well, you weren't coming home anytime soon." His voice is stern, and he is fidget-free. Maybe he practiced on the plane.

"I've been trying to talk to you for weeks. You haven't been taking my calls. Or responding to my e-mails or my faxes. My next step was going to be smoke signals." I keep my voice light, borderline flirty.

"I respond well to skywriting."

"Yeah, priced it out. Way too expensive."

"I have an idea," he says, his tone different from mine. His is laced with sarcasm, angry and tired. "You could have just showed up. Like I did."

"I wanted to. I did. But—Sophie."

"She seems great."

"She's hanging in there. But things have been really rough on her. So, my parents picked a wedding date."

"I heard."

"Yeah, three months from today, actually. I'll come home for that, of course."

"Of course. You'll come home for *that*."

"Can you believe my parents are getting married again?" I ignore his cutting tone and keep mine steady, chipper even.

"They're gluttons for punishment. They must be crazy."

"Phillip?"

"What." A flat statement. No inflection of curiosity.

"Please don't hate me."

Phillip doesn't answer. He lets my remark hang there, his silence revealing its pathetic offering. We once promised to love and to cherish, and now what I feel entitled to ask of him is only this: a desperate plea that he not indulge in its opposite.

We drink a lot of wine. A bottle finished quickly, the fault of nerves and the quiet service, men in white tunics and elaborate belts who match the Thai-themed decor and refill my glass without my noticing. We order a second, another red, and only halfway through this one, once it saturates our blood and numbs our defenses, do we begin to have a normal conversation, back and forth, interrupting each other to carry the conversation forward as we've always done. Awkwardness cedes to comfort, to natural rhythms we both had thought were long forgotten. Discussion about *us* or *the future* is cast aside in favor of simple small talk and attempts to entertain the other. We rise to the occasion, our favorite audience back across the table, an opportunity for the subtle performances for which we are famous.

A potent reminder of why we got married in the first place: We've always made each other laugh.

When was the last time my husband and I sat across from each other in a restaurant, just the two of us, the sole purpose being to spend time together? I can't remember.

Phillip tells a silly story from work—his secretary wearing her skirt backward for an entire day and him spending just as long gathering the nerve to tell her. He agonized—which was worse, to tell or not to tell? He still doesn't know. I side with him in his not telling, though both seem unfairly cruel in their own way.

He asks about my broken arm, and I take him through the names scribbled on the plaster. I introduce him to Claire, who has signed in neat pink cursive and who, in less than one month of dating Mikey, has moved into his studio on Nottingham Court.

"They've gone from strangers to soul mates in five dates or less. I can't believe it," I say to Phillip, and point to Mikey's immature doodlings. An M ♥ C contained within an even larger heart with an arrow. "They're like sixteen-year-olds."

"I know. He said it's love at first sight. He sounds really happy." Phillip is right. When my brother actually finds a moment to call me, his words bleed together, manic and breathless. Everything in him moves a half step quicker now. That's what love does to my brother. He acts like he overindulged in Red Bull. "Funny that she's Sophie's teacher."

"Yeah, Claire is the best. Sophie will have someone else next year, though. School just got out a little while ago. They run till mid-July here."

"And who's this?" Phillip asks, pointing to SIMON, his block letters making his name command attention. I'm not sure we're ready to talk more about Sophie's coming school year, a conversation too loaded right now, too tied up in our own future. Simon seems like a safer option.

"Sophie's therapist. I think he's helping, but who knows? She seems to really like him. I swear she flirts with him."

"Aw, I thought I was the only one she flirted with."

"Sorry, you've got some competition now."

Phillip smiles at me, and for just a second I think we both forget everything, and we are just PhillipandEllie again, living our lives, sharing a delicious pad thai, spearing vegetables off the other's plate.

We continue our aimless, harmless chatter, letting it spin its comforting cocoon. Phillip tells me a neighborhood teenager backed into our car and left behind a small dent. Nothing major, though, nothing that can't be fixed. I tell him about how Sophie and I are reading *The Secret Garden*, which he, too, read once, back in college, when I told him it was one of my favorites. "A little too saccharine," he had said of the book. "But I think it's cute that you like it."

I don't tell Phillip about Lucy's grand plans, about digging through her draft e-mail. Her secrets aren't mine to share.

The check comes too early. It's unclear where we are going with this evening. I hope I'm allowed upstairs, at the very least to sleep in the same bed as my husband, to be given just a little longer with his face, but that's far from guaranteed. He's still wary of me, treading carefully. We jump-rope around conversational land mines.

We have not touched, not once.

And though I don't want to talk about our relationship, don't want to face our continental divide, I do want to touch him and have him touch me. I want to be held, too, maybe more than anything else. I want to lie in Phillip's bed, feel my back against his chest, sit in the chair made by his knees. To lean against him until our edges blur.

Jet lag is beginning to set in. Phillip's face hangs slack. Sad that I find myself here, nervous about approaching the subject of sleeping arrangements with my husband, even after mass quantities of alcohol. *He is your husband,* I remind myself. *Husband, husband, husband,* I repeat until the word has no meaning. I remember when we first got married and I would make up excuses to use the word: *Oh, that's my husband's. I'll ask my husband what he thinks. Have you met my husband?* Then, the term never lost its significance, only gained power in its use. I wanted to advertise our attachment to the world.

I can't tell whether Phillip is nervous or resigned, the latter so much worse, the former bringing me back to that vulnerable place of hope. Hope for what, though, I can't say. Hope that he still loves me, too, that we can make this work on different continents? Hope that he'll tie me up and drag me back home, and then we'll slip back into our old, empty life? Hope that he'll move here, and we can start over in this other country, one where I'm not so sure I even belong?

"I can come with you, right? Upstairs, I mean," I say instead, unable to meet Phillip's eyes. I'm ashamed of the pleading in my voice, but I have no choice. I have unwound us that far.

"We still need to talk, Ellie. We haven't done that yet."

"I know. Upstairs. We'll do that." He looks me up and down. I am wearing my black dress, the one I wore to Lucy's funeral. Crepe, belted, and more conservative than the occasion warrants. I wish I were wearing something daring and red, with a slit maybe, a dash of extra confidence in my new quest to seduce my husband. But I own nothing red in any country.

Yes, the plan is to seduce Phillip. My sex drive is back, the hourglass flipped again and full, the sand beginning a new slow leak.

This dress is not helping matters; right now I look a lot like his mother.

Phillip takes out his plastic key, and I follow him out of the restaurant. We step into the elevator, and then, like magic, we go up.

25

There are two beds in his room. Two. Fucking. Double. Beds. A cosmic joke. An extra negotiation. Lucy is up there somewhere, laughing her ass off at the fact that I no longer know how to make my husband have sex with me.

Two beds in this fussy and tasseled, overtly British hotel room. Two flowered duvets, crimson woven with gold, already turned down, and two notes reminding us to conserve water. Framed black-and-white photographs of London landmarks, Big Ben, Parliament, Tower Bridge, decorate the walls and add an edge of despair. Why go outside when you can see the sights right here in your room? We can get a taste of London just within this paisley-wallpapered oasis, with its impressive selection of complimentary teas and its dangling-pull-string lamps.

"So," I say, and remain standing, not sure which bed to pick and how to do this. Part of me just wants to take off my dress and see what happens. Could he reject me that way? Standing in front of him, naked?

"We need to talk, Ellie."

"Okay, so let's talk." I move closer to him and try to sustain eye contact.

"I think we both know where this is heading." He means our relationship, not the moment. I want him to mean the moment, but he looks so distressed there is no way he is thinking about sex. He is thinking about some inevitable end to us.

"Phillip." The red wine makes me brazen. I am going to flip things; I still can, it's not too late. It's never too late. Lucy's right: We are entitled to as much happiness as we can grab. "Phillip."

I reach up and touch his hair, brown and wavy. My fingers smooth right through it, brush a bit away that has fallen just shy of his eye.

His hand reaches up to catch mine, but it's a cruel gesture. Only a mini-handcuff of thumb to forefinger.

"Don't," he says.

"Please." I ignore my clear desperation, my shame overpowered by my desire to feel his skin. We are almost cheek to cheek now, and he is frozen, holding my wrist in the air, not sure how to play this. We look like samurai warriors in the silent, time-stop moment before the ass-kicking begins.

I kiss his jawline. I do, even though I know he doesn't want to be doing this with me right now. He wants to sit across a table, at least five feet between us, and work through the details. I am not ready yet—to talk about the future, to reap consequences.

"Ellie." His voice cracks in panic. His ears are too sensitive. I am not playing fair and I know it. "Please. We shouldn't."

I ignore him. Since I have no hands—one is still in a cast, the other caught in his—I use my face to turn his, to molest his other ear. He can't help but moan.

Next, his neck. My hand drops, a surrender on his part. He stands there, his arms at his sides, waiting. Just waiting. He has no fight left.

Nature. Habit. Instinct. He finds my mouth. We pick the bed on the right. The one closest to the window, the one with the story-book view of Hyde Park.

Afterward, while he sleeps, I rememorize his face. I trace the shading of his way-past-five-o'clock shadow. The slide from the top of his profile to under his eyes. That spot where my nose fits into his neck.

And when I wonder if it's all too late, if I'm too late, I weep without making a sound.

When I open my eyes, a shaft of sunlight through the drawn blinds, a white line across the center of the room, tells me it's morning. Phillip is out of bed already, showered and dressed and packed, waiting by the door. He is wearing a baby-blue cashmere sweater and the designer jeans with the flap pockets I forced him to buy last year, when we saw them on sale. They make him look ten years younger, like the boy I first saw in the library. His face is shaven, and lined, and I realize the new Phillip is back—the competent adult version, who is perfectly capable and happy to proceed with his day without me. His hand is resting on the plastic handle of his rolling executive suitcase, ready and eager to push it out the door.

"Hey." My voice is creaky. I am very hungover.

"Hey." He's doing that wincing thing again, like my friendly words and gestures are daggers.

"Last night was nice."

"We didn't talk. Ellie—"

"We can talk today."

"Ellie—"

"There's this great breakfast place around the corner—"

"I don't have time for breakfast."

"Come on, it's the most important meal of the day."

"I have a plane to catch."

"Today? You don't have to go. Not yet."

"Ellie—"

"Seriously, not yet."

"We can't keep putting this off."

A beat.

Please don't say it. Phillip, please don't say it. I am not ready. Not yet. Not today. Today is not the day I lose my husband.

"Phillip." I take a breath, ready to dive into my plea, resort to seduction again if I have to, but he beats me to it. "Please don't—"

"Ellie, I've already spoken with a lawyer."

"Please don't—"

"I want a divorce. This is all clearly . . . I don't know, over."

"But last night." I have no words, I have not practiced. Anyone would have known this was coming. And yet, having known doesn't help at all.

"Last night was a mistake. I guess all of our parts still work."

"But it was. I mean. Great. Wasn't it?" I don't wait for his answer, I keep talking. If I keep talking, he can't roll his suitcase out the door. I limit my goals. Damage control. Just keep him from walking out the door. "What about us?"

"This isn't a marriage."

"What was last night, then? Just a . . . a . . . a freaking pity fuck?"

"Ellie." His eyes are pleading, *please don't make this any harder*, but I can't help myself. I am scared, and the fear is morphing into rage. Rage seems easier than total emotional breakdown.

"Is that what I am to you? Someone who you can sleep with and then leave the next day?"

"Let's not."

"Let's not what? Fight? Tell the truth?"

"That's not the truth and you know it. I have better things to do than sit around and wait for my wife to come home. Actually, when you were home you weren't even home. So you know what? I have better things to do than sit around and wait for the woman I married to make a reappearance. I can't even remember the last time I saw her." He sounds like someone who used to be angry and now is just tired. He sounds like someone whose flight keeps getting delayed.

"Phillip—"

"I give up. Okay? Sometimes, you just have to quit. I'm done, I'm done." He shows me his palms; empty.

"So you flew all the way to London to tell me you want a divorce?" The word is still too new, too raw. I don't want a divorce. I want him to climb back into this bed, to make me feel like there is a place called home. To touch him again, reclaim his face.

No, I want to rewind back in time, to when we used to recognize each other. Maybe as far back as pre-Oliver.

"I came here to tell you in person. I figured even you deserved that much."

"Please don't do this." The tears have started and I hurt all over, my body and insides sore.

"Yeah, well."

"But I love you. Doesn't that mean anything to you?" A question, only half rhetorical.

"Ellie, please just let me go. You're not fair. This isn't fair," he says, and I can see now he's pleading too. He is desperate to get out of this room, to get out of this country even, as far as he can get from me.

"Why are you doing this? You know I have to be here for Sophie. You know I can't just get on a plane—"

"You really don't get it, do you? This isn't only about London. Actually, forget it. It doesn't matter anymore. Believe what you want. Good-bye, Ellie." He opens the door, and I see the carpeted hallway of the hotel, the route he will take to the elevator.

"Phillip."

"Please say good-bye to Soph for me, will you?"

He doesn't wait for an answer. A shy wave, and the treadmill sound of his suitcase rolling out the door behind him.

The whole thing takes less than two minutes.

About an hour after he leaves—an hour I have spent trying hard not to vomit up last night's red wine, an hour I have spent convincing myself that it will all be okay, that I can survive losing both Lucy and Phillip in one summer, an hour where I wonder if I will ever recognize myself again—there is a knock on the door. I run to it, let the rush of relief soothe me.

"Phillip! You came—"

"The gentleman ordered breakfast?" A man in a green polyester uniform and long, thin sideburns moves briskly into the room, pushing a rickety clothed table on wheels. When he notices my tear-streaked face, he looks away. "By the window?"

I nod. Look away too.

"Enjoy, madam." The room-service guy leaves quickly, without even pausing for a tip.

Phillip has ordered my favorite hangover meal; he remembered from college, probably the last time I had a hangover before moving to London—black coffee, eggs Benedict, extra hollandaise.

I force myself to eat it, even though the sauce is glutinous and my stomach is in revolt.

Every bite feels like a sucker punch.

26

H ey, where's Uncle Phillip? I drew him the most awesome picture of me and my fake thumb. Look, look," Sophie says, and
tugs on my shirt, moments after I walk in the door. I guess this is
where I live now: Lansdowne Road. Postcode: W11. "Auntie Ellie,
you're not looking."

"Wow, Soph. You did a great job with the knuckles." I glance at
her drawing—a stick figure with a disproportionate turkey hand.
What can I say? She did not do a great job with the knuckles. Sophie
is a terrible artist. She may grow up to be a journalist like Lucy, or a
lawyer like her father, perhaps even a novelist—her obsessive love of
reading has to be worth something—but I am not looking at the
next van Gogh.

"So?"

"So what?"

"Where's Uncle Phillip? I want to show him. Is he hiding?"
Phillip and Sophie used to play marathon games of hide-and-seek in
Sharon. She would explore every nook of the house, while Phillip,
squeezed into the kitchen cupboard, would wait patiently for her to

find him. Now Sophie walks to the hall closet and looks inside at a bundle of jackets: hers, Greg's, and Lucy's also. A heartbreaking gesture. Despite recent events, she has the optimism to interpret Phillip's absence as a form of sport. I wonder if somewhere, in the folded depths of her being, she believes that her mother, too, is just waiting for the right moment to reappear.

"Sweetheart, um, he left. He had to go back home. But he told me to tell you good-bye and that he loves you very much." I deliver my husband's message, kneeling in front of her, the way I've seen parents give children bad news in after-school specials. I am fooling no one with this stoic performance.

"But, but, I didn't even get a chance to . . . We were supposed to . . . Really? He left?"

"I'm so sorry."

"It's okay."

"Soph, you're allowed to be upset. Seriously, I understand if you want to cry or yell or something."

"Nah, it's okay. Really."

"Okay."

"Auntie Ellie?"

"Yeah?"

"Do you want some tea and biscuits?"

Her voice is full of adult efficiency, matter-of-fact and taking control. The tone I used at the funeral, when I realized that I was the one in charge. Taking my hand, she leads me to the kitchen and sits me down in what I've come to think of as our nook. Sophie fills the electric kettle, flips it on, and puts together a plate of cookies.

"Take some," she says, and nudges the tissue box toward me. I touch my face. A flood of tears that I hadn't even noticed or felt.

"So," she says, sitting next to me, patting my shoulder. "You want to talk about it?"

"Not really."

"Okay, do you want to just sit here quietly, then?"

"Yes, please." And so we do, without speaking, just like that night after Lucy's funeral. Sophie rests her head on my shoulder, and just like last time, when our world had cleaved and split in two, we sit here and wait until we have the strength to get back up.

Later, I call my father to give him the news: His daughter is graduating from marriage. I'll tell him first, because then he can tell my mother and I'm spared the psychologist's angle for now. I am not yet ready to analyze this and parse it down to its component parts. To shoulder the blame, which will inevitably fall my way.

My father and I have spent the last half hour discussing the floral arrangements for my parents' upcoming wedding. He has surprised us all by becoming a bridezilla, consumed wholly with the planning process, neglecting his Civil War research to call me up at all hours of the night to debate "signature cocktails." He wants something yellow, to match his tie and the boutonnieres. Personalized water bottles have been bought and secured for every table and labeled in accordance with the "theme": *Reunited and it feels so good*. My parents actually have a theme, like they're turning thirteen and are having a bar mitzvah, and my father intends to have those horrible song lyrics printed on every napkin. He is unswayed by my concerns that the event has taken a terrible turn for the tacky.

"Sweetheart, did you know they have magazines for weddings? Huge ones, like telephone books. An amazing industry. A whole subeconomy. Fascinating stuff."

"Dad, they're not called wedding magazines. They're called *bridal* magazines. For *women*."

"Whatever. I find them informative. There's so much to learn, and we have only three months."

"I know." My mother is rushing back toward the altar; given too much time, she'll bolt. "So, I have some news."

I have waited the hour to tell him, in the ridiculous hope that I can just slip this tiny detail into the conversation. If there is anyone who will let me off the hook with a twenty-second discussion, it's my father, who is much more interested in facts than emotions.

"Phillip left you, huh? I'm so sorry, honey."

"Yup. How'd you—"

"Come on, even I saw that one coming. You okay?"

"I don't know. Sometimes . . . Do you think I screwed up the best thing that's ever happened to me?"

"I think that marriage hasn't been the best thing that's ever happened to either of you for a while now. But, yeah, I do think things changed after you guys lost Oliver. You used to be great together. I love Phillip."

"I know."

"Ellie, I hate to say it, but he did the right thing. I know it hurts, but he had to cut himself loose. You weren't playing fair."

I cough, to shake the tears out of my voice. It's hard to hear that it's universally agreed this breakup is my fault. I had been expecting comfort, not blame. Blame, I've already got covered without my parents.

"Once I read a study about prisoners with a life sentence. The ones without the possibility of parole were happier than those who might get out. Defies logic, but then, not really. Sometimes it's the hope that kills you."

"So what are you saying? Being married to me was like being in prison?"

"Of course not. I'm just saying Phillip couldn't keep waiting. The poor man was miserable wondering when you were coming home. Worse, *if* you were coming home."

"But—"

"Fish or cut bait. Put up or shut up. Shit or get off the pot."

"I get it."

"Listen, honey, if you want to talk more about relationships, you should call your mother. You know she's better at this than I am."

"Okay."

"Sorry, I just realized I need to go. New wedding crisis."

"What is it this time, Dad?"

"I need to redo the seating chart."

"Why?"

"Darling, I need to switch you and Phillip over to the singles' tables."

Greg gets home after ten. Sophie has long been tucked in. A rereading of chapter twenty-five—just thirty pages until the end of *The Secret Garden*, though neither of us is ready—a glass of water by her bedside, a kiss on her forehead. A ritual, like all rituals, clung to and relied upon for relief and comfort.

"Hey, where's Phil—" Greg stops mid-sentence when he sees the bottle of scotch already opened, already poured. This is the second time I've had scotch in my entire life. The first being the Day of the Black Eye. "Oh."

"Yup."

"You okay?"

I shrug and make a silent toast with my glass. "Yeah, I guess."

"I'm sorry. You know I've been there." He sits down on the couch, too, but on the far end, and loosens his tie.

I pour him a drink, much smaller than my own.

"Which part are you going through now? The heartache? The anger? The replaying it all in your mind? Or have you gone straight to the exhaustion phase, when you think about having to start over with someone else?"

"Pretty much all of it at once. But the thought of dating—I haven't even gone there yet. That makes me feel sick. And the anger, yeah, that too. Oh, and guilt. Guilt is currently winning."

"It sucks."

"Yes. It. Does."

We drink in silence for a while, letting the liquid burn its way down, waiting to be anesthetized. I rest my head on the back of the couch and exhale.

"I am going to be okay, right?" I ask, because though this is my fault, I still need to hear someone say it: *You are going to be okay.* I need to know I'll be able to get out of bed tomorrow, and the day after that too.

"Yes. You are."

"But first Lucy. And now Phillip. I know it's not the same and that I sort of asked for it, and forgive me because I know you have it worst of all, but, holy shit, I don't know if I can do this. I really don't. Lose him too?"

"You can do this. You're going to be more than okay. We all deserve more than okay. We deserve all the happiness we can grab." I look at him and wonder if he knows he's parroting Lucy's words. Or maybe it's always been the other way around. Maybe she learned them from him. Took that lesson and used it as a weapon.

My tears start again, and Greg looks alarmed. He is the sort who can be undone by a crying woman. A box of tissues appears, offered without eye contact.

"Sorry," I say, and he waves my words away. "It's just that I'm thirty-five, and somewhere along the way I've lost my life. I don't know where I'm supposed to live. I don't have a career that I care about. I've lost my best friend, and now my husband. The one solid thing—which wasn't solid at all, not really—I don't have him either. What the hell am I doing? How did I get here?"

"I don't know. If it makes you feel any better, I'm a thirty-nine-year-old widower living in a house that I hate—I really hate this place, have I ever told you that? Lucy loves—loved—it, so we stayed. Being a lawyer can be so painfully tedious that every morning I have to talk myself into getting on the tube. And I have an eight-year-old daughter upstairs who it sometimes hurts me to look at. But I know I'll be okay. I can't say that all the time, but right now, in this very instant, I really believe I'll figure this out and I'll be okay. We all will."

"Maybe."

"Better than okay."

"You know what? You're right. We're going to be great." I join his rallying cry with the last bits of my energy.

"Like pigs in shite!" He beams at me, warmth and sunshine and fraternal love, and he brings his glass to clink mine. If our lives were a movie, this would be the scene where the music changes. We'd make eye contact—tentatively at first, then a pact—before we'd rip off each other's clothes and declare our undying love. We'd get to live happily ever after, in this pastel-colored house in Notting Hill, to swelling crescendo. A simple, natural, and, best of all, neat resolution. Sophie gets a mother, I get a child, Greg gets a wife. All solved in five minutes or less.

But this is not a movie, and things are never simple. Besides which I have no interest in seeing Greg naked. We are fellow soldiers at war—he is my brother, he is my comrade—and so there will be no falling into bed and easy cleanup. Our lives are not a puzzle that needs solving but blurry pieces, loose ends, competing loyalties. Resolution has no place in our story.

Instead, I will keep sitting here, sipping my scotch, and wondering who I've suddenly become without the people who most defined me.

27

———

"*There was every joy on earth in the secret garden that morning, and in the midst of them came a delight more delightful than all, because it was more wonderful—*" We are in Sophie's bed, cozy and comfortable, though it is still afternoon. I am in the middle of rereading some of the most moving lines from our book—Mary and Dickon see a red robin darting through the air and Burnett is at her magical best—when Sophie's words burst forth, hostile and without warning.

"Do you think I'm stupid?"

"What are you talking about?"

"It's a simple question: Do. You. Think. I'm. Stupid."

"Of course not. You're the smartest kid I know. What's going on, Soph?" I am not used to her tone, a sophisticated undercutting I don't think I developed until high school. Like her black eye, discordant with the rest of her.

"So if you think I'm so smart, then why didn't you tell me?" She points toward her yellow-sashed drapes, which block the window. I have closed them, hoping she wouldn't notice the commotion outside. The press, with their clipboards and cameras and incessant curiosity, are back for another round of stories. A knife has been found in a trash can behind the council flats in Westbourne Park, and the thing is apparently full of forensic goodies—dried blood and DNA and fingerprints. The final evidence that, fingers crossed, ensures this is an open-and-shut case. The man—who has a name, of course, printed in every newspaper in the country, though I refuse to use it, to dignify his existence that way—is looking at a life sentence. Nigel, our family liaison officer, has suggested we lay low for a few days. He has promised that the media attention will again blow over and has also reminded us that, though inconvenient, garnering sympathy is not necessarily a bad thing. The pictures of Sophie and me holding hands on the way to school, the focus on our linked fingers, have captured the public's imagination, increased both their interest and their outrage. The added pressure on Scotland Yard can only help us.

"Soph, I'm sorry. I wanted to protect you."

"Did you think I wouldn't notice? You haven't bugged me about going to the park in ages. And we haven't left the house in two days."

"It's been raining, so I thought—"

"It's always raining, Auntie Ellie. We just take a brolly."

"How much do you know?" I ask her straight out. She may play tough, but she's still only eight. I do not want her to know yet about the complexities of the judicial system or to ask questions about the testing of dried blood. Maybe I can still shield whatever innocence may be left.

"I know about the knife. I reckon—I mean, Inderpal said it's a good thing, right?"

"You've been talking to Inderpal?"

"Sometimes we talk on the phone. So what?"

"So nothing." I hide my smile and the tiny thrill I get from hearing that perhaps Sophie has a crush. I welcome for her any and all distractions from real life. "It is a good thing. It helps the police."

"Good. Daddy said it's good to help the police. That's why I talked to them, you know, *after*, even though I didn't want to talk to anyone. Not even you."

"Well, I'm glad you're talking now. Are you still mad at me?"

Sophie looks toward the window again and then at our book.

"Don't not tell me things, okay? I'm not a baby."

"I know. You're right." I forget myself for a moment and stroke her forehead, like an infant's, but she doesn't seem to mind. She leans into me, soothed.

"I don't like all those people outside. I know they're journalists, like Mummy, but I wish they'd leave us alone."

"I know what you mean. It's like we're in a fishbowl."

"In a fishbowl. I like that. Well said, Auntie Ellie. I'm going to use that one."

"Why don't we just pretend they aren't out there? Let's just pretend that we're in the gardens of Misselthwaite Manor, with Mary and Dickon instead. We're watching the red robin make his nest, and when he chirps it's like he can talk to us."

"They'll still be out there."

"I know. But we can pretend anyway, right?"

I pass Sophie the book, and she begins to read.

28

The FedEx boxes arrive less than a week later. The first is filled with shoes, and not just any shoes but my favorites, a pupu platter assortment. Flats, heels, sneakers, flip-flops, boots, leather and rain. A dream box. And then the second packs two pairs of jeans, a few sweaters, my fall jacket, some tank tops and T-shirts, my cats-and-dogs umbrella, a complete kit for London life. Phillip carefully picked through my closet, weighing what I might need the most. He even supplies me with a power adapter for my laptop, an extra bottle of skin cream—the same brand I used to export to Lucy because it's twice the price here—and a couple of books, handpicked from our bookshelf at home: *The Portrait of a Lady, Reservation Road, A Moveable Feast*.

The note is short, without sentiment:

For you.

And with that, with those two words, my heart closes again and my body aches for Phillip, literally aches. In my breasts, which throb with love, in my stomach, which aches with loss, until I am back on the floor again, doubled over and replaying again and again the sound of Phillip's suitcase rolling out the door.

29

On Thursday, my favorite day of the week, Sophie and I go to see Simon. Actually, Sophie goes to see Simon and I come along as her escort, lingering longer than I should before and after her sessions. He is handsome and I am now single and he's a healthy distraction. Even before this shift in status, I liked to fantasize about his thick arms and the potential tattoo that might or might not crest his biceps. His bald head makes me want to lick it for luck. No, that's a lie. I want to lick it as an appetizer.

After Sophie's session, which, based on the paper tablecloths I've been forced to admire for the past six weeks, now consists less of drawing and more of chatting, Simon asks to speak with me alone. Sophie is sent downstairs with a couple of pounds for a hot chocolate. I am spared the decision of whether she is old enough to do this on her own, since the child expert is the one who suggests it. I am grateful for this, as I lie awake at nights pondering the many choices I have made during the day on Sophie's behalf, never sure if I've made the right one. Often, I turn to Google searches to soothe my nerves: *eight-year-olds and PG movies; eight-year-olds and* Teen Vogue;

eight-year-olds and American Girl dolls and feminism; British eight-year-olds and tea after three; eight-year-olds and sex. I admit, based on the results, that this last one was a huge mistake, one that gave me nightmares for two weeks straight. If I turn up on any federal watch lists, I'll know why.

"How are you holding up?" Simon asks me as soon as we hear Sophie's footsteps on the stairs. "I heard about your husband."

"Oh, that. Fine. I'm fine. Long time coming."

"Yeah?" He says it in that cute Londoner way, a half syllable and expectant.

"Yeah." I parrot his accent back.

"Good. I'm glad." Simon pauses for a moment and just looks at me. He is a man who manipulates silence, finding bits of Zen in the air of a conversation. If I were married to him, I'd find the habit annoying. Since I am not married to him, I find the habit enviable and charming. "Sophie's. Birthday."

"Yes."

"Is. Coming. Up."

"Yes."

"What's the plan, Stan?"

"I don't know. What do you think? Greg and I haven't talked about it yet, but I was thinking I'd throw a party, like the one she had last year. I remember Lucy saying it was a big hit."

"No one showed up last year."

"What are you talking about? Lucy said all of Notting Hill was there."

"Not according to Soph. She says it was a disaster. She said she'd rather die than have another birthday party. Her words. Not mine."

"Oh." I readjust my thinking. Lucy lied. Not surprising, I am learning, as I've stepped into her life. I feel ashamed that she didn't trust me with the truth. Worse, I feel sick picturing Sophie tucked into a party dress, sitting alone among platters of finger sandwiches, knowing full well that no matter how long they waited the doorbell would not ring. And knowing, too, that she had disappointed her mother.

"Okay, time for a new plan. Any ideas?" I ask.

"I'll have a good think on it, but, Ellie, just so you know, this is really important to Sophie. She's mentioned it multiple times."

"I know. We'll have to come up with something amazing. The kid deserves it."

"How are her nightmares?"

"Still daily. She's better at them, though, if that makes sense. She's grown so used to them, I guess, that she doesn't wake up as shaken. And the bed-wetting has totally stopped, so that's good."

"Good. I'm working through guilt with her right now."

"Guilt? She's eight. What does she have to feel guilty about?"

"She disobeyed the morning of the accident." Interesting that even Simon, an expert on genocide, has adopted that word, *accident*. Maybe it's human nature to want to gloss over the idea of evil, limit our vocabulary to words we can control.

"But what does that have to do—"

"Her mum told her to run, but she stopped at the end of the lane. Sophie thinks her being there, her seeing it, made it happen. She's suffering from a form of survivor's guilt."

"So how do we stop it? How do we make her feel better?"

"I'm working on it." He touches my arm, a gesture of comfort. "It's frustrating. Guilt is such a useless emotion when it's irrational. And yet it's so powerful. Holds us back."

He says it in a way that makes me feel like he is not just talking about Sophie here. I nod my head as if I understand, though I am not sure that I do.

"By the way, reading *The Secret Garden* with Sophie? Absolutely bloody brilliant move. I'm thinking of incorporating it into my grief counseling with some other patients."

"Thanks, I had no idea if it would actually help. I just love the book."

"You know, you'd make a fantastic mother." Simon says it in a clunky manner, like he is handing me a gift that will later require a handwritten thank-you note. I take his words with me and measure them as I walk out the door, the entangled emotions too much to bear. His gift less a gift, more a hand grenade.

His "you'd" implies I am not a mother. Not to Sophie, at least not in the literal sense of the word, and, of course, not to Oliver either. I feel the flare again of guilt and shame. Useless emotions, maybe. Painful, still.

30

Sophie refuses to eat the lamb I so lovingly ordered by number from a fluorescent-backlit menu bar and then transported home in a Styrofoam container. Ordinarily, this wouldn't be such a big deal, but we take in Indian three nights a week and the leftovers spill into lunch the next day, and, yes, lamb kebabs have become a staple of our diet. Without them, I worry Sophie will grow even thinner.

We have created a delicate system of ordering and sharing, a fine balance struck between kebab and curry, spicy and mild, liquid and solid. Above all else, we hold fast to routine in this house. There is comfort in knowing that no matter what, Thursday night will include a fresh-baked piece of naan.

Sophie's sudden refusal to take part in our ritual is upsetting.

The newfound mutton phobia is my fault, of course. Dickon, one of the characters in *The Secret Garden*, finds a motherless lamb out on the moors and nurses her. The description is precious: *It was a soft thing with a darling silly baby face and legs rather long for its body. . . . [W]hen Mary had sat under a tree with its limp warmness hud-*

dled on her lap she had felt as if she were too full of a strange joy to speak.
A lamb—a lamb! A living lamb who lay on your lap like a baby!

Again the orphan theme hitting us from all sides, though Sophie doesn't mind; in fact, we reread that paragraph again and again. We both want to touch its fleece, feel it nip our fingertips, watch it suckle from a bottle; we both want to save this fictional animal and adopt our own motherless lamb.

Sophie takes solace in the fact that there must be other creatures in the world like her. Apparently, dead mothers—mutton and otherwise—abound. Who knew this was the lesson of *The Secret Garden*? Sometimes parents die and the kids turn out okay. Even thrive, in rosy-cheeked and independent fashion. This is something both Sophie and I need to learn: Others have survived what she is surviving.

"Sweetheart, come on. You've been eating this stuff forever," Greg says, attempting to kebab her plate. She keeps returning the skewered meat to his.

"No way. I'm not eating anything that's cute. And sheeps are cute."

I don't join the fight. The kid makes a good point. Why not draw the line at cute? Maybe we need to eat and digest and shit out all of the ugly things in the world and leave the cute to frolic and nibble on leaves.

"I guess that means you're safe, then. Because you're supercute." Greg gobbles up his food in an exaggerated ogre fashion, his Shrek imitation, which results in curry all over his chin. We both do this, Greg and I, go for the cheapest and easiest joke available around Sophie. We would do anything—shame ourselves, even—to provoke a laugh.

She gives him what he wants. A giggle.

"I don't think I'm cute. I'm dorky," she says, slow and deliberate, turning the matter around in her head. "All the kids in school call me 'Sophie the Lesbian Librarian.' What's a lesbian?"

My chicken curry hits the wrong pipe and goes down steaming to my gut. I look at Greg, and we are both thinking exactly the same thing. We need iPhones so we can Google *eight-year-olds and explaining homosexuality* under the table.

"Um, that's because you read a lot, sweetie. That's why they call you a librarian. You know librarians are supercool. Yeah, they used to wear buns and look like Headmistress Calthorp, but now most librarians are smart and beautiful. I'd be excited if you grew up to be a librarian. And, come on, you're the cutest kid in the world."

"Duh, I *know* what a librarian is, Auntie Ellie." She rolls her eyes at me, a habit I assumed she wouldn't develop until age fourteen. "What's a lesbian?"

Greg has gone pale—these are the moments he dreads, the motherless moments, when he has no clue what to do or say to his daughter—and looks at me pleadingly. *Help me*, he says. *Surely you must know what to say? You're a woman. You're genetically modified to deal with children.*

I take the ball, ask myself that same old question, like an evangelical: *What Would Lucy Do?* And answer it the same old way: *I don't know.*

"Um, well, Soph, *lesbian* isn't a bad word or anything. I think they're calling you that because it rhymes with *librarian*."

"Not really. Only the last bit rhymes. Librarian has four syllables. Lesbian has three. But *what* is it?"

"It's a woman who loves other women."

"Oh. You're a girl and I'm a girl, and I love you. So are we lesbians?" Oh, man, if my Googling doesn't get me arrested, surely this will. I picture Sophie announcing to anyone who will listen: *My auntie Ellie and I are lesbians together. She says I am the most beautiful girl in the whole wide world.*

"Nope. I mean loves other women in a romantic way. You know how your mommy and daddy got married? Well, there are some women who want to marry other women, and they're called lesbians."

"That makes sense. But, just so you know, I want to marry a boy."

Greg looks relieved. I am not sure he can handle his eight-year-old daughter coming out right about now.

"Actually, I want to marry Inderpal. He's, like, just the coolest boy I know."

I hide my smile, pleased that Sophie has admitted she has a crush, and on such a worthy candidate—Inderpal is smart and gentle and asks all the right questions, an underrated quality in a person—but Greg's face goes splotchy. Any relief he felt moments ago is short-lived and replaced by paralyzing fear. *Oh, no, the boy stuff can't be starting already. Please, God, not yet.*

No doubt, Greg will be up late tonight, Googling: *All-girls' schools in Notting Hill.*

Mikey calls me at ten p.m., after Sophie's been put to bed, while I'm watching the BBC and trying to understand what's so funny about *Only Fools and Horses.* Greg promises me that, if I give it time, I'll fall in love with the show, like I have with *Big Brother,* but so far the sitcom is not taking. I don't have all that much else to do instead, since I am on sabbatical from my job. No lectures to prepare. So this seems a reasonable pursuit these days: *understanding the British sense of humor.* Life has become a crash course in Londoner ways. Greg has introduced me to Martin Amis and Evelyn Waugh, PG Tips and Marks & Spencer Simply Food, looking right when I cross the street and keeping cool when I meet someone new. I now always leave the house with my umbrella and at least two layers of clothing to take on and off at the whim of the sun, end my sentences with rhetorical questions (*isn't it just?*), and understand that *cunt* and *twat* are perfectly acceptable words in common discourse.

"Ellie?" my brother asks, his voice flatter than usual, all love euphoria stamped out.

"You okay? What happened?" I'll kill Claire. I swear to God, I will chop off her fine brunette head if she has hurt Mikey. Even though she is my new friend and we had a lovely cup of tea yesterday, if she hurt my brother, I'll fucking cut her.

If there is anything I've learned these last few months, it's that you take care of your own. I want no one else to be harmed in the making of my life.

"I'm fine. It's just. The wedding," he says.

"No, please, no. She didn't. Not this time."

"Yup, she did."

"But how? What about Dad?" I ask, as if this is the solution to our mother's insatiable desire for drama, an appeal to my father's feelings.

"She hasn't officially called it off. She says she needs some time. She's currently on a flight to Peru to take part in some sort of retreat. A mystical shaman's thing. A way to explore past lives or some nonsense like that."

"How is Dad taking it?"

"He's in denial, I think. He's still planning away. He just dropped the invitations off at the calligrapher. I only found out she bolted because I happened to call him."

"Is he okay?"

"Funny, he asked me the same thing about you. When were you planning on telling me about the divorce?" My stomach knots at my selfishness. Of course my brother would eventually find out about Phillip and me; trying to protect him from the news was just an excuse to put off saying the words out loud again. If I brought it up with him, I would have to talk about it, and I don't want to talk about it.

"I'm sorry, I just . . . I was going to. It just happened."

"Are you okay?"

"No. Yes. I don't know. How are you and Claire? Please tell me at least someone is in a healthy relationship in this family."

"We're . . . Yeah, we're pretty great."

"I'm so glad. I'm putting my faith in humanity in you two."

"Well, fortunately, she's nothing like you or Mom."

"What's that supposed to mean?" I know exactly what he means. I feel nauseous, lamb kebabs and chicken curry revolting in my gut, and worry I might throw up. He ignores my question.

"What do we do?"

"What can we do?"

"I don't know."

"Me neither, Mikey."

"What do we do about you, then?"

"What can we do?"

"I don't know. But it seems like such a waste. Phillip, he's good people, and I know I've said this a million times before, but you were good together. Before everything happened, you guys were happy. Obnoxiously so, if I remember correctly." *Everything happened* is code for losing Oliver, like *the accident* is code for losing Lucy.

"Yeah, well. It's sad, but what can you do?" I don't mention that it feels like whatever comes after *sad, sad* is too light a word; I am crushed by a quiet pain. Sounding flip seems to be my only option.

"I don't know."

"Me neither, Mikey. Me neither."

We continue chatting and get nowhere. There is nothing to be done about the Lerner women. My mom will climb mountains in Peru, and maybe she'll come back and maybe she won't. And Phillip has already spoken with a lawyer.

I wonder if it is human nature to always want what doesn't belong to you. Is that why Lucy kissed Stuart Tannenbaum and wanted to run away with her married Frenchman? Why my mother enjoys the noise of New York, a city on loan, indulging in the temporary burden of other people's problems? Why I am here, in this house, cruelly, kindly, ambivalently borrowing Lucy's child?

But when I flip the question, try to embrace what I do have, what I can hold on to—*what does belong to me*—I come up empty. It doesn't surprise me, then, that as soon as I hang up the phone with my brother, I am on the floor of the second of the Staffords' four bathrooms, losing my lamb kebabs. Apparently, even they weren't mine to keep.

31

My arm is finally set for liberation the week before Sophie's birthday. She comes with me to the hospital, eager to see how they will manage to chop off the fiberglass without chopping off my limb.

"How will you know to stop?" she asks the doctor, who, within ten seconds of me sitting on the patient's table, already has his blade out. "You know like how magicians saw people in half? Wouldn't it be cool if you cut off Auntie Ellie's arm but it wasn't bloody or anything? And we could just take it home. I would take it everywhere, and be like, see, this is my Auntie Ellie's arm. Want to shake it?"

Her excitement flows off her in waves, and she bounces in the pink high-topped Converse that she's taken to wearing during this nonuniformed summer break. The doctor demonstrates how the blade can't hurt me, that the cast will catch the safety before it can cut flesh; I still don't like the idea of it being so close to my skin. I begin to sweat, and I make Sophie hold my other hand, the good hand, the one I will leave here with today, no matter what.

The doctor, a young Brit, with surprisingly perfect teeth and a wedding ring, powers up the saw. The noise is piercing. The dentist's drill is nothing in comparison to this spinning blade, which is not much bigger than an electric toothbrush. It's way too small to make so much noise.

"Stop!" I yell, to make myself heard above the churning engine. I don't want that thing anywhere near me. "I think my arm needs more time to heal. It still hurts. Let's leave the cast on. I want to leave it on."

"Sit back and relax. I promise, I won't chop off your arm," the doctor says, polite enough not to laugh in my terrified face. Sophie squeezes my hand—she's scared, too—and I realize suddenly that this may not have been a smart move, taking her here. "Just look at your beautiful little girl and concentrate on her instead."

So I do, I look at Sophie and don't bother to correct the doctor's possessive. It happens too often these days, anyhow, to keep correcting. Even though she called me Auntie right in front of him, he wants to see a mother and daughter. Everyone seems to do that, fill in a parental relationship for the sake of convenience. Like we are one of those psychological tests where you can read the sentence even though most of the words are missing.

Sophie and I make eye contact, and I hold her gaze; neither of us watches as the saw spins and churns its way through the fiberglass.

Of course, the doctor doesn't chop off my arm. Doesn't even snag the skin. But the noise—like a scream, because it's all I can hear—and the spinning blade, and the final cracking of the cast with something like reverse pliers, leaves me shaking and breathless. My arm, when it is finally rerevealed to the world, is shrunken, scaly, and heavy and light at the same time. A puny, useless thing, like a dead fish.

"Peeyooo, you stink!" Sophie says in glee, maybe even happier than I am that I still have two arms. "It's like your arm farted."

"It's from sweating under the cast. A quick shower will take care of that in no time." The doctor is kind, a child himself, no more than twenty-five. He makes me clench my fist, wiggle my fingers. Puts my new X ray up on the light board.

"You see that fine white line," he says to Sophie as much as to me. She's much more interested in the medical side of all of this; I just want to take my arm and go. "That's the fracture point. That line is going to be there for a while. Like an internal scar."

"Why?" Sophie asks.

"The body needs to remember where it has been broken. Even though the bone has fused, it still needs time. Healing doesn't happen overnight."

"Well, unless you die, right? Then you heal immediately. You don't go to heaven all bloody and scarred, do you? Do you?"

The doctor catches my eye above Sophie's head, not the *save me* look Greg gave me over dinner the other day, but the alarm-bell look, the one that says *this kid better be in therapy.*

"Of course not, Soph," I say, jumping in, because if the doctor isn't careful about what he says here, we may be looking at nightmares for another two years. "That's what's so special about heaven. Everything is all better. No blood, or guts, or any of that gross stuff. No casts in heaven, or stinky arms for that matter."

I move my arm toward her so she is forced to jump away to avoid smelling my sweaty flesh.

"Eewww, stop, please stop," she says, laughing and holding her nose, her attention successfully averted.

The doctor runs through his tests and gives me a few exercises to strengthen my atrophied muscles. Sophie gets a gold-star sticker and a lollipop, "for being patient with the patient," and the cast, too, because she wants to keep her drawings, and I get my arm back. I keep looking at it, like it's a phantom limb. I still don't recognize it as my own.

"Off you go," the doctor says to us. "Almost as good as new."

Almost, but not really, I think, picturing the fine white line that if I could strip off my flesh would be visible to the naked eye. Everyone would be able to see the exact spot where I've been broken.

32

Only one chapter from the end of *The Secret Garden*. We will finish today and end this two-hundred-page project at the real Secret Garden, the actual place where Frances Hodgson Burnett once lived and later wrote the book about, when she was homesick while living across the pond in a house on Long Island. Greg and I have arranged for a private tour of the grounds in honor of Sophie's birthday—no easy feat, considering the land is not open to the public. The manor house has been transformed into lush carpeted flats for retired aristocrats, who get the distinct pleasure of spending their final years puttering and rambling on the moors. But when I called and pled, the estate manager listened to my story—it turns out he had read about the "murdered American journalist" in the tabloids, a "tragedy," he had said, "she was quite the looker," he had said—and was moved by Sophie's desire to see the place firsthand.

I explained that the book is no longer just a book to us, and he seemed to intuit that we were not mere tourists, looking for a fancy picnic spot. We were on a pilgrimage to the motherland, the novel having been elevated to biblical proportions, one-stop shopping for entertainment, philosophy, comfort, guidance. I didn't tell him that in our free time we play "Secret Garden," a game Sophie has designed, where we each pretend to be different characters and act out the scenes in the backyard.

"I get to be Mary this time," Sophie said yesterday, when we took advantage of a bout of afternoon sun and wandered into the patch of grass behind the house.

"But you were Mary last time."

"Yeah, but I'm the kid here." She had a fair point.

"Fine. Then I'll play Susan Sowerby, mother to fourteen beautiful children and wisest woman on the moor."

"Which scene should we do? When Susan brings fresh bread and milk to the kids playing in the garden?"

"Sure. Just promise you won't laugh at my Yorkshire accent. Aye, nowt, tha' mun take it from tha' top."

Now it's 0800 hours on Saturday—I have embraced the British use of military time—and Operation Perfect Birthday starts without a hitch. Sophie's favorite people have been gathered: Greg, Mikey, Claire, and Inderpal (whose parents have become big fans of Greg's since he stood up to the headmistress; based on their enthusiasm about today's events, it seems like Inderpal gets invited to birthday parties about as often as Sophie). We are all buckled in and ready to go in this rented minivan, snacks and lunch packed and presents in the "boot"; Greg, in the front seat, chauffeuring; me next to him, as navigator. I feel in charge and in control, a supergodmother at the helm.

Sophie and Inderpal are in the first row, just behind us, and Claire and Mikey sit in the back, the two of them still at that stage where all their seams need to be in constant contact. Whenever they kiss, the kids—and, yes, sometimes Greg, and I—bring them back from oblivion with loud and immature heckling: "Gross!"

Now that the arrangements have been sorted—we will tour, then picnic and read—the anticipation is palpable and electric in the minivan; we are buzzing with *are we there yet?*s. When I told Sophie my plan for her birthday, she was equal parts excited and relieved: "Seriously? The real Secret Garden? And I can invite whoever I want? They don't have to be kids? Are you having a laugh?" My mother would probably say I'm skirting the issue, that we should force Sophie to interact more with other children. Not sure what the "right thing" is here, I just know that if I were to stop time and freeze this shot, zoom in on Sophie in her front seat, she is smiling in anticipation and as far away as she can get from the looming darkness and trench-coated shadows.

And seeing, being in, the actual Secret Garden? I have no doubt there will be magic there, or Magic, as it is referred to in the book— what I have come to think of as a child's word for God. The God I don't believe in, but have no trouble summoning up and bargaining with when the need arises.

"So there's this boy named Dickon, and he has this way with animals and people and birds and everything, and he is only thirteen but everyone loves him. And once Mary discovers the key to the garden, they become best friends, and he helps Mary make things grow," Sophie says, with animation and delight, the look she always gets when we talk about our favorite book. "And guess what? No one has been in the garden for, like, ten years, since Colin's mum died in there, which was really sad. And Colin, see, he's Mary's cousin, and he lives in the big house on the moor too. And he thinks he's disabled and hunchbacked, and he never gets to leave his room. But then—"

Sophie stops, dramatic pause, an effect I have no doubt she learned from her mother. Lucy told a mean story, every encounter spun into comedy or tragedy, the learned narrator's punctuation of desperate beats and cheap punch lines.

"Then he meets Mary, and she takes him to the Secret Garden. And they all get fresh air and gain back their appetites and become like children again," Sophie says.

"And the wheelchair," Inderpal cuts in, apparently well versed in this classic as well. "Remember, they call Colin a rajah because he acts all like an Indian prince and stuff. That's what they called princes in India. Rajahs."

"Right. But Colin doesn't need a wheelchair. He's just convinced himself that he does, because he's been told all his life he's sick. He's not, though! He's not! He's perfectly fine. He's a perfectly fine little boy. Like everyone else. That's the best part, when they turn out to be just like everyone else. All they need is food and fresh air and some time in the garden."

Sophie looks over to me in the front passenger seat, for approval. I give her a big grin.

"Exactly, Soph. Great summary."

"And Mary actually gets pretty from doing all that good stuff for her. She starts out all sad and sickly and ugly, but then she gets a little fatter and stuff, and by the end she's a pretty little girl." Sophie takes off her glasses and cleans them with her T-shirt. "And my favorite thing is, she makes friends. People stop not liking her."

We drive through Kent, a region called the "Garden of England," and stare out the window at the rolling green fields that cause a hush after breaking free of London's sprawling metropolis. This is the other England, the England of those BBC miniseries Phillip always makes fun of me for watching on PBS, ninety-five percent of which are adaptations of Jane Austen novels. I imagine all of the women here wearing late-eighteenth-century gowns, their busts bound and blooming, spending their evenings twirling away at neighborhood balls, sizing up potential husbands in a choreographed dance. Hands meet, palms barely touching, and the rest of the candlelit room blurs away. No matter that she has a measly dowry and he's a rich nobleman. By the final scene, they'll figure it out.

I do understand that this world has been updated—I even saw a woman walking by wearing 7 For All Mankind jeans and designer wellies—yet still I imagine life here is somehow better. I can picture myself living in one of the tiny stone cottages, with an antique four-pronged chimney—chimneys are as much a part of the landscape here as the monochromatic grass—and roaming my impossibly green farm. I'd befriend the horses and cows and sheep. Become an animal whisperer. Someone, too, who could have a long conversation about the growth of my anemones and the best fertilizers.

"Look, Dad, sheeps!" Sophie exclaims, as we pass a farm with about fifty roaming fluff balls. I grab my camera and take a picture. They look placed there for our amusement, a postcard image of what the English countryside is supposed to look like. "What are those numbers on their sides?" Sophie's eyes are already filled with water, waiting.

"Just to keep track of them, love. So another neighboring farm can't steal them," Greg says.

"They aren't going to become, you know, food, are they?" she asks, her optimism willing her tears to retreat.

"Of course not," Greg says. "They shave them for wool, that's all."

I try to catch his eye, to see if he is lying. Are these the animals that go into my lamb kebabs? Greg refuses to look me in the eye, though, and that tells me everything I need to know.

At 1100 hours we pull off a windy country road and arrive at Great Maytham Hall, which is what the Brits call, in typical understated style, a manor house and what I would call a mansion. Enormous and made of faded red brick, the place unfolds on both sides, giving the impression that it has been extended from the center building twice, construction that must have happened about a century ago. The driveway stretches across the expanse of the front lawn straight to the middle of the house, and as we get closer and closer, the building grows in front of us until we are right there, parked at the mammoth front door. I feel dwarfed by the scale.

We start the festivities on the front lawn, enjoying the cupcakes I brought as a mid-morning snack, a resting moment that only heightens the anticipation for what's next. I have three, fast and in a row, stopping only to admire how pretty they are—pink tops, yellow stars. My speed and nervous hunger just outpace my dizziness from the intestinal country roads.

"Auntie Ellie?" Sophie walks up next to me and takes my hand. "Do you think things will be better in there?"

She points to the house—which has, at first count, at least ten chimneys and thirty windows in masterly symmetry and too belongs in a BBC miniseries. Sophie, though, means just beyond: our garden out back.

"Like, do you reckon being in the garden will make us feel better?" she asks.

"What do you mean?" But I know exactly what she means. She is hoping to find some answers and some peace among the four ivied walls and the rosebushes. She wants to know how she can stare down evil every single night in her dreams and yet pretend to be a normal kid during the day. How she can wake up every morning to a world without her mother and still get dressed and brush her teeth and eat Weetabix. Or maybe she's asking the universal question that's reflexive when the world seems too heavy for our given pair of slim shoulders: *Why me?*

I hope she is not asking for something more: that her mother will somehow reappear in the garden. If Colin can walk out of his wheelchair, surely people can rise from the dead there, re-souled and blood-filled, resurrected and ready to resume the reins of parenthood. Has Sophie been led astray by the false hopes of magic? The world is full of happy tricks—quarters hidden behind ears, flowers tucked into sleeves, love, love, love—but there will be no miracles here today. The Virgin Mary will not be etched in the mold of our sandwiches. I don't know how old you have to be to understand that when mothers or babies die, they stay that way. Worse, that those left behind don't get their shot at redemption, no matter how hard we reach for it. No matter how many oceans we cross.

Nine is too young. So is thirty-five.

In fact, I would love to be finally rid of all of my empty promises and my fake God-bartering. I am exhausted by my pile of empty vows.

I'll do anything if you'll bring Lucy back to Sophie.

Empty, nonsensical promises of sacrifice that echo ones I made, but never kept, almost two years earlier.

I promise to die if you'll bring Oliver back.

I promise to do anything you want if you'll bring Oliver back.

Take me. Not him. Take anyone else but him. Please, please.

Last week I found Sophie on the floor of her bedroom, surrounded by a photograph of her mother taken by me three Fourth of Julys ago, a credit-card receipt with Lucy's signature, and an old hairbrush, Lucy's strands pulled out and collected in a small heap. Sophie's magic kit was open, and she was circling her black cardboard wand above the pile of junk—or now, in the wake of loss, Sophie's salvaged treasure.

I had been in the exact same spot once before. Two days after Oliver died, Phillip found me in our living room, surrounded by one hundred chain letters addressed to our wedding invite list. I was guaranteed, somewhere in the not-so-fine print, that if I mailed the note one hundred times, *all of my wishes would come true.* One hundred first-class stamps, one hundred copies at Kinko's, the embarrassment and shame of having one hundred of our closest friends and family open up a chain letter from me, seemed a small price to pay for a shot at my wish. I didn't even need *all* of them granted. Just the one. A sucker is born every day out of grief.

When Phillip asked what I was doing, I lied, even though I knew he already knew. I could see it in the line between his eyebrows, a line now permanently etched there. The body needs to remember where it has been broken, the doctor said.

So when Sophie asks her question, do I think things will be better in our Secret Garden, I don't need to Google to know what I should say. I give her the truth, even though my answer will make Frances Hodgson Burnett turn over in her grave on Long Island.

"I don't think so, Soph. It's just going to be, you know, a garden. Nothing more."

33

I am in paradise, and paradise smells like jasmine. Tight pink buds and bluebells line the stone walls, and a canopied walkway splits the garden in halves. The morning light is cut by a roof of pink roses braided with overgrown ivy perched above the path—a narrow corridor from one end to the other. The garden, while not quite secret—the walls are only about five feet high—is nonetheless sacred ground. I understand now why this has been turned into a retirement home. One of the few places I've been where I imagine innocence can be re-earned.

Lucy would hate it here. One look around and she'd be bothered by its gnawing perfection, the pinks and the blues and the greens too exact and sentimental. Like an old English painting of a garden, only worse, because the flickering of the leaves renders the sunlight just slightly out of focus. A canvas you'd find leaning against a fence at an amateur art fair.

Sorry, L, it's just too pretty to be interesting, I can hear her saying.

I disagree. I can't stop looking, at the tiny shoots of hot pink that are growing in the seams of the stone wall. At the sheer abundance of *bloom*. A line from the book repeats in my head: *I want to see all the things that grow in England.*

"Which ones do you think are crocuses? What about snowdrops and daffodils like Mary finds in the book? Which are which?" Sophie asks me. She is walking the perimeter with Inderpal, letting her fingers run along the warmed stone. Her jaw is slack with awe, her expression so naked, it's a parody of wonder. There is so much to be explored. Sophie is just getting started.

"I wish I knew," I say.

"I think those may be crocuses. My mum has them at home," Inderpal says, and points to a small group of flowers in the far corner. They are little cups of pale pink, with a dab of yellow in their center.

"Those are happy flowers," Sophie says, and manages to speak out loud exactly the same two words I had been thinking. My mind has slowed here, my thoughts simplified: *happy flowers.*

"So which tree do you think is the one that killed Colin's mum?" Sophie asks, looking from one tree to another, as if to find a culprit. I had forgotten about that part of the book: The garden is locked away because it is the place where Colin's saintly mother died.

"You know the book is fiction, right? It's made up. No one died here. No one has ever died here," I say.

"Of course I know it's *fiction*. I was just wondering what tree Frances imagined Colin's mum falling out of." Sophie and I are now both on a first-name basis with Frances Hodgson Burnett. When we're being silly, we call her Frannie.

"That one," Inderpal says, and points to the biggest and grandest tree in the garden. Too tall and old and proud to be ignored. I'm sure it has been here for hundreds of years. "Just look at it. Right there. That's where Colin's mum died."

Sophie and Inderpal wander off on their own to explore a line of ants climbing into a flower bed, examining them with Inderpal's magnifying glass. They use their hands to shield the insects from the light, so there will be no accidental cooking. I seek shelter under the canopy; summer has reemerged today, hot and sunny. The smell of flowers and trees and rich overturned earth fills my nose, and I taste the thin film of sugar left behind from my yellow-starred cupcake overdose, and next thing I know I am on the brick path, head between my knees, fighting nausea. I cannot—I will not—throw up in the Secret Garden. That would be sacrilegious.

"You okay?" Mikey asks, unlinking arms with Claire to come to my side. I wait a moment to answer, bite down hard, hoping the rush up the back of my throat will back down, and it does.

"Yeah, just ate too much. I'm fine."

"I think bringing her here was a good idea," he says, motioning over to Sophie and Inderpal playing entomologist in the corner.

"Yeah?"

"Yeah. You're really good with her." My head drops a little lower. "Hey, you sure you're okay?"

"I think so," I say, except for the fact that I'm not. The vertigo has passed, but I still feel unrooted, floating above myself in the one place I thought, like Sophie did, that I might feel better. "I mean, besides the fact that I lost my best friend and my husband in the course of a summer. And that I clearly haven't yet learned basic portion control."

"Well, there is that. Remember when we went to Sizzler that one time when we were little and you ate so much of the cubed ham that you threw up on the car ride home?"

My family loves that story, even told it at my wedding.

"For the record, I got sick on bacon bits, not ham. And they were undercooked. Mikey, seriously, though? I have no idea what the hell I'm doing here. I'm not sure I've ever been this lost."

"Look at her." He points again at Sophie. "You made this happen today. Honestly, I think you seem much less lost than you've been in a while."

"But I just feel so powerless. I can't bring Lucy back, and that's what Sophie really needs. Her actual mother. And I'm living in this godforsaken country. I am so tired of having wet feet and eating everything with mayonnaise."

"You need to get some wellies. They'll change your life." I don't hear him. Apparently I have started something and I can't stop. Finger out of dam, camel crushed under the weight of its straw, egg will never be whole again. I forget where I am, that the sky is actually a piercing blue all the way until it meets ground, an idyllic summer day, and I am wearing sunglasses. The garden is as beautiful as it was in my imagination, flowers bursting forth as if freshly born. We are in a land far, far away.

"I bet Phillip already has a new girlfriend. Please tell me she's not twenty-two and blond and hot. And precocious too. I hate that type. I really hate that type."

"Actually, he just called me yesterday. Said that since he dumped my sister, he's found himself 'a nice piece of ass.'"

"That's not funny."

"I'm kidding. Phillip would never say 'nice piece of ass.' Tail, maybe, but not ass."

"Mikey."

"Sorry. Bad joke. Go on. What are you freaking out about?"

"We are all such messes. Mom is jilting Dad, *again*, and there is nothing we can do about any of it. And you know what? I haven't waxed my eyebrows since I got here. I look like a freaking wildebeest. No wonder my husband doesn't want to stay married to me. Who wants to be married to a freaking wildebeest?"

"Phillip mentioned that to me. Said he was divorcing you over the 'eyebrow issue.'" Mikey uses ridiculous air quotes.

"I'm serious. I feel like I'm losing my shit. Phillip left me. For real."

"I know." There is something new and tender in his voice, he's finally stopped joking, and the fact that it feels like something to latch on to causes me to break—that point in a meltdown where I feel my body surrender to the hysteria, surrender the ability to harness or control anything. My emotions, my fear, my guilt, my bladder all under the power of the wildebeest within.

I now have tears streaming out of my eyes and snot pouring from my nose. I need to run away, to the other end of the globe, but I have already run, I am three thousand miles from home, and it seems to have gotten me nowhere.

Mikey steers me by the elbow out of my stone-walled paradise—better yet, out of eyeshot and earshot of the rest of the group—to another garden just beyond, this one with a water fountain. The water collects and gets pumped to the top, just to be dribbled down again for our amusement. It is spectacular. Because of Mikey, my fit will only have a single witness, and when I realize this, how my little brother has come to my rescue, saved me from letting the rest of our party see me fall apart, I want to weep in gratitude. The switch from desolation to sentimental weepiness happens so quickly, I have trouble keeping up.

"Sit here, just take a breath," he says.

"Okay." The humiliation rises in my gut with the three cupcakes and the Ribena juice box I called breakfast this morning.

Somehow, Mikey knows what's next, and he jumps out of the way before I even see what is happening. My head opens, and I throw up. Some of the frosting stars are still intact, and I have managed to produce perfect constellational vomit.

Mikey looks at me, and I look at him, and now he grins at me; he can't help it.

"Oh, shit," I say, because I have been here before, have felt this all before, though last time it ended too soon, like in a horror movie where you think there may still be time for the dead to be resurrected but there isn't. Last time it ended with a black-and-white photograph taken off the fridge. "Oh, no. Shit, shit, shit. I can't be. I mean, it's not really possible."

But sure it is. Possible. If Lucy can be butchered in an alley at eight a.m. on a random Thursday morning, just before she was planning to run away to Paris with her also-married lover—if life can be that bloody messy—then I can be pregnant from a one-night stand with my estranged husband while I am playing godmother to a motherless lamb.

I put my head in my hands, too nauseous and shocked to use the muscles in the back of my neck to support my cranium. I flop like a newborn. The terror is pointed and sharp and painful. A spinal tap.

Mikey is still grinning. My Jerry Springer life is hilarious to my staid brother. This kind of stuff never happens in his carrel at LSE.

"Well, I have to say, Ellie, things just got a little bit interesting."

About twenty minutes later, I have collected myself enough to return to the group, resigned to the fact that there will be no answers while I'm gallivanting around Kent with this multigenerational birthday party. There will be no sneaking off and buying a pregnancy test and peeing on a stick in a porta-potty off the M25. Nope, the word *baby* will be tucked away safely inside the deep scars in my brain, nestled there where I have been cracked for so long that my memory sometimes can't stretch back to the before. I will smile at Sophie playing in the dirt, smile at the love pheromones wafting between Claire and Mikey, smile at Greg watching his child in wonder—*I created that*, he's thinking. I'll smile, smile, smile, hold down my position, and fix it in time.

Maybe things are different in the Secret Garden—maybe things do grow here. Barren, scorched landscapes turn lush; flower buds replace cacti. Pinned butterflies pump back to life, flutter out of an airless box.

"You okay?" Greg asks, when I join him next to the grand tree. He looks at its deep roots, a circular web around the trunk.

"Yup. You?"

"Yeah. Today is one of the good days." Sophie and Inderpal sit on the wet grass about ten feet away, not caring that their pants' bottoms are soaked through. They are now interested in the dirt, in worms in particular, and the adults are occasionally summoned over to inspect.

I cannot think about what happens next, about what it means if my recent display was what I think it was, where that will lead me. I cannot think about Phillip. About Lucy's choice to leave, my recent commitment to stay, my mother fleeing the best thing that has ever happened to her, again and again.

"Sophie asked me the other day about how you lost a baby," Greg says, his tone gentle, and it's clear he can tell my mind keeps drifting far away from here.

"Really? Sophie knows about Oliver?"

"Yup, I guess Lucy must have told her at some point."

"Lucy always had a big mouth," I say, my tone jokey. Lucy's big mouth was one of my favorite things about her. And suddenly the missing-her part hits me, the constant steamroll of grief. I am flattened and lost without my best friend. *Lucy, what would you do?* And the next question, the new one: *Would I do what you would do?* She was always braver than I was, more reckless, and at the same time, so much more alive. If I could have picked who to be, me or her, I would have picked her every single time. Even now, even knowing she was going to walk away, even knowing how it all ended.

But I am not her and never will be.

"You know, having been through something like that, losing Oliver, I don't think I could ever do it again. I really don't think I could survive it twice," I say, and look at Greg, but from the way his mouth is drawn tight, I can tell he knows that I am lying.

The truth is, I didn't really survive it the first time.

34

When Oliver died, I didn't cry at first. I was eight months pregnant, and then I was told I wasn't anymore, as if pregnancy was merely a stop on the way to a potential and I hadn't fulfilled mine. Oliver was deemed *unviable*, a cruel word, a sentence, an even crueler verdict; the doctor seemed to prefer it to *dead*, though, as if this medical euphemism would make any of us feel better.

Oliver was removed via a lifeless C-section so that my own baby couldn't poison me. Not only was Oliver unviable, he was suddenly dangerous. He was only eleven inches long. Less than a foot. I still did not cry.

Instead, in an advanced state of denial, I asked if they could keep him inside me a little longer, let me surround him a little longer, let us be one thing a little longer, but the doctor wouldn't allow it. For medical reasons, we had to cleave off the dead, before it could render me the same.

Based on the reaction, a flinching chorus, it seemed my request was a first; I found out later that most women upon discovering they have lost the nine-month race, want their baby out. Out for me meant lost, and I wasn't ready to make the switch that quickly. Less than twenty-four hours earlier we were debating the benefits of an overpriced stroller and a wipes warmer, whether I'd be able to slug through the delivery without an epidural. Now, the word of the day was *removal*, not *birth*. We weren't going to have a welcoming party—connected letters across the mantel, *It's a boy!* No, the event had turned ugly, surgical, a cutting.

"Death is contagious," they had said. And they were right.

I held my baby for a minute, sixty seconds, thirty of my own breaths taken in and out, almost mocking his stillness, and then they took him away. Phillip watched but couldn't touch. That would be crossing a line into making Oliver real, and Oliver couldn't be real now that he was gone. He touched me, though, and then I did the exact wrong thing, a reflex that later morphed into habit. I shrugged his hand away.

One of my biggest regrets in life, one of the cruelest things I have ever done: that first flinch. I still see Phillip's face just then. The horror and the fear and the loneliness. In that moment I violated the basic tenet of our marriage; what happened to me happened to him, and vice versa, and here I was, refusing to share. I often wonder where we would be if I had let him touch me, if I'd absorbed whatever comfort his warm hands could impart and hadn't made visible the invisible line between us. Who would we be now?

A coffin was picked out, a baby-sized coffin—they actually have those, one of the many things in this world that shouldn't exist but does, one of the many things that if you let yourself think about in the morning, you would never get out of bed—and Phillip and I still don't know who did the choosing. It wasn't us; we were too drugged, too caught in the undertow, to make something like a decision. Come to think of it, I bet it was my mother, who did what a mother should never have to do for her daughter but in this world she sometimes does. We had a funeral with just the family and Lucy, who flew in and stocked our fridge with soup and macaroni and cheese and other thick and fatty comfort foods and packed up the half-finished nursery. She hid the mobile Phillip and I had spent hours picking out: dancing monkeys. I remember we had fun in the store, taking turns dangling it over each other's faces, deciding what we had wanted our baby to see each night before he closed his eyes and again each morning when he opened them.

"Definitely the monkeys," Phillip said, when we had narrowed it down to two. "For some reason, I just love their purple pants."

I'm sure some thought having a funeral was melodramatic, unnecessary. How can you send off a life that never actually made it into the world, never took a single breath on the outside? What can you say? He had baby hands, and baby feet, and a tiny baby mouth? He looked like a doll? We didn't know if he was smart, or funny, or if he would have turned into one of those angry teenagers who smuggles a gun into the school cafeteria. No anecdotes to share other than the fact that he gave me indigestion for eight months and had a preference for kicking the right side of my rib cage.

All we knew was that he was ours, and he was beautiful, as all babies are, alive or not. We knew I had failed him, we knew that, too, but no one said that out loud. The tears came, heavy and for weeks, and then months, and from the start I felt that the rest of the world saw my grief as overblown and indulgent. We had lost the potential of a baby, not a real baby, another universal thought shared but not said aloud by those who hadn't lost a thing. Instead, the words stayed etched on their confused foreheads when time didn't snap me back into Ellie Before. They were wrong, though, in their failed attempts at empathy, at the faux-enthusiasm and high voice usually reserved for dealing with sullen kids. They were wrong in thinking this some small setback.

I had held him. He existed before he didn't. He was mine.

The guilt, too, came, in suffocating waves. The guilt that sometimes, still, late at night, when the raw edges of sleep are too far away and the reality of daylight not there to smooth out the irrational, consumes me and I imagine the hundred ways in which I failed him. Turns out when I had my nine-month shot, I was a terrible mother. I count the rules I broke. There was that cheese I ate, buried in a lasagna, that tasted so good I didn't want to ask if it was pasteurized. I drank, too, a glass of wine here or there, feeling European and modern. Lucy had; I thought it was okay.

There was the time I tripped on the sidewalk—I shouldn't have gone out, but I was antsy and bored and found myself flat-back in the snow. A teenage girl, hiding her face behind too long, too curly, too blond hair, offered a shy hand, no eye contact. I took it, and before I could say thank you, she ran away. I remember feeling bad about that, the not saying thank you to my good Samaritan, but I didn't for a moment feel bad about not calling the doctor.

I didn't want to be one of those crazy OCD mommies-to-be, who rendered the experience of pregnancy unbearable and without charm, who lectured the rest of us who hadn't yet read all the books. My desire to be a certain kind of person—above the paranoia and the fear, to be cooler than the worriers—left Oliver exposed and unprotected. That's who Ellie Before was, someone who felt immune to tragedy and loss, felt strong and invincible, if only because I had never before been tested.

The doctor attempted to soothe me with platitudes: *These things happen; they are nobody's fault. I promise you, it wasn't the lasagna or a glass of wine.* But I didn't believe her. I had one job for those forty weeks, to create a snow-globe world for my baby, and I somehow shattered the glass. Some things can't yet be answered with medical rationales. Perhaps one day a team of scientists will prove my theory—that ego, and doubt, and naïveté, and presumptuousness— those are the charged chemicals, the delicate pH balance, that can tilt your world upside down.

Now I find myself in the Secret Garden on this sunny afternoon, in charge of a child's birthday party. We have lunch and then cake, bought at a fancy pastry shop in Notting Hill, unsecured from its box and decorated with nine candles. We all know and do exactly what we are supposed to do: We sing "Happy Birthday," and Sophie closes her eyes, takes a moment, and blows. Her breath extinguishes the light to claps and cheers. I don't ask about Sophie's wish. Just a few days ago, she had a magic kit and a lock of her mother's hair. There is only one thing she wants, and she won't get it.

"I can't believe you are nine. I am so jealous," Inderpal says. "I still have to wait three months."

"I can't believe it either," Greg says, and ruffles both kids' hair. They swat his hand away, since they are too old for that. "My little girl is nine. One more year and you'll be a decade. Double digits."

"In only ninety-one more years, I'll be a century. Triple digits," Sophie says, and looks elated at the thought.

A hand tentatively touches my belly. My hand. My belly. No curve yet, at least no curves attributable to a zygote. I fight the grip of fear, Ellie After, knowing all that can unravel, minute by minute. Will there be more birthday parties in my future? A celebration, too, if a child comes out live and whole and breathing? And how do I lose the terror that accompanies the mere accumulation of days— if I'm even lucky enough to get that far—that something will turn, that my protection, even at its most vigilant, may not be enough?

The sheer responsibility—no, the flip side of responsibility: The vulnerability of it paralyzes me. If something happened to my child, or to Sophie, too, since she now resides within the folds of me, there would be nothing left.

The group gathers on the grass in a semicircle around us, partially shaded by the large tree. Sophie is sitting in my lap; her thin legs perch over my knees and pin me in place. She feels less frail than she did when I first came here almost three months ago: a solid, real-life kid who can talk and walk and run circles around a garden. The book is already in her hands, the green tattered cover a testament to our overuse and abuse. I tune out the tsunami in my head and focus instead on the birthday girl.

"Chapter Twenty-Seven, 'In the Garden,'" she announces, and does that thing she always does, her puppy reflex. I nod and smile and give her the pat on the head she needs, my best impression of Lucy, maybe, in her quieter, more indulgent moments. Sophie begins to read the last part of our book to the group.

As usual, I get lost in the words, caught up in the sentences, laid word by word toward our happy ending. Today, though, I see it being acted out in front of me, just beyond this semicircle of interested, or at the very least, humoring observers. Little Mary, all plumped up and rosy-cheeked, uses her trowel to dig up dirt. Dickon is playing the flute in the corner under a low-drooping tree. Colin, practicing the still-novel use of his legs, is running from wall to wall, slapping his bare palm across the stone, where it has already been warmed by the midday sun. I'm not sure if any of this is on the page, but that doesn't matter.

"One of the new things people began to find out in the last century was that thoughts—just mere thoughts—are as powerful as electric batteries— as good for one as sunlight is, or as bad for one as poison. To let a sad thought or a bad one get into your mind is as dangerous as letting a scarlet fever germ get into your body. If you let it stay there after it has got in you may never get over it as long as you live," Sophie reads, slowly, making sure to get each word right, and I am drawn right back into the book again. This is why I love *The Secret Garden*—the self-help message so casually snuck into a children's story, like putting vitamins in soda.

A flush of bliss passes through me. I feel the weight of Sophie in my lap, smell her hair—she uses baby shampoo, just like Lucy did because she once read in a magazine it was good for curls—hear the birds chirping in the distance, and all of it combines into a sedative. The anxious stirring that has kept me alert and stiff in the back since hearing about Lucy—amplified this morning—slows down and releases. Maybe I am exactly where I am supposed to be. Maybe this is what it means to be home. Real internal quiet, the voice in your head turned to mute, a momentary lapse in consciousness and expectation.

Right now I am free to play in dirt and run in circles. The burden of life—and that's how I've thought about it these past two years, life as a burden, an awareness of the literal weight of my body as I schlepped from one place to another, the driving desire not to make a single mistake—has lifted, been replaced by nothing more than a peaceful lightness.

"Ellie?" Sophie brings me back to the here and now, to the garden, where my fictional characters are no longer putting on a show for my amusement.

"Yeah?"

"I said, 'The End.' You didn't clap. Everyone else clapped, but you didn't." I look up at the semicircle of people, almost all strangers before Lucy, cheering for Sophie's reading. Greg has gotten on his feet to give his daughter a standing ovation. The look on Inderpal's face as he smiles at Sophie tells me that he, too, is relieved to have found a friend. My brother and Claire whistle their approval, their faces flush with new love, their happiness contagious.

"Sorry, sweetheart. Got caught up in the moment. You were wonderful," I say, and beam at the girl in my lap. Nine years old now; just shy of ten years since I came here and talked Lucy off the ledge. Sophie was so tiny then, just a bundle of a baby.

"I'm sad we've finished it," she says. "I wish we could start all over again."

"We can."

"It won't be the same." Sophie looks around the garden, as if she knows it is her last time here and she must soak it all up before her day wanes to a close.

"Of course it will be. We've done it loads of times. We'll just turn the book over and read it again." An edge of panic shades my voice. I am not ready to let go of our evenings tucked into her mini-bed, the green book in hand offering up an alternate universe. We have a routine, like the lamb kebabs. Headmistress Calthorp was wrong when she told Greg that Sophie needs consistency to deal with her grief; it's we adults who do.

"It won't be the same. We've read it. We know what happens. There's no such thing as starting all over again."

"But we can pretend—"

"Right. We can pretend, but that won't get us very far, will it?" She uses that rhetorical flourish owned by the British: *Will it?*

"I don't know."

"Auntie Ellie, it's no big deal." Sophie looks at me with palpable curiosity, her hand patting mine in that comforting after-school-special way. She can't figure out why I'm shaken up all of a sudden. "It's over."

35

Two postal surprises await when we get home after Sophie's party. My parents' wedding invitation has arrived. No matter that the bride is MIA, last heard from somewhere outside Machu Picchu. Red blooms, etched into the thick paper, sprout from the corners, the kind of image intended to celebrate a different sort of union: fresh, innocent love. My parents have already married and divorced, have reconciled and crushed each other so many times I have now lost count.

I am not sure what my dad is thinking in mailing an invitation at all, any invitation, since this form of combat warfare is not his usual style. When my mother retreats, his patterned reflex is to do the same. This time his pursuit is aggressive. He has just told one hundred fifty of their favorite people to make plans for fall nuptials regardless of whether my mother appears to be on board. Denial? Or maybe he's attempting to shame her back from the mountains of Peru. A perverse form of emotional blackmail that she deserves. Either way, I hope it doesn't backfire and that my poor father is not stuck at the top of an aisle waiting for a runaway bride. We will all accept the verdict long before he does.

The second: a huge box for Sophie airmailed from Phillip. Of course he didn't forget her birthday. She squeals when she opens the Professional Deluxe Magic Kit, an all-in-one magician's toolbox, with a collapsible hat, tapered card deck, a book with one hundred different sleight-of-hand tricks, and a follow-along DVD to teach her the moves. The scale of the gift dwarfs mine. I bought her the Harry Potter boxed set, all of the hardcovers nestled side by side into a cardboard treasure chest. The ultimate escape route—a box filled with countless hours of reading pleasure and a chance for Sophie to sample a fantasy world. My gift was courtesy of AmEx, a card whose tread is running thin now that my income has shrunk to zero. My dot-com savings are a comfort, no doubt, but they'll take me only so far.

"OhmyGod, ohmyGod, ohmyGod. Look, Auntie Ellie, it's absolutely brilliant. I have to call Uncle Phillip now. Can I call him now? Please, please, please," Sophie says, jumping up and down the way she usually does when we are in the park and she has to pee and there isn't a bathroom within a five-mile radius.

"Sure." I grab the phone and start to dial, the number second nature. I am calling my own home, a place where, though it houses my letters, my photographs, the buttons and hairspray and old business suits that comprise the accoutrements of my life, I am no longer welcome. What if the test is positive? Would I be welcome then?

"Wait, Auntie Ellie. Is it okay to call?" Sophie's face has sobered; she has descended from her magic high.

"Of course."

"But you guys are getting divorced." I flinch. I can't help it. I re-

peat the word to myself as often as I can. Nonetheless, it still stings.
Divorce.

"But he's not divorcing you, Soph."

"Will he still be my uncle?"

"Of course he will. He loves you, and that won't change regardless of whether Phillip and I are still married."

"Are you sure?"

"Yup."

"But he used to love you, too, didn't he?"

"Yes, he did."

"But he doesn't now?"

"I guess you can say that."

"Then how do I know he won't stop loving me too?"

She's the master of unassailable logic. I pause long enough that
my answer loses credibility.

"Because you're a kid. People never stop loving kids." And without looking at her, I hand the phone off to Sophie so she can say all
the words I used to say out loud to my husband: *I miss you. I love you.
Thank you.*

While I'm pouring our breakfasts and wondering how I'll manage to
sneak out to Boots today to buy a plastic stick to urinate on and then
likely cry over, regardless of my verdict, Sophie pads into the
kitchen and throws her arms around my middle. She is warm from
sleep.

"Good morning to you too," I say, and kiss the top of her head.
I'm not quite sure what this rush of affection is about; Sophie's a loving kid, yes, but not a demonstrative one. She is, after all, half British.

I wonder if she has a sixth sense about the hypothetical tadpole swimming in my belly, its primordial pull so strong it could throw me back across the Atlantic.

"Hi," Sophie says, her voice low and shy, the right pitch, considering I haven't yet had my coffee and am still debating whether I'll allow myself a cup. "Guess what?"

"What?" I resist the urge to pick her up—she is too heavy for that—but I want to feel her arms around my neck.

"Guess."

"You did a cool magic trick?"

"Nope."

"You lost that tooth you've been playing with?"

"Nope."

"You decided to give dreadlocks a try?"

"Nope. What are dreadlocks?" she asks, though her fingers are already on her head, smoothing out her unruly bedhead.

"A hairstyle. Like Bob Marley's."

"Mummy and I used to listen to Bob Marley." Sophie surprises me by breaking out into "One Love," with a matching dance, no less. The moves, a simple translation: a forefinger upright, a number one, and then crossing her hands at her heart. She looks exactly like Lucy when she does it—Lucy, who danced her way through our childhood, making me put on "shows" with her for our disinterested parents, full of Michael Jackson crotch thrusts and a subpar moonwalk. Sophie throws me back in time, and I wonder how I can be there, in Cambridge, giggling and skating backward on the bed, Lucy alive and trapped at nine, making so much noise that her mother yells at us to "pipe down," and how I can be here, too, looking at Sophie, Lucy's doppelgänger, barefoot in Lucy's grown-up kitchen, not an Easy-Bake Oven in sight. Lucy gone and not gone all at once.

Me, age nine, echoing Lucy's moves. Me, age thirty-five, echoing Lucy's life.

"Marley rocks. So I give up. What am I guessing?"

"I did it."

"Did what?"

"You really didn't notice, Auntie Ellie? You've been acting so weird lately."

"What are you talking about?"

"I slept all night." She doesn't make eye contact, looks at the kitchen tile, swallowing down the emotion of the accomplishment. The nights have been cruel to her, leaving a swath of blue under her eyes, like a brand.

"Oh, my God! You did it! I can't believe I—Soph, you did it!" This time I do pick her up and dance her around the kitchen. She is heavy, slipping down my hip, but I don't care. We belt out "One Love," the first time I have sung before a cup of coffee in at least a decade—the first time I have sung out loud at all, come to think of it, for as long as I can remember. "You did it! You really did it?"

"I did."

"I am so happy, I don't know what to do with myself."

"And guess what I dreamed about instead?"

"What?"

"Mary and Colin and Dickon in the Secret Garden. They didn't call me a Lesbian Librarian or make fun of me or anything. Instead, they let me play with them."

"Really?"

"Yup. They even let me feed the lamb."

36

The last time I shopped for pregnancy tests, Phillip was with me, and we chose based on which was the most expensive kit. "Only the best for my baby," he had said.

I didn't know if he meant me or the potential inside me, but either way I laughed. When we got home, he came into the bathroom—he wanted to be part of things every step of the way—and he made us do a fertility dance during the three-minute wait time to make it go faster. The made-up ritual involved some chicken moves, and when my elbow smashed against the sink, he kissed the exact right spot. The test was positive, and for the first time in our lives we both cried tears of happiness.

Today, standing alone before the display in the pharmacy, I choose the cheapest option. A generic brand with a white box and zero promises.

"Stephen, put that back right now," says a woman whose back is to me, but I recognize the voice, the blond bun shimmering under the fluorescent lighting, the familiar Transformer noises. Stephen's mother, the zoo bitch.

I start to walk away, quickly, quietly, to avoid a confrontation. Part of me wants to step on her expensive-looking shoes and punch her La Mer–pampered face; the other part of me is shocked to discover I feel sorry for her. I recognize the defeated hang of her neck, the resigned tone, the exhaustion coming off her in waves; she is a woman who is one hair away from losing her shit.

"I said put that back or when we get home you're having another time-out. And for God's sake will you quit making those noises for five minutes?" Her voice now totters on the edge of disassembling. She's trying hard not to cry. "Mummy and Daddy just need to pick up a few things. Please. Just. Stop. It. Stephen James Devereaux, I beg of you. Stop it!"

Wait—*Mummy and Daddy?* I whirl around, wanting to see the object of Lucy's affections, the man who broke Greg's heart, and almost Sophie's. There he is, hair long, past his ears, brown and shaggy; funky glasses; too tight European jeans.

And, of course, I was right. The Parisian reporter, the one who had the nerve to keep asking, again and again, the voice in my head, *But who are you?*

How dare you? I want to say now, want to slap him for preying upon—for destroying—a family. Surely, had there been no Paris, there would have been no mews *accident.* Surely, this man and Lucy's death are tied in that bizarre cosmic way: A butterfly flaps its wings in Tokyo, there is a tornado in California. Surely, had there been no René, I would be back home, working on my curriculum for next semester. Phillip would be home in a couple of hours, and we'd take in pizza for dinner, half eggplant for me, half olives for him. If there was a test to be bought, to be taken, we'd be buying it, taking it, together.

And what does it mean that as soon as Lucy is gone, conveniently out of the picture and now not even on the cover of the *Daily Mail*—the country has moved on to a missing five-year-old with a bowl cut and one front tooth—René surrenders his Parisian fantasy and returns to his family life? I notice that his face has a scar, a faint line from his bottom lip leading out to his jaw, and I wonder if Lucy felt ownership over that scar, the way I feel ownership of the small birthmark on Phillip's left hip. And then I see the blond woman again and remember that Lucy was claiming what didn't belong to her, and if it ever did, if even for a moment, it wasn't for very long. Suddenly it seems that everything about Lucy was fleeting.

I look at him one last time; I want to be able to conjure up his face again the next time I wonder about those parts of Lucy I didn't know or understand. But he sees me; of course he sees me.

"Ellie?" he asks, and with the word his wife's head jerks up.

I can't face them, and I feel the flush of shame and rage. Shame for Lucy's overreaching, as if her actions are one and the same as mine; rage for my Sophie—how dare they hurt her, all of them, in their different, perverse ways.

So I do what any normal person would do. I drop my basket and I run.

René catches up with me two blocks later, on Notting Hill Gate, the only part of the neighborhood designed for practicality—a main street of chain restaurants, pharmacies, coffee shops, and supermarkets right near the tube, where bustling bodies check off to-do lists on the way to and from work. He takes firm hold of my upper arm, a finger and forefinger around the new extra flesh that mocks me in the mirror, and leads us into the doorway of a hardware store. The cataract skies are misting in that way that they do in London, where the rain particles defy gravity and stand still, bouncing on the noth-ingness of air. We are no better shielded under the awning.

"Please," he says, when I shrug off his hand—*how dare he touch me?*—with more force than I need to free myself of his grasp. "Please, may I talk to you?"

René is looking at me with such intensity, I can't help but look away. I examine the drills on display in the window, the industrial-strength oven cleaner, fifty percent off. What do I have to say to this man?

"A cup of tea? Look, there's a Starbucks right there. Please, just one cup of tea." His accent is lighter than I imagined, and his des-peration is palpable. Though he may be reunited with his family, he has not let Lucy go. I can feel it in the way he held my arm.

"Why?"

"Because," he says. "You know. Because for Lucy."

I nod, too tired to speak, shocked at how my world has gone from a satiric portrayal of suburban malaise to the drama of a soap opera in what feels like minutes. He leads again, this time without touch-ing my arm, and I follow him the half block to the fourth Starbucks I have counted in Notting Hill.

"So," he says, once he has bought our drinks and two packets of shortbread cookies and brought them to a table by the front win-dow. "I . . . I don't even know where to start. I'm sorry about Stephen at school. And I'm sorry about bothering you back when, you know, it first happened. I'm just—"

His voice breaks, and he runs his fingers through his hair. A prac-ticed gesture once, maybe, but now a reflexive one. He takes off his glasses and breathes into each lens.

"I'm just . . . I'm sorry. And I can't believe I didn't realize it was you. The famous Ellie. Who else could you have been? You just looked so different from how Lucy described."

"She talked about me?"

"Of course. All the time. You were sisters. I mean, I knew you weren't related, but she had said you two looked alike. That you were practically, um, what's that expression? Where two babies stick together?"

"Siamese twins?"

"Ah, yes. She said you were Siamese."

"Lucy said that? We don't—we didn't—look alike."

"*Non*, I see. She never felt quite good enough to be your friend, you know? She'd say that all the time. Especially after, you know. After. Us."

"That's ridiculous."

He leaves my words hanging. Sips his tea and stares at me some more, as if just looking can give him answers to questions he has not yet asked.

"Is she all right?" he asks, his tone urgent again.

"Who?"

"Sophie. I need to know if she's all right. It would kill Lucy—" He stops, examines his hands. "It would have hurt her to know she wasn't."

"She's all right. She's tougher than she looks."

"Good. I'm glad."

"Yeah."

"You should know that it was real. Our relationship. I loved her."

"I know."

"I mean, now that she's gone I can almost make believe it never happened. Like she was a dream or something. Like that whole time wasn't, you know, real. But it was." He looks out the window, and his wife is right there, steering Stephen down the road, pharmacy bags in both of her hands and tears streaking her face. She doesn't see us, and he looks away. Neither of us wants to watch the collateral damage. The life out there, trekking in the rain, fighting a ghost she can't compete against, looks like an alternative destiny. "I guess that's why I wanted to talk to you. To remind me that she existed. I have no one else to do that for me."

René looks older than Greg, maybe forty-five, and his eyes are tired with grief. He wears a weariness that makes him look the part of the widower too.

"I wanted to go to the funeral," he says now. He holds a stirrer like a cigarette, then breaks it in half with two fingers, and then in half yet again. "I felt horrible that I couldn't go. Can you imagine? Not being able to go to the funeral of the woman you love? I bring flowers to her grave, but, *non*, it's not enough."

Since the funeral, I have not been back to the cemetery. I should go, I realize now, if it means one more way to honor Lucy. I'm grateful suddenly to this man in front of me, her lover, who has made sure that her grave doesn't sit unadorned. I bet he brings her tulips, her favorite, in simple and elegant bouquets.

"How was it? The funeral? Would she have liked it? I mean, would she have been happy with it?"

"Not really. We just weren't, you know, ready. Prepared, I mean. None of us knew what to say. It was too much." I think of the little boy I saw playing in the private garden that day, and I think of his red plastic shovel. "The food was good."

"Good. She would have liked that." He closes his eyes for a minute, and I am not sure where he goes. Maybe to Lucy, maybe to the funeral he wasn't welcome at. "I know you probably think I'm a horrible person."

"I don't think you're a horrible person. I don't even know you. I just can't understand. I mean, how could she have? How could she have left Sophie? An affair, okay, I get that. But leaving? Moving to Paris?" I feel on the verge of tears again. But not for me: for Sophie. She got left behind not once but twice.

"It's not that far."

"That's not the point."

"I know."

We look out the window again, at the gray that shades the city daily and can make this place feel hard and cold and lonely too.

"Have you ever just wanted to start your life over? That's how Lucy and I felt. We just wanted a second chance. A clean slate. Until Lucy, I felt like I was just getting through the days. After Lucy—" He stops, takes a breath, picks up a new stirrer to fiddle with. "I felt alive. Like there was a whole other world out there. And then the job in Paris came up, and the timing seemed so perfect. We always talked about running away."

For a moment, I let myself believe that there is another universe where they get to see their story through, where they reach for more happiness, maybe more love, than they had each thought they deserved. For a moment, I'm even willing to sacrifice Sophie and Greg, leave them to pick up the shards, for Lucy to live in Paris with this man. To be silly and madly and shamelessly in love. To attain that elusive dream of a do-over. Heartbreaking to think she had her life taken at the exact moment when she thought it was just getting started.

"Thank you for bringing her flowers," I say.

"She wanted to tell you. About me. She said she tried a million times but was always too scared."

"Lucy wasn't scared of anything, least of all me."

"She was. She was scared of telling you. She thought that by leaving Sophie, she'd be losing you."

"That makes no sense."

"She said you'd never understand. She said it was the one thing."

"The one thing?"

"Yes, *je ne sais pas*, the one thing—the only thing—you could never understand."

37

When I get back to the house, Sophie and a woman I don't recognize at first are sitting cross-legged on the floor around the coffee table, chatting about yesterday's birthday party. Sophie is still in her pajamas, her head hidden under the tall black magician's hat Phillip sent. The woman has her graying hair pulled back in a messy ponytail and is dressed head to toe in sweats; both the matching pants and top are decorated with a large and absurd decal of the Union Jack. She wears no makeup, and her face—defeated and lined—reminds me of a desert photo, all scorched earth and fine intersecting lines. Unyielding terrain, tired and dried up.

Upon seeing me, her features reorganize into a smile, blood flows into her cheeks, and she now almost looks like my mother. If my mother wasn't a beatnik New Yorker who loves tunics and saris but a Midwestern tourist who forgot her fanny pack and Nikon. I am frightened by this approximation.

"Jane? What are you doing here? Aren't you supposed to be in Peru? And what the hell are you wearing?"

"Nice to see you, too, Eleanor."

I draw my mother into a forceful hug, a gesture that surprises her even more than it does me. Though she looks too different, like someone I used to know but have lost touch with, I am relieved just at the sight of her. My mom is here to rescue me.

"She lost her luggage in Lima," Sophie says, apparently already up to speed on my mother's resurfacing. "And instead of taking a flight back to New York after the ashram, she wanted to see you. So she thought, why not? You only live once. Next thing she knows she's hailing a black cab outside Heathrow."

I love when Sophie parrots back adultspeak. She gets the intonation spot-on, a mirrored reflection of your own verbal tics, like hearing your voice on an answering machine. My mother's *why not? You only live once.* Her *next thing I know* filtered through the mechanics of a little girl.

Jane looks me up and down, paying special attention to my chest. My boobs haven't gotten bigger already, have they? She takes in my hair, frizzy from the humidity, my jeans, T-shirt, and sneakers, hastily thrown on this morning, the new lines on my face, the younger version of hers.

"Sweetheart, are you okay?" she asks, her surprise betraying her agenda. She is not here to rescue me—she didn't know I needed rescuing; how could she?—she is here for me to rescue her. "You look, um, terrible."

"I know. So do you. You okay?"

She shrugs. "Been better."

"Hey, Soph, why don't you go upstairs and start that Harry Potter I got you?"

A pout.

"We need some grown-up time," I say, and smile at her, though she still stomps off. I've been here long enough now that it doesn't break my heart.

"So it seems both of us are at a crossroads," my mother says once Sophie is out of earshot and the two of us have settled on the couch. We are leaning into each other as we talk, the way Lucy and I used to at fourteen when we'd gossip about boys. "You're getting a divorce. And I'm supposed to be getting married in two months."

"Your invitation is beautiful, by the way."

"The invitation?"

"Are you serious? Did you really not know Dad sent out the invitations?"

"I didn't even know he'd picked them out. I'm so screwed," my mother says, and slouches like a boy unsure of how to deal with his growth spurt.

"Or you could just go back and marry Dad and get it over and done with already. Stop messing up both your lives."

"Or I could do that."

"Sounds like a plan to me," I say, as if it is as simple as my mother getting on a plane, and perhaps it is.

"So what's going on with you? I don't think you've hugged me that hard since I bought you that beat-up station wagon on your sixteenth birthday."

"I think I may be pregnant."

"But you don't know?"

"Haven't had a chance to take the test. But I've been throwing up and moody, and my boobs kill, and I've been here before. With Oliver, this is what it felt like. Except then I was happy about it. Until I wasn't."

"The father?" No judgment in the question.

"Phillip."

"Huh."

"Yup."

"Well, I guess that's what you get for having sex with your husband," my mother says, and laughs too hard at her own joke.

"Funny, Jane."

"We sure are messed up, aren't we?" She now rests her head on my shoulder, as if she is too tired to keep it lifted.

"We sure are." And then we both close our eyes—my mother's head on my shoulder, my head on top of hers—and let ourselves take that accidental fall into sleep.

"Did you know I proposed to your father?" she says later, when we are back in the pharmacy, shopping for a new stick for me to pee on and prenatal vitamins, *just in case*. Before we headed to Boots, my mother forced me to stop at the nearest eyebrow waxer. Apparently she couldn't stand me looking like, as she put it, "one of those hairy wolf boys from the Mexican circus."

"You proposed this time or the first time?" I ask.

"This time."

"Seriously?" I stop walking and face her straight on. She looks nonplussed.

"Seriously. I have this client; she's a couple of years younger than you. Anyhow, she had an amazing boyfriend, and as soon as she sensed he was about to propose, what did she do? She dumped him. So I'm listening to her tell the story, and it's so obvious that she has all these commitment issues because she lost her mother at a young age and she's still a kid herself in so many ways—so textbook, it's ridiculous, right? But it suddenly hits me that I need to grow up, too, you know? How can I tell this girl to get some balls already if I don't have a pair of my own? You know what I mean? I'm sixty years old, for God's sake."

"Yeah. I hate to remind you, but Grandma's still alive. So what's your excuse?"

"I dunno. My dad was a rampant philanderer. Does that count?"

"Maybe. I always forget that about Grandpa. He always seemed like such a nice guy."

"He *was* a nice guy *and* a rampant philanderer. Apparently you can be more than one thing. "

I read the back of the pregnancy test. I can have results in as quickly as two minutes.

"Anyhow, I have this major realization that I need to change the way I'm living my life. So that night I took the shuttle up to Boston, surprised your dad, and proposed. Out in the garden in the gazebo. Right where you and Phillip got married, come to think of it. And guess what? Want to hear the hilarious part? He said no."

"Go Dad."

"Yeah, then I spend the better part of three months trying to convince him to say yes, and you know what happens as soon as he does?"

"You run like hell."

"Exactly."

"Mom, what do I do if the test is positive?" For perhaps the first time in my life, my mother doesn't correct me and ask that I call her Jane. Instead, she puts her arms around me and draws me into our second hug of the day. A daily record for us.

"You know what you'll do, Eleanor."

"I do? Take care of the problem?"

Another ugly euphemism, and my voice catches as I use it. She gives me a look that speaks a full sentence without saying a word: *You are thirty-five, financially solvent, and this may be your last shot; I am not even going to waste my time having that discussion.*

"I know: We'll move in with you." I am joking, but as soon as I say it, I feel shaken by my own use of *we* so quickly, so naturally. I have already co-opted this seed—which may not be a seed at all—into a *we*.

My mother smiles. She won't even let my father, her fiancé, move in; their long-term plan was a long-distance marriage. Me and Hypothetical Baby are not welcome in the small two-bedroom in the West Village.

"Nope. You're gonna do what you do best."

"What's that?"

"My dear Eleanor, you're going to grow a pair."

We spend the one-hundred-twenty-second wait time playing charades. My mother goes first. Two words. A movie. She gets into it: starts gesturing wildly, fake-punching herself in the face, falling to the floor of the three-by-five bathroom, and closing her eyes.

"Punching. Um, hitting. Knocked out."

She points at me and then at the ceiling.

"Heaven. Sky. Up," I guess.

She smiles and points again. Gestures for me to put the two words together.

"Knocked Up!" My voice triumphant for a moment, before I get her joke. My mother has always had a bitchy sense of humor, an amazing ability to crack me up only to discover, twenty seconds too late to be angry, that I am laughing at myself.

The cell phone beeps time.

My mother looks at the stick, hands it over, still in mute charades mode, and just points at me and smiles.

And then she motions her hands in a big round arch over her belly.

I breathe in and out of one of Sophie's old lunch bags, which smells like ham, whenever I need a break from crying. I'm not taking this like an adult. I've mastered guilt and nostalgia and grief; we've all been friends for years. Fear, though, bone-shattering and stomach-cramping visceral fear, renders me unprepared and trembling. I feel like I've just strapped on the dynamite backpack for a suicide mission.

"Do you know why I've always asked that you and Michael call me Jane?" my mother asks, apropos of nothing. We have not communicated much since I passed my big test with a plus sign. She just sits next to me on the couch, rubbing my back and keeping an eye out for Sophie and Greg, who went for ice cream a while ago.

"Why?"

"Because I didn't want you or anyone else to see me *only* as a mother. I didn't want to be *only* your father's wife. I thought it would be good for you to see me as a whole person. Jane, not Mom."

"That's stupid. That's not what I'm afraid of. This isn't an identity crisis."

"It's not?" she asks. "Then why is this such a tragedy?"

I look at her, amazed that my own mother—a psychologist, no less—doesn't get it. She assumes everyone else approaches their own life with the same amount of self-absorption.

"I never said this was a tragedy."

"Okay, then, what's the problem?"

"What's the problem? Are you seriously asking me what's the fucking problem?" I put my forehead against the cool glass of the coffee table, take a deep breath. I know my mother happens to be the closest target, but I can't keep myself from showering her with stray bullets. With Lucy gone and Phillip opting out, I feel so lonely, it's almost an out-of-body experience. One Ellie floating above, watching the proceedings with interest, another going through the motions of sitting on this couch, hyperventilating, inappropriately cursing at her mother.

"Yes, I'm seriously asking you what's the fucking problem. You're pushing forty, you've always wanted to be a mother. You've been screwing up everything good in your own life lately. The way I see it, this is the best thing that has ever happened to you."

Blunt-force trauma to the head.

"First of all, I'm not pushing forty. Not yet, anyway. And putting aside for a moment the fact that the father of this future baby is filing for divorce, and, you know, I'm here to take care of Sophie— putting those eensy-weensy matters aside for just one second—do I have to remind you of what happened last time? How that turned out? I can't go through that again. I can't. I won't." I start to cry again, but this time the tears are full and loose, a total body release.

"What if I promise that everything will be okay? That this baby will be perfect and healthy?"

"But you can't. You can't promise that."

"But what if I could?"

"But you can't. That's the whole point. You just can't."

"You won't lose two babies. I know it in my soul. I do." She takes my hand and looks into my bloodshot, brimming eyes. My mother, despite her ridiculous dress sense, tends not to use words like *soul*, or *universe*. I guess a couple of weeks on an ashram in the mountains of

Peru could infect anyone's vocabulary. Or maybe she has lost her clinical distance, and her daughter is sitting next to her on the couch, and she wants to make it all okay.

"Your soul, seriously? I am supposed to relax and trust your soul? Oliver died, Mom. Inside me. And then Lucy died, walking down the street. You can't promise me everything is going to be okay. You just can't. Sometimes things are not okay. Life isn't like a movie."

My mother lets me cry a little bit more, rubs my back in the concentric circles of my childhood. I give in to the sensation, spiral down into the last pool of comfort, the fatigue finally overriding my adrenaline.

"But sometimes they are, Eleanor. Sometimes things do turn out okay. Can you at least accept that? That sometimes things do work out in the end?"

"What, like you and Dad?"

She meets my sarcasm, my glare, first with her own secret smile, the one she uses with her patients, the one that says, *Fine, I'll humor you*, and then it switches, the smile turns real and wide, her eyes filling with tears to match. Her face plays out her realization, much like Sophie's, the thoughts pulsating so loudly they broadcast without anyone saying a word.

"Yup," she says. "Exactly like me and your father."

My mother books a flight leaving tomorrow morning, direct to Boston, where she will rendezvous with my dad, beg and receive his forgiveness, and then indulge him in the final wedding planning. She promises that she will be there in eight weeks' time, walking down the long aisle in my dad's backyard, the very same one I once walked.

"You know what's interesting? No matter where you go—an ashram in Peru, to visit your beautiful daughter in London, even New York—you're still stuck with yourself at the end of the day. I know it's cliché, but it's true: The voice in your head doesn't change with geography," my mother says as we take a "ramble" on Hampstead Heath—my mother's idea, since we must use all words and do all deeds British while we're here. I don't know how a ramble is any different from a walk. Nonetheless, it feels different today as I link elbows with my mother on the paved path through the green grass.

Next to the pastel houses in Notting Hill—I've grown to love how their fairy exteriors refuse to give in to the gloom, whimsical enough that I often feel like I'm on a stage set—the Heath is my second-favorite place in London. Japanese-style trees, fine and pointed, contrast with meadows and hills and glittering ponds. It reminds me of Kent but without the sheep and the cottages; I'm again tempted to put ribbons in my hair and walk with a lace-lined umbrella to shield my fair skin from the nonexistent sun.

Deep thicketed woods bracket the landscape, adding an ominous quality—the green of the rolling hills that much greener, that much brighter, because of the deep forest shading its edges, and because you know the deep thick of the city is breathing its choked breaths less than a mile away.

"Yeah, I guess."

"And I'm not just talking about place either. I'm talking about circumstances. You know, they did this study of people who became paraplegics later in life and found that just a few years after their accidents they were back to their original selves. If they were happy people before they lost the ability to walk, they eventually became happy people again. If they were depressed before, they went back to the same level of depression. We can't escape our nature. We are who we are."

"But you're going back to Dad. If we are who we are, shouldn't you be getting on a plane tomorrow to go anywhere but Boston?"

"Nope. I love your father, I've always loved him, even when I wanted to kill him, and no matter where I go on this planet, that never seems to change. Might as well accept it already. It's time you went back to being as happy as you were before, too."

"Go back to being as happy as I was before what?"

Now she gives me the look reserved for insubordinate patients, not one that is in any way *patient*; her jaw sets rigid, her nostrils flare, her eyes go cold and hard.

"Enough, Eleanor."

"No, seriously, Jane. As before what?" She looks at me tenderly now, almost as if to say, *You really don't know, do you?* And then she unlinks my arm from its perch under her elbow. She holds my hand now, the way I used to with Lucy when we were six, both of us in our OshKosh overalls, me shy, her giggling, as we took a tour of her backyard:

"There is the tree where I fell when I was four but got up and didn't cry. And that's the slide that my uncle gave my parents when my cousins got too big for it. And here is my armpit. I can make fart noises from it. My dad taught me," Lucy would say, the master of ceremonies even then.

"Before Oliver, Eleanor. Before Oliver."

"Who's Oliver?" Sophie asks. I had almost forgotten she was here, since she has been walking and skipping a few feet in front of us, lost in the scale of the Heath, an outrageous-sized version of her own Secret Garden.

I am about to say, *Nobody*, but I remember my mother is with me, and a therapist, and she'll look down upon my dodge.

"My son. The baby, who, you know, died."

"Oh, right. I didn't know his name was Oliver. I wish I'd got to meet him. I bet he would have been cool and would have played with me."

"I bet he would have." This is the most I've said out loud about Oliver in two years. I touch my stomach. A reflex.

"You think he's hanging out with my mom in heaven?" Sophie asks.

"I hope so, sweetheart. She'd take good care of him." And for an instant I picture it, Lucy and Oliver together, taking a tour of someone's backyard.

"Just like you're taking good care of me here." I feel the guilt multiply and breed in my gut. Can she sense the gravitational force, that something may take me back across the pond? Can she tell I am making pro–con lists in my head as we speak, deciding what it is I am supposed to do? My competing vows amplified and in direct conflict. What I owe to Lucy, and to Sophie.

What I owe to the dividing cells in my stomach, and, by extension, Phillip.

And, yes, what I owe to myself too.

38

I buy a single pregnancy book. The one everyone tells you not to buy when you are pregnant because it will horrify you with its litany of things that can go wrong in the womb. I eat the forbidden book whole, devour the dismal forecasts, swallow each one, each warning sign, until I feel them nestle in my gut. I am not naive this time. I ignore the happy, optimistic books I used to read; I will leave nothing to chance. Statistics comfort and haunt me. Daily inspection of my skin, my teeth, my urine, the shape of my belly helps me sleep better at night. No one can say I am not watching, not taking the best care I know how.

I read the book again and again. My new bible, now that Sophie and I have moved on from *The Secret Garden*.

The doctor—part of the UK National Health Service—tells me not to worry, that what happened before will not necessarily happen again. My second pregnancy is no riskier than any other. She doesn't tell me what I want to hear, that my bad luck the first time acts as insurance. That I've already paid my premium and used up my deductible. That I can't lose twice.

Greg looks at me strangely when I refuse a glass of wine with dinner, when I ask for chicken teriyaki no MSG when he orders in sushi, when I touch my stomach like it's something delicate.

He doesn't ask, and I don't tell.

Three months. I give myself three months, the first trimester, to keep my secret, to jump through the first hoop of security, before announcing the situation to anyone, and that—*please forgive me*—includes Phillip. Other than my mother and my new NHS ob-gyn—and I guess my brother—no one knows about the cells multiplying and coalescing, somersaulting in my belly. No one knows it is now almost half an inch long, has elbows and toes. Already, the gods have decided the sex—there are miniature testes or ovaries tucked inside the tadpole tucked inside me, organic predictors of a potential future. They will grow and unfold and drop, and one day, in thirty-two weeks, assuming—*don't assume, don't jinx it, don't get your hopes up*—assuming this doesn't come undone, I will hold a baby in my arms, a tiny boy or a tiny girl, and he, she, will belong to me.

Phillip hasn't called, and I haven't called him. When I think of him, I feel pure guilt about my silence. But I'm too scared. Not only will talking to him require me to make necessary continental decisions and own up to my literal Sophie's Choice, there is the possibility that he could reject us both—me and the baby—wholesale. Even worse, telling him feels like making the same mistake twice—indulging in that toxic presumptuousness. I *should* wait until after the three-month mark. Right now is too soon to start talking about something that may not even be real.

Instead, I will relish my twelve-week reprieve. I've never had a huge secret before, never known the pleasure of keeping a part of yourself hidden and unavailable, protected from others' parasitic impulses. In my hopeful moments, the ones I try to keep tamped down to not let them overwhelm the fear—the fear I've become comfortable with—I want to hug my fishbowl belly and scream: *Mine!*

I wonder if this is how Lucy felt during her time with René. Did she walk around with this whole new life tucked into her pocket? A reservoir of excitement and love and giddy warmth amplified because it didn't yet have to be shared? The one part of her not ripe for picking from her husband, from her daughter. Did she enjoy the romance of the undercover world? The fact that she could keep a secret from me if she needed to? That where she ended and I began, and where I ended and she began, was much clearer than we had ever thought?

Do you know I'm having another baby, Luce? I think to myself, words sent out to a destinationless universe. *Do you now know my secrets, too, the ones I don't even get to know yet? Boy or girl?*

I don't expect answers, and I laugh at myself, unable to even attempt to hold my news close and locked under my skin. I still try to tell Lucy, even though she can't hear me.

I'm lousy with secrets. Which may be why, unlike my best friend, I've never really had any until now.

We watch the news every night at six over dinner. Greg comes home early most days—early meaning after a full ten-hour workday—to spend time with Sophie. He tucks her in now, after we've eaten and put our time in with BBC One and she and I have read together. He's taken on the responsibility of her nightly glass of water. The nights are routinized and relaxing. A well-choreographed dance that begins with Greg sweeping through the door at five, running straight to Sophie as he loosens his tie: *How was your day, love? Give us a kiss.*

She still has nightmares. Fewer, though. Less painful. The grip on her dreams has softened, her reaction dulled from the nightly repetition. She has them once a week, at the most.

When we last saw Simon, I asked what had caused the change.

"I think she's grown bored with her own horror. She is a resilient kid," he said.

I felt a flush of pride then for Sophie. She even gets As in Therapy.

"The last known living American veteran of World War One has died today, at the age of one hundred ten," the pretty BBC presenter with the posh accent and the Botoxed forehead says now. Behind her on the big screen we see color pictures of the man, with his four kids, six grandchildren, and four great-grandchildren. His skin ropes around his tiny frame, the teeth too big for a retreating mouth.

"Is World War One the war where America got free from London?" Sophie asks.

"No, Soph. The American Revolution was a good one hundred fifty years before that. And America fought and won its independence from the British Empire, not *London*. London, as you already know, is a *city* in the *country* of England," Greg says.

"Right." Sophie's attention is drawn back to the television as they show pictures of the funeral. A row of men in uniform point large rifles at the sky, like they are aiming for God.

I am trying hard to keep my tears silent, wiping them away as quickly as they come. A period of history over and done with, eventually swept clean with the death of every veteran. Not just an erosion of memory. A complete wipeout. I twist the event into something dramatic and devastating and within reach: *They're gone. They're all gone.* As if I am watching a flattening bomb, twin buildings collapsing, an explosion on the tube—events that I can relate to, that twist my gut, that conflate time via burned televised images.

One man has died, a ridiculously old man, no less, a universe away from what we now casually call our "terror threat."

I see his picture, and his teeth, and his family, and I remember reading about the Battle of the Somme, where almost twenty thousand men died in a single hour, and my heart breaks for the march of history. For the world my baby may one day join, the one that Sophie already lives in, a world unrecognizable, and yet the same as it has always been: people killing one another with the closest tool at hand.

"Auntie Ellie, why are you crying? You're such a dork. Yesterday you got upset at a nappy commercial," Sophie says, crushing any illusion I may have had that my frequent tears have been well hidden.

Greg looks at me, more concerned than bemused. I have no idea if he knows I'm pregnant. Certainly, there haven't been any gentleman callers as of late to indicate I've been up to some baby-making. Other than when my parents visited, my pay-as-you-go phone rarely rings, and when it does it's either my brother or Claire, my brother to gush, Claire to thank me again and again for setting them up. Phillip's out of the picture—no calls, no packages, no e-mails, no faxes—more radio silence. He makes only late-night appearances. I dream of him, mundane dreams in which we do things normal husbands and wives do, movies and dinner and loading the dishwasher; they fill me with such comfort that I have trouble escaping out of bed in the mornings. I want to stay tucked in my head, warm with my own boring memories that aren't boring to me at all.

"You all right?" Greg asks me, handing over a paper towel, presumably for me to use as a tissue.

"Yeah, he just looked like a sweet man."

"He lived to one hundred ten! We should all be so lucky."

"We should all be so lucky," Sophie echoes, but softly, as if she's inputting the expression into her brain.

"I guess. I dunno, it's still sad. That's the dream, right? To survive something like a war and do something you love and live that long and have lots of kids and grandkids," I say, thinking of my stomach, which hasn't grown all that much. I look like I recently indulged in a bit too much Chinese food.

"My dream is to grow up and marry Inderpal and have lots of kids, at least ten, and be a news anchorman like that lady," Sophie says, pointing at the screen. "She has a cool job. Or J. K. Rowling. I kind of want to be her too. I want to be lots of things."

Greg smiles at Sophie, no longer concerned about her burgeoning interest in boys. He's heard the marrying-Inderpal thing enough times that he doesn't react. Now that he's met the kid, heard Inderpal's adorable adultspeak, listened to him talk about his rock collection and how he now wants to be a doctor *and* an astronomer and why he thinks Gordon Brown is underperforming as prime minister, Greg can't help but approve. We are just relieved that she has found a real friend.

I take Sophie for playdates at the park, where she and Inderpal sit at the bottom of the slide, she with a Harry Potter on her lap, he listening to an audiobook through his iPod. Occasionally, Inderpal bops his head to make it look like he is listening to rap or Panjabi MC. We all pretend to be fooled.

"What do you want to be when you grow up, Ellie?" Greg asks. He gives me a nostalgic look, one that says, *Are we there yet? Are we actual grown-ups? Because this isn't what I dreamed about when I wore pajamas with feet: to be a lost widower, a bored lawyer, a confused parent.* Sophie laughs at us, her assumption that we are too old to be fantasizing about our futures. Ours have arrived long ago.

"I have no idea. I used to want to be a CEO. That's what I would say when I was little. I was rebelling against my mother. Now I don't know. Definitely not what I was doing before I came here. Maybe an elementary-school teacher? What about you?"

"I want to live on a big farm and throw out my BlackBerry. Have one of those movie moments where I get to chuck the thing in the ocean or something. Maybe burn my ties too."

"Your ties? But you like to look formal."

"Not really. I just live in a formal world."

"So why don't you? Trade in that Beamer for a tractor. Put on some overalls and call it a day. Wake up and smell the manure. You can afford it." Greg doesn't answer me and doesn't smile. He just looks away. Changing your whole way of life is easier said than done.

"Can we have sheeps? If we live on a farm?" Sophie asks.

"Sheep," Greg and I both correct her in unison.

"Sheep," she echoes, happy to have learned something new. I can't help but think of the baby and know, with a guilty certainty, that he or she will never be this easy to please. "We should all be so lucky to have sheep."

39

Sophie and I read *A Little Princess.* Not quite as good as *The Secret Garden*, but it does the trick nonetheless. We again have an orphan, which now seems to be a prerequisite for children's literature, and again she's a little white girl, born in India. Poor Sara Crewe must endure the ultimate twist of fortune: She goes from being the favored student at a fancy boarding school in England, when her rich father was alive, to being a lowly servant, when he dies and leaves her penniless. We blissfully ignore the imperialistic undertones in the book, as we did last time, Sophie not quite ready for a lit-crit discussion of the implications and lasting effects of the British Empire's complex relationship with pre-independence India.

After we finish chapter five, where we learned about Sara's mesmerizing storytelling capabilities, and I'm leaning to turn off Winnie's torch, Sophie says my name—"Auntie Ellie?"—with a tone I've come to recognize. It's her *I have a big question* voice.

"Yes?"

"Um, I have a question." Greg should be up in a few minutes to smooth her forehead and to say good night. I wish he'd hurry up.

"Shoot."

"Do you think Mum knew she was going to die?"

"What makes you say that?" I try to keep the alarm out of my voice. Pretend like I can grow accustomed to the reality of Lucy's death, just as Sophie has become increasingly numbed to the terror of her dreams. I can be a grown-up too.

"Well, that day—you know, *That Day*—we were talking at breakfast, and Daddy went to work super early, and so it was just Mum and me, and she said that no matter what happened she would always love me. Even if she wasn't around every day to say it. She even let me have Lucky Charms. She *never* let me have Lucky Charms."

"I don't think so. I mean, there is no way she could have known. No one could have. Just like no one could have stopped it."

"I guess."

"But it's true, you know."

"What?"

"That she will always love you, even if she isn't around to say it every day. Just so you know, I love you too. Every day. Even if I'm not around to say it."

"Okay. But you're not going anywhere, are you?"

"Nope."

And I lie straight to her beautiful face.

40

After Thursday's therapy, I give Sophie a couple of pounds and send her to the coffee shop downstairs for a hot chocolate again. In a few minutes, I'll find her sitting at the counter chatting with Gus, the owner, who has a covert agreement with Simon to babysit his patients whenever they retreat downstairs alone; this way, Simon can give the parents an update and the kids the sweet gateway drug of independence.

"Sophie seems better, right? The nightmares are almost all gone," I say.

"She's doing great. This is a lifelong thing, though. Grief. Loss. She is not just going to wake up one day and be cured."

"Well, that's great news." I'm tired, which sharpens the edge of my sarcasm. Even though I haven't gained that much weight yet, every day now feels like moving day; this new working body feels like heavy equipment that follows me around. I want to lie down and sleep for the next seven months. "Sorry. I'm cranky."

"You okay?" The sun is shining through the bay windows, and in the bright spotlight of day, Simon is less attractive, his rough edges exaggerated. His muscles are almost too big, bulbous ropy knots and hard-earned, and he seems a good ten years older than I had originally guessed. Nearer to fifty than forty. This new, less handsome Simon is easier to talk to.

"Yeah, but I need to ask you an important question. Will Sophie be okay if I go back?"

"What's going on? You going home?"

"Well, it turns out I am . . . I guess I should just say it. I'm pregnant. But please don't tell. I haven't told anyone yet. My husband—my soon-to-be ex-husband—is back in Boston, and I'm here. And Sophie—"

"Sounds complicated."

"Yup. It is."

"So what happens now?"

"I don't know. Any advice, Doctor?"

Simon looks pensive.

"You do what you got to do," he says, in the worst faux–New York accent I've ever heard, but I give him points for the hand gesture: a good shake, mob-boss style.

"Yeah? What's that?"

"I don't know. Just trying to do a *Sopranos* impersonation. I just got the DVDs. Hey, did you know that I have three kids?" I have been staring at the big sheet of white paper spread across the table. Sophie's drawing. A picture of her and me and a birthday cake with nine candles. A few sheep dot the background in white swirls of crayon.

Simon again has made hand turkeys. He apparently has a limited repertoire.

"Three? Wow. How old?" I am rearranging my vision of Simon's life. Before, I pictured him young and single, taking those big arms and his bald head to the bars of London, swigging beers and bedding women; a plunderer, with a tender side. In the last five minutes he has aged a decade and spawned three children. Still no wedding ring.

"Two girls and a boy: six, nine, and twelve. My partner, Steve, and I adopted from Cambodia."

I do my best to keep my face from betraying my surprise. I have been out of the dating world so long that it hasn't even occurred to me to wonder if he's gay. The revelation makes me like Simon even more, because his arms are no longer threatening.

"I guess my point is, when you start a family, you make real trade-offs. You just can't do everything. I've given up my work in Sudan for my family. Hardest thing I've ever done, but I'm not sure I had a choice."

"But Sophie. I mean, seriously, will she be okay?"

"I'm not sure what you want me to say, Ellie. Yes? No? She'll be heartbroken, she'll miss you. No doubt about it, mate. But will she be okay? Yeah, she'll be okay. She's a fighter, that kid. And I assume you'd just be leaving the country, not her life entirely."

"She needs me. How could I? How could I leave her?"

He doesn't respond. Lucy, I realize, would tell me to go home. Chase the happiness to which we are all entitled. She may even disagree with Simon—that we all have a choice. And Phillip. What will Phillip say? *I don't know, I don't know, I don't know. What will Phillip say?* is a new refrain for me, like my old standby, *What would Lucy do?* Both make my stomach hurt.

But Sophie—and I imagine her right now, just below me, sipping her hot chocolate in a deliberate manner, enjoying the heat of it, the sweetness as an ephemeral pleasure. I should teach her that word, *ephemeral.* She'd like it.

But Sophie. But Sophie. But Sophie.

I've thought through the variables. The tidy ending we all hope for. Boarding school in New England? Phillip loves me and wants me back and transfers to the London branch? I spend six months here, six months there? None works.

I want to smuggle Sophie home, make her belong to me.

But she doesn't belong to me.

"I miss Mum," she says now on a daily basis, the words bubbling up when we least expect them. Like cartoon speech: a circle of air between us, a string of letters. When she says it, she doesn't look like a nine-year-old girl, doing normal nine-year-old things—playing in the leaves that have started to fall and gather, reading Harry Potter, waiting in line for a Flake 99—she looks like a resigned adult.

"I miss her, too," I always parrot back, because it's the truth, and there is nothing else to say. I try to tamp down the visions that come up unbidden; Sophie making her way through adolescence and then on to the marathon of adulthood without a mother. Sophie's first heartbreak, her first business suit, her wedding, and also the everyday, every day, the sweet beat of life that beats us down. The alarm clocks, the apologies, the passive–aggressive put-downs. Canker sores and menstrual cramps. The stomach flu, the good old-fashioned flu, and that thing that is almost-but-not-quite a flu. And the victories, too: the season finales, an e-mail back, getting the job, falling in love. The possibility. All that possibility.

Here is the truth, again, unbidden. The one thing that will never be said out loud: Sophie needs—will need—the only thing in the world I can't give her. And this, too, a destructive confession that I have no choice but to make out loud, soon: I need—will need—to go back, to leave behind that which doesn't belong to me and finally take charge of what does.

* * *

We take a long, nonsensical route home and lap up the surprising heat of the day. Sophie and I follow Portobello Road to its end, loop through Westbourne Park, and then take the big hill down until we reach the mansion blocks of Holland Park, identifying the flags that salute us from the guarded embassies. We then make our way back east through the Notting Hill side streets, allowing ourselves detoured circles around the grandest private gardens. Sophie decides to play one of the games we usually reserve for the school run. She points out her favorite houses and makes up stories about the people who live there.

The pink one on the corner is an orphanage for seven kids whose parents were wiped out in a hurricane. (Note to self: Consider limiting Sophie's news-watching and orphan-reading.) Next door is a childless couple who wants to adopt. We imagine the two groups meeting; one day the couple will buy lemonade from the stand the kids set up to make some money for shoes. *We've always wanted seven children!* they will say. *We've always wanted parents to take care of us!* the kids will say, and then pack their meager belongings into plastic bags and carry them next door. Of course, everyone will live happily ever after, riding away into the sunset in bunk beds. We're both suckers for *happily ever after.*

"You know what I figured out today?" Sophie asks, after we send our fantasy family on a trip to Hawaii as an alternate director's-cut ending.

"What?"

"Magic isn't magic."

"Huh?"

"I mean, I've always known it wasn't *real,* that they were tricks.

But they're not even tricks. They're secrets. According to that video that Uncle Phillip sent, 'Magic only works when the magician knows something the audience doesn't.'"

"Give me an example." This is a teaching tool I picked up from Claire. The real-life equivalent of *show your math*.

"Okay, that card trick I did yesterday? The secret was that I hid the queen of hearts in my sleeve. But you didn't know my secret. And if you knew it, it would have ruined everything."

"That's a clever way to look at it. But what about *real magic*? Do you think that exists? Like how Dickon can talk to animals? Or is that just like a card up the sleeve?"

"I don't know. Dickon is a character in a book."

"So?"

"So he doesn't count."

"Why?"

"Because he's not real either, silly. Frannie made him up."

"Maybe she did, maybe she didn't."

"Come on, Auntie Ellie. A little boy who can talk to animals? And if magic existed, my spell would have worked."

"What spell?"

"The one I did for, you know, Mummy. I tried twice. Even on the day of the accident, I tried to make it a trick. I even believed it was a trick. But it wasn't a trick."

"No, no, it wasn't." I put my arm around her, move her closer to me. Always more for my comfort than hers. She's the bravest person I've ever known. Even braver than her mother.

"So, to tell you the truth, Auntie Ellie? I'm not so sure about magic. I think I'm pretty much done with it."

"But don't you think certain things are magical? And if we believe certain things are magical, maybe then it's easier to believe in magic?" I am not sure why it is important to me that she believe, but it is. She's been forced to surrender too much of her childhood already, told to accept as fact the unacceptable: Her mother is not coming back. The least I can give her—the bare minimum—is something to hold on to.

"Like what?"

"Well, for starters, the Secret Garden."

"The book or the actual place?"

"Both."

Sophie smiles. "Good one. What else?"

"You?"

"Me?"

"Yup. You, my favorite goddaughter, are pure magic."

"I'm your only goddaughter."

"Still my favorite."

"And I'm not magic."

"Yes, Sophie. Yes, you are."

41

After Sophie's gone to bed, Greg suggests we have a drink out-side in honor of the clear skies, and he pours harmless lemon-ade for both of us. Not much attention has been paid to the landscaping in the backyard, which is a rectangular patch of green that mirrors the shape of the house. Long and skinny. We lie on twin wooden chairs padded with waterproof pillows and keep them at the angles we find them, almost flat-backed. Lucy was likely the last one to sit out here, and I picture her relaxing on a rare sunny day last summer, feeling decadent for taking the time to do nothing but warm and darken her skin. A human surrender to the sun, and that reflexive inclination to face the heat straight on.

"Nice night," Greg says, staring up at the cloudless sky, at the stars that are somehow still there though we haven't seen them in a while.

"Perfect." I rest my hand on my abdomen, and in my head I talk to the baby. *You feel that air? It's kissing our skin. Appreciate nights like these. They don't come often.*

"Ellie? We need to have a chat." Greg sounds nervous, and I

wonder if I should be too. But the chair is too comfortable, I am sinking into my cushion, and I feel far away from his words. There is the outside me and there is the inside me now, and I am reveling in the bubble of the inside me. I don't even have to look at him, not with the sky stretched before us like a canvas.

"What's up?" I ask.

"I don't know how to say this."

"Just say it. Like ripping off a Band-Aid." My tone is casual, almost flippant. I feel invincible, as long as Sophie is safe in her bed, the baby safe in my belly. Nothing can touch me as long as those two things remain fact.

"I, um . . . well, here's the ten-thousand-foot view: I sold the house." Invincibility broken, so clean and fast that I don't even get a moment's satisfaction at his finance terminology—*ten-thousand-foot view*. My heart blinks, drops clear down into my stomach, and I grip the armrests to fight the vertigo. The strange part, though, is that I can't say why. I hadn't even known I loved this house. But I do, with a ferocity that frightens me. *You can't sell Lucy's house.*

"But. I mean. Why?"

"Don't worry. It's not like I'm going to throw you out or anything. You can stay with us for as long as you like. Even after we move. You know you're always welcome. You're family now."

"Thanks, but I wasn't even thinking about me. It's just . . . it's Lucy's house."

"No, Ellie. It's *my* house."

"I'm sorry, I know, I know it's yours. But it's her, this house, if you know what I mean. This house screams Lucy."

I picture the white couch in the living room, so optimistic, a symbol that the world can be kept as clean as you like, as beautiful and ordered as you choose it to be. And then her office, the exact oppo-

site, an embracing of wear and tear, of the shabby chic, of the fact
that the relics of our lives—the diplomas, the books, the pictures—
add up to something worth displaying, if only to ourselves.

"Exactly. I need to get the hell out of here. Enough of seeing
Lucy everywhere. I'm just tired. I'm tired of missing her, and hating
her, and then missing her all over again. It's killing me. I found a
Post-it note yesterday with her handwriting on it. At first I almost
kept it; you don't chuck out that sort of thing, anything to remember her by, you know? And then I thought, *What if it's* his *number on
it?* But it doesn't matter, none of it matters." His voice revs up and
then gives out, broken. "No, none of it matters, not a whit, but it
still feels like it does. Is it so wrong to not want to feel so much all
the time?"

Greg squeezes his eyes shut, as if even looking at the stars is too
much. His face says what Sophie said out loud less than a month
ago, when she again woke up wet with the residue of her nightmares: *Please, make it stop. Please. Just. Make. It. Stop.*

"I'm sorry. I sometimes forget . . . I don't know, that you're not
allowed to just miss her. That's it's more complicated than that."

"But want to hear the sickest part? It's like she gave me a gift before she died. It's so much easier to be angry at her than to miss her.
When I forget to be angry, it's almost too much. And when I look at
Sophie—" Greg's voice breaks, and he drifts off into silence as he
composes himself. When he speaks next, he is back in the confer-
ence room, cool and controlled. "There are just too many memories
here, good and bad, for both of us."

"You should go. A fresh start. We all deserve those once in a
while." But even as the words come out, I wonder if they're true.
Not the deserving part, but the possibility of starting over. Cleaning
the slate. And whether we are all just missing the point when we

reorient toward a new place we decide, sometimes arbitrarily, to call home.

"Ashford," he says, when I ask where he's found a new neighborhood. "It's a tiny village. As picturesque as the English countryside gets. Sheep and cows, and everything is green and lush. But it's only sixty miles from here, so Soph can still see Inderpal and go to sessions with Simon, if she wants to."

"Sounds great, Greg."

"And there's this amazing school, just up the road, where they have special gifted classes. Here's the best part—" He pauses to build up the suspense, the silent equivalent of *drum roll, please*. "Tomorrow I'm going to announce to the partnership that I'm going part-time. I'll work only a couple of days a week, virtually commute from a home office and be there when Soph gets home every day. I think she'll love the countryside, getting out of the city. It's not all that far from where we went for her birthday. It looks just like that, actually. She'll practically have her own Secret Garden in the backyard." He says it all at once, his practiced spiel for everyone who will ask in the weeks ahead where they are going. A practiced spiel that he's in the process of refining for Sophie.

"I am so happy for you." And I mean it, even though there are now tears dripping down my face. Even though I feel like someone has stepped on my chest and forced me to lose Lucy all over again. There is the loss, and there are the million side losses, and this house is one of those. "And I'm happy for Soph too."

"It's the right thing, Ellie. It is." Greg announces it as if he is convincing himself and the universe at once. "It has to be."

"I know. It will be." I swat at my eyes with the backs of my hands.

"And the garden? It's a proper one, not like this box but one with vegetables and herbs. I think Sophie will enjoy playing out there."

"I'll have to buy her a book so she can identify all the plants. She's going to drive you crazy with all the scientific names. Just you wait."

"L?" He says it just like Lucy did. Short and to the point.

"Yeah?"

"You're going to make a great mum."

"You think?"

"I know," he says, and I finally turn to look at him, to see if he is saying what I think he is saying. But his eyes are closed again. "Please just tell me that it's Phillip's."

So he knows. Of course he knows. I haven't touched a cup of coffee or a glass of wine in almost twelve weeks.

"Yes. It is. Of course."

"Are you scared?"

"Yes."

"Have you told him?"

"No."

"Are you leaving us?"

"I'm sorry," I say, and now the tears come again, this time, loud and gulping, remorse-filled tears. "I lied to Sophie. I said I wasn't going anywhere."

"I see."

"I'm a coward."

Greg doesn't say anything for a while. He just lets me cry. He's a different man from the one he was four and a half months ago. He is resolute, less brittle. He can endure a woman's tears.

"You'll still be in her life, though, won't you?"

278 / Julie Buxbaum

I nod my head yes, because I can't form words. Imagining my life without Sophie now is like how it once was imagining my life without Lucy, like how it would be to imagine my life without my left arm; unimaginable.

"You'll visit, and she can visit you?"

"Of course."

"Could we do all the holidays together? I want to give her a sense of family. I don't want it to be just her and me against the world. That's how I grew up, and it wasn't good." Greg is now a man with a plan; I imagine he has a list typed out somewhere, ways to get their lives back in control. Ways to be a better parent, to be both mother and father to Sophie. Action items.

"Please. Yes. We can be a transatlantic team. A transatlantic family. I may be leaving, but I'm not going anywhere. You're stuck with me."

"Okay," he says.

"Okay," I say, both of us making vows to the sky.

Fifteen minutes later. We are still lying here, awake, looking straight ahead, as if the stars are a puzzle that we are capable of solving. The stillness of the night settling around us like a duvet.

"Ellie, you know you have to tell him. Soon. It's not fair. All these secrets you women keep."

"I will. I'm . . . I've just been . . . gathering my strength. I kind of wanted to wait until it looked like things were pretty safe; I didn't want to jinx it. And now I'm just too scared. I don't even know what to say. The last time I saw him, he asked me for a divorce. He's going to freak out."

"Are you kidding? Have you met Phillip? The man will be thrilled. He was so crushed before, when you lost the baby."

"Oliver."

"When you lost Oliver." Greg repeats after me, without judgment, with understanding of why I need his name said. "He was calling here every day, talking to Lucy, even asking me, trying to figure out how to help you when he could barely handle it himself. He was a mess."

"I didn't know that."

"Now you do."

42

For my thirty-fourth birthday, shortly after I lost Oliver, Phillip gave me the only gift that had a shot at cheering me up. He flew Lucy in for the weekend. She arrived on a Friday afternoon with an overnight bag and two bottles of wine she bought for us at duty-free; she was unwrinkled, looking not at all like she had just spent six hours on the plane. But that's how Lucy was, someone who could spend the day in a tsunami and come out with her hair a little tousled, a natural I-just-had-great-sex look. She hugged me with the same ferocity that I hugged her, a mutual clinging, a reminder just by seeing each other's faces of who we used to be, who we maybe still were.

"I'm here!" she said, in a *ta-dah* voice, as if she had done a magic trick just by showing up.

Phillip had booked us a day at the spa—again, another perfect gift—one of the fancy ones on Newbury Street where, after your massage, you got to spend hours slipping in and out of a terry-cloth robe, reveling in the release of the hot tub, the steam room, and the sauna. We deemed it the Day of Our Pore Opening.

"I would rather die than get old," I remember Lucy saying, while she stared at the mirror and poked at her skin. Stretching it hard across her cheekbones and letting it relax back to its normal state.

"Stop being ridiculous. You're beautiful, and, as much as it pains me to admit it, you'll always be beautiful."

"No, I really won't. Did you see those girls in here earlier? How old were they? Twenty-two? Did you see their asses? My ass will never look like that again."

"My ass has never looked like that."

"And their skin. It glowed."

"They just had facials."

"I just had a facial. Seriously, L, every day I'm getting a little less attractive, and Greg, the bastard, is getting more attractive. I know it's a cliché, but it's true: Men have it easier. And it's not fair. Maybe the answer is to die young."

"That's the stupidest thing I've ever heard. There is more to life than whether you look twenty-two." I remember it occurred to me for the first time that there was a price to be paid for beauty like Lucy's; I had never before seen the downside, except for maybe the fact that it made other people always assume you were better— smarter, nicer, more spectacular—than you actually were. I could think of worse things than high expectations and the benefit of the doubt. But seeing Lucy look in the mirror, the way she poked at the burgeoning crow's-feet around her eyes—which I had noticed but acted as if I hadn't—I realized it must be hard to let go of something that everyone has always patted you on the head for. Something that was ninety percent out of your control.

What happens after beautiful? Sad, ballooned lips and plastic-surgery scars? Desperate attempts to reclaim what was only one draft of you, though somehow the defining draft?

"Is there? Really? Can you imagine even ten years from now, being right here, with a new crop of young girls, and seeing how they'll look at me? They'll feel sorry for me that I can't leave the house without a tub of cover-up under my eyes and a scarf because of my stupid neck. Have you seen these lines? I have started the descent. And eventually people are going to stop seeing me at all." Her eyes brimmed with tears, and she blinked them away, embarrassed that something as trivial as necklines could trigger such passion, particularly in light of the circumstances. I had just lost a baby. "I know, I know. I'm awful, and small-minded, and my values are all screwed up. I know what you're going to say. I grew up in Cambridge too."

She grinned at me, trying to erase her tears: *Of course I don't mean it. I don't really care about necklines.*

"I wasn't going to say anything. I can list a hundred things I hate about myself that are only going to get worse. I get it," I said, and just like that a list pooled, almost written in the air. The line between my eyebrows; my hips and ass, which hadn't yet had a chance to recover from pregnancy; the line on my belly, where they cut Oliver out. The flaws all felt heavy, like guilt, like an inevitable disappointment. "But there is such a thing as aging with dignity. There is no shame in getting old."

"But maybe I just don't want to do it. Maybe I'll die young and glamorous like Marilyn Monroe." She put her hand to her forehead, her familiar *I know I'm being melodramatic* gesture, turning her statement into something silly.

"She OD'd. That's not glamorous."

"When you think of Marilyn Monroe, what do you think of?"

"Her holding down that white dress."

"Exactly. Not her taking enough barbiturates to kill a small town. You think of her white dress."

"So?"

"So I wouldn't mind being remembered for something as simple and as beautiful as a white dress."

Lucy got what she wanted. Because of the diabolical nature of the Internet, a new form of indelibility has arisen: Lucy Stafford will be remembered for being the rich Notting Hill mother and journalist who got stabbed in a mews less than a mile from her multimillion-dollar home. The photograph that accompanies every article—now almost an emblem—was taken moments before her wedding ceremony; it's a reflection shot, two Lucys, one looking at the other, as she puts on her earrings in the mirror. I have no idea where they got the picture from—probably one of the nannies—but it's the one she will be remembered for and the one Sophie will see a couple of years from now, when she learns the magical powers of the search engine.

Lucy would be happy with the picture. She looks beautiful and alive. She's wearing white.

We, of course, the ones who loved her—who can still imagine her at the age of nine, decapitating her Barbies' heads to string them along some fishing wire, who can imagine her at the age of twenty-four, talking through chipped white plasterboard in our "two"-bedroom apartment in New York, who can imagine her at twenty-seven, exhausted and teary after childbirth, who can imagine her at thirty-four, tracing the lines on her face in a mirror, who can imagine her at thirty-five, dancing to Bob Marley with her daughter in this kitchen—when we think of her, we will think of all these different versions. When you spend a lifetime with someone and then they are gone, *whoosh*, *just like that*, all the incarnations bend time and stay suspended in a line, not simply stuck in what came last. Still and constant, memories an unfolded map, like the timeline in Sophie's history textbook. Memories we will cling to and origami, until they fade out, colorless. Until one day we, too, are left to Google for a hit of that spectacular woman we once knew, the image we find superseding all others. The final draft; Lucy in a white dress.

43

Before we start, I've got to tell you something." Sophie is tucked into her mini-bed, a safe place, perhaps a manipulative place for me to spring my news. *The Secret Garden* is open on her lap. Now that we've finished *A Little Princess*, which we enjoyed but it didn't grab us by the throats, we want to go back and revisit our favorite just one more time. We've missed Mary and her transformation; we want to watch her unfold from her numb ugliness into full childhood glory.

I'm nervous and sweaty and my brain is spinning too fast. I'm scared that I'm about to lose my favorite person in the world. Greg and I have decided that I'll tell Sophie I'm leaving, and then he'll get her on board with Operation Move to the Countryside. We are throwing a lot at her, maybe too much, at once.

She looks up at me, open and trusting. Even after this year, she still retains the expectations of a child—most news is good news; parental figures will never hurt you. If you do what you are told, everything will be okay. My chest feels tight; my imminent betrayal will not be lessened by its unburdening. It will be magnified when I see the shift in those eyes. From love to anger.

"You're not going to like what I have to say, but I need to tell you the truth. And I hope you'll be able to understand. If not today, then one day."

Sophie scoots down lower in the bed. Winnie-the-Pooh casts his golden light over her, and the rain drums the rooftop, a steady background beat.

"I lied to you the other day."

An audible gasp. In her world, there are categories of people: *good, bad.* By lying, I have gone to the dark side.

"And I lied because I didn't want to hurt you. It was stupid and I was scared and I'm sorry."

Sophie doesn't speak. She's frozen in anticipation.

"I'm going home—back to the US, I mean. I want to stay here with you, I want nothing more than that, but I have responsibilities, and if I stayed it wouldn't be right."

No answer. My tears start now, heavy curtains around my face.

"I love you, Soph. And I will always love you, and I will always be here for you, even if I'm not here, here. You know what I mean? If you ever need me, I'll be a phone call away, and I'll get on that plane no matter what. No matter how small the problem is. We'll talk every day, and we'll see each other. Of course we'll see each other. You're my goddaughter, and nothing is going to change that."

"But. But you said." Her own tears have unleashed already, and her face is wet, just like mine. She's furious and sad and will not pretend otherwise. She is too small, too fragile a package to hold that much in.

"I know I did. Have you ever said something you knew wasn't true, but you said it anyway because you wanted it to be?"

"Maybe."

"I want to be here, stay here with you. But something happened, and it means I need to go back and at least be near Phillip. See, I'm . . . well, I'm pregnant. I'm having a baby."

"What? Why?" She looks disgusted.

I am not sure how to tackle that one, leave the birds-and-the-bees discussion for another day. Even with that part taken out of the equation, the answer is no more clear: *I am having a baby because I got pregnant, which seemed like a one-in-a-million shot from a round of pity sex with my soon-to-be-ex-husband, but there it is, it happened. And sometimes it feels like a miracle, like magic. And sometimes it feels like the universe is playing a cruel joke on me.*

"Well, I'm not sure how else to say it. But there's a baby growing in here, and because of it—him or her—I need to go back. I haven't even told Phillip yet." I feel another stab of betrayal, the guilt just stacking up; Phillip will be the last to know information that first and foremost should be his. The sort of information that cannot be told over the phone. The longer I wait, though, the more impossible telling him seems to get.

"So there is a baby in there, right now?" Her curiosity in the *how* of everything is getting the better of her. She tilts her head, puts her ear to my belly, and I take the opportunity to smooth her hair down.

"Yup."

"I don't hear anything."

"You will, eventually. It's still pretty small. About this big." I spread my thumb and forefinger as wide as they'll go.

"I thought you'd just gotten fat."

"Thanks."

"You eat a lot of biscuits."

"I do."

"But you can't, I mean, you can't have a baby. No, it's not fair." She has drawn herself in until she is at her smallest, tightest kernel of self. "Absolutely not. You can't go. What about me?"

"Soph—"

"No. No." She turns away from me now, so all I can see is her pa-jamaed back and the hiccuping of her shoulders. She has moved from bracing, to tears, and now to full-blown anger. It's sinking in. I'm leaving and there is nothing she can do about it. "I hate you. I fucking hate you."

She says it in a whisper. No need to scream, since she is tasting the power of those words for the first time. There is nothing funny about them; she, unlike me, isn't going for a cheap laugh. She turns what had before been our inside joke—my foul mouth—into a weapon.

"I fucking hate you," she says it again, this time yelling, the repetition not lessening her sting. Her fists, her whole body, is clenched.

"Can I say something?"

"No. You're a liar. A big fat fuck shit liar. I never want to speak to you again."

I'm still crying, again trying and failing to be the adult. I don't know what I'm doing, don't know what I should be doing, and the thought that I'm hurting Sophie, that I've chosen to hurt Sophie, turns my fear, my confusion, into horror. I stare up at the ceiling, the closest approximation of heaven or the beyond I don't believe in: *Lucy, what do I do? What have I done?*

I am a big fat fuck shit liar—I pulled the old magician's trick of a bait and switch on her, and I shouldn't get away with it. I deserve her tears and her yelling. What I can't handle, what I've never been able to handle, is her pain.

"Soph, it's important you hear this. Just because I'm having a baby, that doesn't mean I'll love you any less. You need to know that. No matter what happens in this world, I'll love you with all my heart. Nothing, nothing can change that."

I'm met with dreaded silence, no noise except the desperate gulping of tears. I have lost her for now. We have regressed back to mute Sophie, back to me being more stranger than family. Any satisfaction I may have felt by doing right by her, by Lucy, has been erased; my scales have tipped now. I've done this family more harm than good.

"I'm sorry," I say, my voice broken and hoarse, one hand on my stomach, already a divided loyalty, a traitor, since I whisper to it in my head, even now: *We're okay, we're okay, we're okay.* "I can't tell you how sorry."

Sophie sits up, her back still to me, and wipes away her tears with her sleeve. And then she does the thing I least expect. She picks up *The Secret Garden* and throws it as hard as she can against the wall.

"Stupid fucking book."

Sophie cries herself to sleep. I sit on her bed, rubbing her back, until her breathing evens out and her tears dissolve into dreams. Before I leave, I kiss her forehead and turn off the light. My movements are slow, methodical. Careful. My job so far has only been to protect, and I keep failing. I want the robustness of Susan Sowerby on the moors, able to feed and care for and love an entire brood, never making promises that are really compromises in disguise: *I'll visit every few months; we'll use this thing called Skype; I won't miss a thing.* I pick up our book, take solace in the fact that the spine has not been broken, and decide to bring it to bed. I want to dip into the warm pool of fiction and let it coat me.

Before I allow myself the respite, I take my second step of the evening toward righting my upside-down world. I reach out to my husband.

To: phillip.klein@excesscapital.com
From: ellie.lerner@yahoo.com
Subject: Please

Hey. My guess is I am the last person you want to hear from right now, but I need to ask you for a favor. You owe me nothing, and I'll understand if you've already stopped reading. I'll ask anyway, though, because I have to, and I need to, and I want to, and I owe it to both of us to.

As you know, I am coming home for the wedding. Rumor has it you'll be there, too, and I hope you will set aside some time to talk to me. I have some things that need to be said and that need to be said in person. Actually, that should only be said in person.

So here is what I am asking: Please don't file anything. Can you believe I can't say it, even now, the D-word? Please don't, if you haven't already. Please not yet. I know I've asked too much of you these last few months, maybe the last few years, but just one more thing. Please give me a fourteen-day reprieve.

Much love,

Ellie

PS—Yesterday I was thinking about how we used to go to Best Buy to play video games. That was fun. Why did we stop doing that?

The horror of the BlackBerry. Its flattening of language and the death of reflective thought. I get a response in twenty seconds flat.

To: ellie.lerner@yahoo.com

From: phillip.klein@excesscapital.com

Subject: Re: Please

Already filed. You'll get the papers later this week. We stopped going to Best Buy bc you said it was stupid.

44

I am going to see the spot where Lucy was murdered. I want to know if the ground is still red. If there are permanent cracks. With Sophie left in the capable hands of her father, I venture out into this borrowed city and take that forbidden path we have ignored every day on the school run. I draw my jacket tighter, as the city has made the shift from filmy summer to unfolding autumn; the air has turned sharper, the leaves losing their green first, soon their bearings. Palm cupped to flesh, I hold my stomach, as if to keep the baby inside, praying the jelly roll that surrounds it is enough protection for this horrible place.

A pilgrimage for a nonbeliever.

At first, I think I've gone the wrong way. This mews is charming, at least in the noon light under the broad blue sky. The homes are dollhouse-sized, with flower boxes and streetlamps, shared walls lining the cobblestone streets. This block could be in a guidebook—*the real London for free!*—maybe even make the cover photograph: a curve of a road, some of the stone walls decorated with a tangle of roses, the jagged roofs like English teeth, the lack of a sidewalk part of the attraction. The string of homes, converted eighteenth-century stables, are now occupied by millionaires, not horses, happy to pay the premium for living on a cobblestone street in the back alleys of a Dickens novel or perhaps Sherlock Holmes territory. A place for fictional characters and fictional crimes a good century ago. Nancy Drew would fit in as well: pint-sized houses, filled with pint-sized mystery for the pint-sized Girl Detective.

How did Lucy die here? The mere thought of it—that she was brought to her knees in a place like this—seems impossible. Too cute. Too rich. Too movie set for this to be it. I half-expect to see a chalk outline on the ground, a smug, good-looking detective measuring for some cop-show antics. The street lacks the hectic atmosphere of the market stalls on Portobello Road, where the charm is tinged with just a bit of desperation and the sheer number of people passing by suggests you might want to keep your hand on your wallet, an engagement ring turned around, diamond-shaped diamond to palm.

Lucy died here, on a beautiful street, in a beautiful neighborhood, and there is nothing to show for it. The potted plants still bloom, alive, like a splash of color in a doctored black-and-white photograph. The ground is dry, the stones old enough to make you think of horse-drawn carriages and women in gloves.

I allow the *if only*s to taunt me. The infinitesimal increments of fate that added up to something so significant it can be described only with an absence. If only Lucy and Soph had taken a little longer getting out of the house that morning, if only the man had chosen a different street, left not right, or vice versa, if only, if only. If only these two beings had never collided on a quiet mews at eight in the morning, mass against mass, anger to passion, the hungry bottom of addiction, the hungry high of love, and how that somehow devolved into this: a cutting. The opening of flesh, and the stopping. God damn it, the infinite, inglorious permanence of the stopping.

I stand here. Long enough that I get a strange look from a guy decked out in hipster regalia—skinny jeans, a Danger Mouse T-shirt—who passes me while walking his wirehaired terrier. Paralysis has set in; I stare at the ground, hoping for a porthole that will allow me to talk to Lucy. I still have her voice in my head, though I know that, too, will go with time. Sophie has already lost it, asking me on a daily basis to remind her what Mummy sounded like.

Tired and heavy and swollen all over, my body has abandoned me wholesale and is tuned only in to its baby-manufacturing responsibilities. I am no longer important. Mere rubbery shell, expanding to fit the needs of the swimming creature within.

I eat for it. Walk for it. Hurt my goddaughter for it.

I'm going home, I say to this bit of ground on which my feet are planted. As arbitrary a piece of land as any other, this place where Lucy died.

I'm saying good-bye and going home and trying to recover whoever I was before. You remember, right? The Old Ellie. I know I'm leaving bodies in my wake, and for that last bit, Luce, for that part, I am sorry.

"Do you live here?" I ask the guy with the dog, my voice finding its way outside my head, where it had felt locked and boxed. Speaking only to steady myself.

"Yes. You another journalist?"

"No."

"Oh, too bad. Thought I could get in the paper or on the news again." He laughs, a short staccato spurt, as if he is sharing the fact that he is the proud owner of a chuckle-snort. His free hand goes to his heart, a *dear me, isn't that a hoot?* gesture. It is not a hoot.

"Excuse me?"

"Well, when that lady was murdered, I got to be interviewed on BBC and ITV. Have it taped to prove it." He motions with his thumb to one of the houses, yellow and petite, white-shuttered, almost an invitation. For some reason, the place makes me think of Goldilocks: I imagine going in and passing judgment on every room. *Too small.*

"Good for you," I say.

"You heard all about it, didn't you? It happened right over here, right about where you're standing."

"Yeah, I heard." I curl my hands into fists, the anger coursing through me so fast, I start to shake. How dare he speak so casually? Like it was fun and exciting that Sophie was here watching the unspeakable.

"Biggest thing to happen to this neighborhood since that bloody stupid film, if you ask me."

But I didn't ask him, and then I can't help it, the rage coils to the blistering surface. This man is why Lucy has morphed from person to story, a warning tale told in self-defense classes around the city. Or a piece of gossip: *You hear what happened to that pretty lady?* This man is all that is evil, all self-interest and self-glorification; a man with a cute dog but no shame. He is a surrogate, and I'm okay with that. I hate him with every molecule of my body.

I forget Lucy, and Sophie, and Phillip, and even the baby for a moment. I am rage, and rage is me, and there is no stopping it.

"Listen, you little shit, how *dare* you? Who do you think you are?

Someone died here, and you think it's okay to laugh and brag about being on television? Screw you." I look at him again, and for a minute I pretend he's the man in the trench coat. Here's my chance to stop him from following me. "Her name was Lucy, by the way. L-U-C-Y. She was thirty-five years old, and she was somebody's mother. Don't you for a moment—not one single moment—forget that. You hear me?"

The guy looks at me, maybe a little scared. I take a step closer.

"Her daughter is only nine years old. It should have been you," I say. "It should have been you here, dying like a dog in the street. Not Lucy. Never Lucy."

And then, for the first time in my life, I do the exact right thing, the brave thing, the stupid thing, and it feels as good as I imagined it would. No, it feels even better.

I slap him hard against his face. Palm to cheek. My wedding ring—which I had turned around a few blocks ago, near the bottom of Portobello—cuts a thin line into his skin.

When he bleeds, he drips onto the pristine cobblestone.

Not my proudest moment when Greg picks me up from the police station. He arrives solemn and in lawyer mode, all business with the police officers, until he sees me around the corner, shamefaced and rubbing my chafed wrists, sitting next to a cuffed 250-pound man with facial tattoos of tears. His demeanor shifts in an instant. Greg tucks his chin to his chest, puts his hand up to cover his mouth, looks around the dingy, fluorescent space. Anything to hold it back until we get out of here. Still, the backs of his shoulders tremble and he covertly wipes away a tear. He can't help it, the scene is too much, the need to keep it tamped down amplifies the need for release, and, despite his best efforts, his smile breaks through, and then the laughter comes next, booming and filling up the room. He doubles over, trying to mask the noise with a cough, until he's able to take it down a notch into girlish giggles.

His first words to me are not *don't worry, I know your rights,* or even *are you hurt?* Instead: "Damn it, I can't believe I didn't bring my camera."

I get off easy, since this is my first offense in any country, and, let's face it, all I did was slap a guy. I am freed after a short period of time during which I was handcuffed, which was more uncomfortable than I would have imagined, and forced to wait in a cell with an intoxicated prostitute, which, as these things go, was surprisingly pleasant. She and I chatted about her last client, a well-respected politician with two kids, who pays to be burned in his armpits and other discreet places his wife likely won't notice.

"The secrets I see," she said. "You'd be amazed how little people actually know each other." Her voice was so casual—this is her life, indulging other people's demons—that part of me admired this sad woman. I almost wished I was still wearing my cast, so I could ask her to sign it.

After my time *behind bars*—an expression I will definitely use when I tell this story to my mother, who, no doubt, will be very proud—I am given a stern lecture about assault and battery before I'm released into Greg's custody.

Apparently it's illegal to go around slapping people. No matter that the wound was superficial and the guy didn't need a single stitch. No matter that the asshole deserved it.

The officer is merely putting on a show, though, since it's clear there will be no charges. We both know I won't do this again. This was a one-time-only, a freak occurrence, something I can check off my list of things to do before I die. I don't hesitate to use the tadpole here, when it seems I am a little too unrepentant for the police officer's taste. I plead pregnant insanity, which means one more person knows I'm having a baby before Phillip does.

"Sorry," I say. "It was the grief and the hormones talking."

"Sorry, sorry, sorry," I told the guy, too, once our scuffle was over, which wasn't much of a scuffle at all. I slapped him, he called me a "twat" and other beautiful and elaborate and British swear words, and the fight pretty much ended when he stepped out of arm's reach and called the police from his cell phone.

"I can't believe you did that. Just slapped some guy off the street," Greg says on the car ride home, after we sit for ten minutes in the police-station parking lot because he is laughing too hard to drive. He laughs the way I used to—instinctual and guttural, no reservations, no posturing—so different from how I've been laughing lately—tired and resigned. His is contagious, though, and I start to laugh, too, deep and with my whole body, until we both have tears rolling down our faces.

For some reason, it's hilarious that I just got arrested.

"Yeah."

"And you made him bleed."

"Apparently. But it wasn't a big deal. Just a small cut."

"And after you slapped him, he called the police?"

"Yes."

"What a wuss."

"That's what I said."

"Out loud?"

"What?"

"You called him a wuss out loud *after* you slapped him?"

"Um. Yeah."

"You are out of your bloody mind. You could have been hurt."

He's right. We've seen where false bravery can get you. Then again, he didn't get a look at the guy. You can't really be afraid of a schmuck in a Danger Mouse T-shirt, walking a tiny terrier, no less.

"Sorry about you having to pick me up from jail, Greg." I feel bad about dragging him out of the house with yet another emergency phone call, forcing him to come to my rescue.

"Are you kidding?" Greg says, his shoulders starting to heave again, and then mine do too. The giggles once more taking their hold and rising to the top. "This is the most fun I've had in years."

The first thing I want to do when I get back to the house is call Phillip and tell him about the way the handcuffs cut into my skin and about the cell I got locked in, albeit for less than twenty minutes. I want to tell him about the baby, and how I am coming home for good, and that I miss him, and that I slapped a stranger. I want to tell him I won't teach our tidy little swimmer to hit, and I promise to never even tell about my criminal record; nonetheless, I know I will be secretly proud for the rest of my life. That was the messy, dirty guts of real existence—hand-to-hand combat—which has given me new appreciation for why some people, usually men, enjoy watching boxing and Ultimate Fighting Championship. Less than twelve hours ago, I found organized fighting abhorrent.

I feel high and light, released. Absolution through a damn good palm-to-cheek slap. I feel brave for the first time in my life. Bigger than I actually am. Bigger than I ever thought I could be. And a little bit more like the old me.

Phillip is too far out of reach. My big announcement will be made in person, face-to-face, and so the phone and e-mail are not options right now. I've waited this long to tell him, I can wait one more week, seven more days, until I flash a passport and get on a plane and watch my parents get married in the backyard and ask my estranged husband: *What do we do now?*

Sophie is sitting on the stairs when I get back, as if in judgment. Greg has promised to keep quiet about my indiscretion, since it would further push me off my role-model stool. I have fallen enough in recent days. She looks like she knows, or knows something, the way she is sitting with her arms crossed, her eyebrows drawn into a crease down the middle of her forehead. Her glasses perched low.

"Are you ready to talk to me yet?" I ask her, reaching out to smooth down her ponytail. I take comfort in the fact that she doesn't move away.

"No."

"Well, that's a start, at least. You said no. You didn't just shake your head." She nods at me, serious and solemn. I should know by now that little of what Sophie does is accidental. She never lets a word slip. "How about this? You don't have to talk at first, but I'd like you to listen. Do you think you could do that for me?"

"Okay."

I move over to the stairs and sit down next to her, so we are shoulder to shoulder.

"Did you know that when you love someone as much as I love you, it makes you more capable of loving other people? It makes you more generous with yourself. I have even more love to give now. Do you know what I mean?"

I get a head shake negative, her eyes on her knees.

"Okay, what I'm trying to say is that being here with you and taking care of you has made me a better person. You have literally grown my heart bigger." My eyes fill up when I realize that hitting that man was a product of her, too, an awakened life. I have taken so much more from this child than I will ever be capable of giving back. "So, when I have this baby, that doesn't mean I'm going to love you or care for you any less. It does mean I'll be farther away, which stinks. But that's just simple geography. You and me? We can handle geography."

Sophie sometimes plays that game with the big plastic globe in her room that we all have played, a finger tracing its edges as it spins, and a verdict wherever it lands. *Where do I go?* And maybe a close corollary, the one I used to play as a kid and sometimes do even now: *Where do I belong?*

"Know what else? Since I'm your godmother, guess what? You're going to be a godsister."

"I am?"

"Yup."

"I guess that's pretty cool."

"Serious responsibility, but I know you can handle it. And we'll get to talk every day. I found this neat thing where we can see each other on the computer while we talk. So it'll be like we're in the same room."

"Skype."

"How do you know about Skype?"

"Mummy told me about it."

"Oh." What a waste of anticipatory pain, which reverberates now, hearing Sophie show a hand she doesn't even know she was dealt: all of Lucy's groundwork for a different kind of departure.

"Too bad you can't use Skype in heaven."

"Yeah."

"Auntie Ellie?"

"Yeah?"

"You won't forget about me, right?"

"How could I forget about you, Soph? You're my home."

"People can't be home. Places are home."

"Nope, people can be home too."

Sophie stands up, takes a quick look around the room, and then looks at me, really looks at me—a sweeping of my eyes with her eyes, a long deliberation, as if mining my soul for bombs. When she's done, she still looks pensive. She's not quite convinced.

"I need to think more about that," she says, and then walks away.

45

Today's airport departure will be clean and clinical, all business. Greg drops me at the curb, since I can't handle the waving good-bye as I disappear into a security line, my laptop out, my shoes ready to be placed in the plastic bin, as I feel myself in literal retreat. Getting smaller and smaller. I want my farewell to be quick, three minutes or less of hugs, and I love yous, and I'll see you soons, because the alternative is too real and too painful. If I admit what is happening here—I am leaving Sophie behind—I am not sure I can do it. Put the one foot in front of the other and lead myself thousands of miles away from her. How did Lucy make her Parisian plans and buy tickets and rent an apartment? Maybe René was right; maybe I could never understand, even though I find myself in the exact same place, making an identical decision. I want to pick Sophie up and run as fast as I can toward Gate 43B. Steal her away, as if she were mine to keep.

We say good-bye, and I smell Sophie's hair and watch her push her glasses back up her nose. We high-five. I give her an extra hug. I give Greg a kiss on the cheek, and we say over and over again how we'll see each other next month, for Thanksgiving; this isn't good-bye, this is so long for now, even though we all know a certain stage has come to an end. We are all saying good-bye to something, even if it isn't me.

I put my arm around Sophie's shoulder and look at her to memorize this incarnation, since she'll grow even in these few weeks apart. Looking at her, I see Lucy and not Lucy at once, as if thirty years of friendship aren't lost but saved-up love for this new person, who is so much more—braver, smarter, more intuitive—than we ever were.

"Did you know that the formal title of the House of Lords is actually the Right Honourable the Lords Spiritual and Temporal of the United Kingdom of Great Britain and Northern Ireland in Parliament Assembled?" Sophie asks me, just as I am about to walk away. She's showing off.

"No, I didn't. But that's hilarious."

"Is it?" Her face, as usual gives her away; she's wondering whether she has lost me already, another adult laughing at what she doesn't understand.

"I don't know. I think so. It's just so fussy and formal. What do you think, Soph?"

She takes a moment to answer, her lips moving as she turns it over in her mind.

"I know what you mean. I reckon it's a little ridiculous." And then she smiles, that irresistible smile, and I smile back, until my cheeks hurt.

"You be good," I say, nodding, smiling, tightening my jaw, tightening my heart against the current of tears. Stupid words, though I have no others.

"I'll try."

"I know."

And then she says one last thing to me before I get eclipsed by the sliding doors and sucked into the madness of Heathrow, one last thing that tells me we might be okay, that perhaps our world can be re-righted, that some things, at least, can take us back to the better parts of the before: "Auntie Ellie! Don't forget to send me presents."

Flying in a metal machine over the Atlantic, wrung out from crying, I fall asleep with my head against the windowpane. I dream I am in a children's story, but this time it has little to do with gardens and redemption and overcoming obstacles. I am Peter Pan leaving behind Neverland, that beautiful far-off island nation, hurtling through the air away from my Lost Boys, leaving them to fend for themselves against Captain Hook. The wind pushes against my skin, and I soar through the night clouds, dodging the brilliant searing stars, too fast to stop and make a wish. I have abandoned all dreams of escape, of never growing up. I fly back in relief.

When I get to the airport, my dad is there waiting in baggage claim, with a sign with my name on it. My *i* is dotted with a heart.

"Dad, you didn't have to come all this way. I could have taken a cab. I bet you have a million things to take care of."

"I just wanted to see my darling daughter."

I eye him with suspicion. My dad is loving, absolutely; doting, not so much. Airport pickups are usually out of bounds.

"Fine. You caught me. I needed to get out of that house. I have clearly lost my mind. I freaked out because the personalized napkins I ordered haven't come yet. When did I become someone who cares about napkins? And that signature cocktail tastes horrible. I'm not sure what I was thinking."

"You're just excited, that's all. Anyhow, I'm glad you came." I kiss my father's cheek, loop my arm through his, and let him take the suitcase right out of my hands.

"Me too." He sizes me up, and for a second his eyes turn watery. "Sweetheart, you look great. If I didn't know any better, I'd say you're positively . . . glowing." And then he winks. So quick and fast, I almost miss it.

In the car, the blue Volvo that has been in the family so long I'm amazed it still runs, my dad doesn't ask me any questions about my "situation." Instead, he talks with nostalgia about the Big Dig, the construction headache that has terrorized the city of Boston for two decades.

"Can you believe they finished it? I swear, I almost miss all that mess. I loved the reliability of the traffic. You could count on it being a nightmare," he says.

"You're crazy."

"I must be. I'm marrying your mother again."

"You said it, not me." I grin at my dad. Today, him marrying Jane seems like a good idea. I'm hopeful in a way that I haven't been for a long time. "I actually think it's great. You two. I'll keep all my fingers crossed for you tomorrow."

"And toes too. I need all the help I can get."

"You'll be fine."

"It's not me I'm worried about." Since I can make no guarantees about my mother—no one, not even she, can—I keep quiet. "By the way, I seated you and Phillip at the same table. I figured you have a lot to talk about."

"Thanks. We do."

"It's going to be okay," my dad says, almost a mutter under his breath, as if he is convincing himself of something.

"What is?" I ask. I don't know if he means his marriage or mine.

"The napkins, silly. No one's going to die without personalized napkins, right?"

As soon as I get back to my dad's house, I call Sophie from my childhood bedroom, or my "other room," the one I slept in three days a week after their divorce. The decor is unchanged—pink wallpaper, white Formica, an over-the-top interior-decorating attempt by my father to get me not to hate him for leaving, even though he never left, not in any meaningful way, and it never occurred to me to hate him. He was always only a few doors away. I'm on the same phone I would use to talk to Lucy when we were teenagers and we would gossip late into the night. The phone, a relic; one of those beige plastic clamshell ones with a forever knotted cord.

Sophie and I spend most of the time talking about Inderpal: how he has read all the Harry Potter series and will rent the movies again with Sophie when she catches up; how he gave her astronaut ice cream; how he called her his BFF in a recent e-mail.

"How many days again?" Sophie asks now, with a certain drawn beat that indicates we are starting a new sort of routine. We will be doing this countdown daily, a substitute for the nightly tuck-in.

"Twenty-one."

"Okay."

"Twenty-one is not so bad."

"Yeah, you're right."

"There are worse things than twenty-one."

"What? Like twenty-two?" And then she giggles—pure and contagious—like all nine-year-olds do when they think they have just made the funniest joke in the world.

46

My parents are getting remarried in less than three hours. A leap of faith, if I've ever seen one, their history so gnarled and complex and painful, it's amazing they can be in the same room, no less retake vows that they have already once failed to keep.

The backyard has begun its transformation. White chairs fan out from a center aisle, where the lawn is covered by a white runner. The chuppah is four sticks of wood canopied with my paternal grandfather's tallis and a sprinkling of multicolored leaves. The effect is autumnal and rustic, with a dab of modern flair. Should my father ever tire of academia, wedding planning may well be a viable alternative. The house looks spectacular, and I touch my hand to my belly and wax sentimental, as it seems I'm prone to do in pregnancy: *This is beauty and love and hope.*

Claire and Mikey arrived just a little while ago; they've been visiting New York for a couple of days, since she has never been before. They played the role of tourist, fanny packs and all, electrified by the bright lights of Times Square, sobered downtown at the gaping mouth of Ground Zero. Later, they kissed at the top of the Empire

State Building, ignoring a smirk from the security guard, who has seen that same kiss a million times before. My brother has hinted there is a proposal pending, most likely at the comic-book convention in Vegas sometime this spring. I can think of nothing more, and nothing less, romantic than that: my brother asking Claire to stand next to him for the rest of their lives while they are geeking out among hordes of people dressed like superheroes.

My mother gets ready in my bedroom. Her long gray hair is pulled back into a low bun, with a few loose tendrils. She wears an ivory suit, pin-tucked at the waist, with short matching gloves.

"What, no sari?" I ask, after I get my first glance at the bride, fighting back the mistiness that comes too easily.

"Not today." She looks misty herself, come to think of it, which is as unlike my mother as her suit.

"You look beautiful." And she does. Foreign, yes, and an anachronism too: She's dressed like an ambassador's wife at a state dinner fifty years ago. Nonetheless, looking at her is like looking at an old photograph, a one-second moment of an easier, simpler time captured in a frozen image.

"I'm scared," she says, her eyes catching mine in the mirror.

"Of what?"

"Of absolutely every single thing. I'm about to marry the man I have loved for about three quarters of my life and the man I have fought with for just as long. What if tomorrow morning I wake up and want to run as far as I can away from him?"

"You probably will."

"And then what?"

"I don't know. You don't run. You push through it. To borrow your horribly antifeminist phrase, you grow a pair."

"Okay."

"You're going to show up, right?"

A tiny, almost imperceptible pause. Small enough that I choose to believe it didn't happen.

"Of course I'm going to show up."

My dad walks down the aisle first. A couple of flutists play a whimsical tune, light and buoyant, like a morning bird's song. He wears a gray suit I have never seen before. Tailored. Expensive. Careful in the way a suit should be. He looks like a different man, a dapper man, without his characteristic arm patches and frayed edges, no coffee and pen stains just above the pocket. His silver hair parted on the side and combed back, like a little boy's for Christmas dinner. The thought of my father buying a new suit for today charms me, and I have to hold myself back from running to give him a hug once he is already standing up there. Destination reached under his father's tallis. He waits for my mother to arrive with a brave smile, which does little to hide his naked vulnerability.

I take a quick scan of the guests, who have now completely filled out the one hundred or so chairs set on the lawn. All of them are smiling either forward or backward, at my dad, or at Mikey and me, waiting at the end of the aisle. I see Claire making eye contact with my brother, their faces filled with the wonder that weddings seem to bring forth in new lovers. *This will be us one day.* I feel a happy twinge when I see how sincere they both seem and how absorbed in each other.

The rest of the guest list skews older, a crowd that has seen as many divorces as marriages. They are still capable of being expectant and ready, enjoying that delicious moment before the start of a play, when they don't yet know if the show will be good or bad but they're optimistic nonetheless.

I notice some family friends I haven't seen in years, lots of faces I don't recognize, none of which belongs to my husband. I know Phillip is here, though. I can feel it, in the weakness in my legs, the noticeable tremble in my bouquet. The way I keep compulsively re-assuring my belly: *We're okay, we're going to be okay.*

Next, Mikey and I walk, arm in arm, slowly down the aisle, just as we promised and practiced for our father; he took seriously the bridal magazines' warning against a gallop. Apparently a measured pace helps to build tension, he said, and we were kind enough to keep our mouths shut. Neither of us reminded him that we didn't really need any extra tension-building at this particular event. My mother has yet to come out to follow us, and so I clench my bouquet and Mikey's elbow and hold my smile tight across my face. What if she can't do this? Maybe the run gene always wins in the end.

At the front, Mikey and I split. I go to stand on my mother's empty side—*Jane's* side—and my brother, looking sharp and bou-tonnièred as best man, stands next to my dad. I look over at them, ready to give my father an encouraging thumbs-up—*she's going to show up; of course she's going to show up*—but he's looking straight ahead. Pale and covered in beads of sweat. He looks like a man awaiting sentencing. This, a tug on the very last bit of petal: *She loves me; she loves me not.*

I glance back out at the crowd and I spot Phillip, sitting front and center, his eyes studiously trained away from me.

The bridal music starts, Pachelbel's Canon in D Major, and there my mother is, *thank God*, smiling a brave smile almost identical to my father's, as all of the eyes turn to stare at her. Murmurs erupt— *she looks beautiful; how lovely*—cameras click and flash, and Jane con-tinues to take one step in front of the other.

I am watching my mother, and my mother is watching me, and I am talking to her with my eyes: *Only a few more feet now. Almost there. You can do this. You are doing this.* And her response: *Damn right I am doing this. Oh, no, please help me do this.* We are lost in our own conversation, this motivational dialogue with our eyes, and so neither of us sees what happens next. We only hear it—Phillip, above all the others.

His panicked voice, which has a male-hero pitch: calm and reasonable and on the wrong end of hope. The sort of voice that gets people moving in an organized yet speedy fashion toward the designated emergency exits.

"For God's sake, is someone here a doctor?" he yells to the crowd. And there my husband is, my soon-to-be-ex-husband, at the front of the aisle, looking handsome in a suit and tie, at the exact spot where we once stood and said our own vows. *Phillip,* I think, and almost tap the baby—*your dad*—before my brain catches up and realizes what is going on here.

His BlackBerry is out; he has already called 911.

I hear but don't understand the words he says next: *Emergency, down, not sure if he is breathing. Fast.* And this: *Please. Help us.*

Everyone is on their feet and gasping, frozen in group-fear.

Phillip stands over my dad, who is no longer standing at all. He has crumpled to the ground, passed out, his hand on his heart.

"Please, please," I say over and over again, a mantra, my pleading with God or the universe second nature, a reflex now. I try to stay calm. The books have warned me of the simple math: If I upset myself too much, I hurt the baby, and I cannot hurt the baby. We are in the waiting room of Mount Auburn Hospital, the same one where Oliver was born and lost, lost and extracted, and the way Phillip stands, stiff and alert, the heavy and expectant quality to his waiting, tells me he is remembering it too. Our last memory of this place a blurry nightmare. One of us got left behind.

"Please, please," I say again, though I can't tell if I am saying the words out loud or just in my head. The paralysis and blurring from fear. I don't know where I stop and the world begins.

My mother sits next to me, gripping my hand. Silent. She is still in her ivory suit, but her hair has unraveled. The other people here look at us strangely, our formal clothes so at odds with the clinical surroundings, the flashing lights that pull up at random intervals and streak our faces red, then blue. So much activity, the ambulance roaring up the driveway, fast, they were fast, just like Phillip asked, I think. All slow motion and hyperspeed at the same time, there is no time, just a string of events, backward and forward, losses and gains, a never-ending tally, and then we were here, how did we get here again? I don't remember. A car, the backseat; I can't tell you whose car. My dad left to the care and transport of experts, and we followed through the parting streets, the traffic like the Red Sea, and right through the yellow lights, and then he was wheeled in, on a stretcher, the stretcher the worst part of all.

We were told to wait.

I'm sorry. We have no information at this time.

We are waiting.

We have lived in this waiting room all of our lives.

Phillip gets tired of pacing and sits next to me, on the other side, and bumps his shoulder against mine, a light tap. A gesture of solidarity. His touch means so much, it burns. I look at him, and he gives me a half smile. There is nothing happy about it; he is saying, *I am here and you are here,* and *we are here and this is going to be okay. Today is not like that other time; we are not leaving here with less.*

He can't promise me that, though. We may leave here having lost it all. And my mother showed up, she actually showed up, in ivory no less, and there was supposed to be dancing and for dessert red velvet cupcakes that my dad loves from the bakery in Somerville. And it's like there were two futures, one in which we are all still at the party, where vows were said with fear and conviction, food was eaten, and good-natured jokes and toasts were made about my parents' unlikely re-union. And there is this one, where we are sentenced to wait while doctors perform tests on my sixty-five-year-old father, to make sure his heart—the most resilient and forgiving heart I know—keeps beating.

"Thank you," I whisper to Phillip. There is only one hero here.

He shakes his head, *no need*, and squeezes my hand, so we are now a chain, Claire, Mikey, my mom, me, and Phillip, in these ridiculous plastic chairs that bear the weight of so much pain, day in and day out; these chairs should be destroyed. These chairs, like baby-sized coffins, should not exist in the world.

"Mom?" I say.

"Yeah." Talking right now is the hardest work we've ever done.

"He's going to be fine. He will."

"Please, please," she says, out loud, but, of course, not to me.

A doctor eventually comes out, a middle-aged man in a white jacket, with a stethoscope around his neck and a beer gut. He has some-thing white at the corner of his mouth, probably mayo, which makes me distrust him. When did he stop for a sandwich? Before or after they rolled my father in? Who does he think he is, eating at a time like this?

"Mrs. Lerner?" he asks.

"How . . . ?" She can't finish her sentence. She is trembling with her whole body, and so I stand behind her, to hold her up, to absorb as much of the fear and the pain as I can. I will take it but not let it pass to the baby. I don't know how I will do this, but I will.

This is what adults do. We absorb and we shield. This is what parents do.

"He's going to be fine. Absolutely fine." The tears come now, the ones we hadn't let ourselves shed for fear they could have meant something; they would have allowed room for the unimaginable. "Has your husband been under a lot of stress lately?"

"We were supposed to get married today," my mother says, and motions to her ivory suit, which now looks dirty and deflated, like a Halloween costume the morning after.

"That explains it," the doctor says. Phillip takes a step forward, a defensive maneuver, since the guy is obviously a bastard. What's that supposed to mean: *That explains it*?

"Was it, you know, a heart attack?" my brother asks, finding the words we have been unable to say until now. Claire is behind Mikey, too, mirroring my body language with my mother, her arms literally holding him up, and that's when I know for sure, if I ever had any doubt, that she will say yes, whenever or however Mikey asks.

"Nope. We did an EKG, blood tests, a chest X ray. His heart is in pretty good condition. Honestly, we're not sure what happened. My best guess, though, is that this was a panic attack."

"A panic attack," my mother repeats, her voice calm at first, taking it in. "You are telling me he had a God damn panic attack at the altar? That's what you're telling me?"

"Yeah, I think so."

And then she starts to laugh and cry, all at once in a rush of release, the two sounds blurring until they sound like, until they are, exactly the same thing.

* * *

Later, we all stand around my dad's bed, a half circle. He is spending the night at the hospital for observation. He looks embarrassed
to have found himself like this today, without his designer gray suit,
him the one in a gown, papery thin and mint green, his skinny white-
haired limbs on display, betraying the truth that none of us can bear
to see: He is getting older, and one day he'll stop doing that.

"So," he says to my mother, who, as soon as she sees him, kisses
his whole face, again and again, forehead, cheeks, eyes, nose, lips,
until the rest of us look away.

"So," she says. "Don't you ever d— Don't you dare ever do that
on me."

She can't finish, she won't finish, because there are some vows
you can make and some you can't, no matter how hard or how much
you want to be able to.

And there are some three-letter words that can't be said on days
like this.

"I'll try my best," he says.

My mother shakes her head at him, scoots herself into his bed,
so they are body to body and I don't know where he ends and she
begins under the white hospital sheet. "Not yet."

"Not yet."

"Honey?"

"Yeah."

"I told you so."

"Told me so what?"

"We totally should have gotten the wedding insurance."

47

Phillip drives Mikey and Claire and me back to the house. The hospital has given my mother a cot, and she will stay there by my father's side until he is discharged tomorrow morning. Though she will not sleep—the terror still clings to all of us, just like the antiseptic smell of the waiting room—I know she will not have a single instinct to run. She will ride that fine line between exhilaration and claustrophobia that comes along with finding yourself exactly where you are supposed to be.

From the look of the backyard, it seems the party dispersed itself in an orderly fashion. The tent is gone, the chairs returned to the rental company, the dance floor that was laid out in the far corner of the grass packed up, leaving behind a square of flattened green. Only the chuppah remains outside, my grandfather's tallis still tied down across the top, the tassels flapping in the wind.

The food is left waiting for us, Saran-Wrapped, half in the freezer and the refrigerator, half laid out on the table. My dad went traditional on the menu, chicken or beef or vegetable, mini hot dogs and crab cakes to start. The flowers, too, have been brought inside and decorate the house. Looking through the back window, it seems someone either recently wed or died.

Phillip and I sit in the living room, just the side-table lamp on, the way it was left this morning. Claire and Mikey have gone upstairs, after a wave good night and Mikey giving Phillip a hug and a "Thanks, man."

I feel a rush of pride that I married someone like this, even if he no longer wants to belong to me. He was strong and capable and fast, calling 911 at the same time he loosened my father's tie, cradled his head. Gliding through traffic, fearless, like a car thief, which it turns out he sort of was: When the ambulance came, he grabbed a random set of keys from the valet. We found out later, from an understanding answering-machine message, that the borrowed Prius belonged to one of the flutists.

After Oliver, too, Phillip was the one who paid all the bills and dealt with Blue Cross Blue Shield, and went back to work, and still made sure I was eating and there was dinner on the table that included a vegetable. At the time, what appeared to be superhuman seemed like a slap in the face; it seemed *wrong*, somehow, that he could be okay, when I could barely brush my teeth. Didn't he notice that our baby—that Oliver—had died? His ability to function only highlighted all that I was incapable of, seemed like evidence that he had managed to bypass the pain. I couldn't understand how he found a way to lose less.

Now I realize, sitting here in the half dark of the living room, that I left him with no choice. Just like when I found myself making tea for Greg and breakfast for Sophie after Lucy's funeral, someone has to be the adult. Phillip was keeping his vows, *in sickness and in health*, and he was taking care of me in the only way he knew how. I used it to divide us, because we seemed too far apart, unequal to the task at hand, and somehow, along the way, I forgot how to talk to my husband. And he forgot how to talk to me.

"You were, um, great today. I don't know what we would have done without you," I say, hoping my voice tells him how grateful I am. No matter what has happened or what happens between us going forward, my family was lucky to ever count him as one of us.

"Please, stop. I'm just glad he's going to be okay." Phillip puts his head against the back of the couch and closes his eyes. The anxiety still hasn't left us, despite the doctor's reassurance and seeing my dad look almost the same as he did this morning, though decidedly less dapper. That sort of emotion doesn't just go; it sits on you, has aftershocks. All of us, except Phillip, cried at least once during the car ride home. "I am so tired. I feel like I'm a hundred years old."

"I know what you mean." I stare into the dark corners of the room, where the built-in bookcase lines the wall. I can't see the books, but I know they are there, as they always have been, installed and filled by my dad right after he bought the house. As if keeping all that knowledge around could protect us from real life. Maybe that's why my father has never seemed to fear his own mortality. He thought his books protected him. Who knows? Maybe they do.

"Phillip?"

"Yeah?"

"We need to talk."

"I know. Please not tonight. I'm just . . . I'm out of strength for the day. I'm all tapped out." This is the closest Phillip has ever come to expressing weakness, humanness, and it makes me want to crumble. I want to take him in my arms, kiss his face like I saw my mother do to my father not too long ago. Kisses that say, *You are mine, and you are loved.*

"Fair enough. You're welcome to stay here tonight. You shouldn't drive home. I won't, you know, try anything," I say. He smiles at me, a tired smile, somewhat charmed despite himself by our regression to high school terms.

"Okay."

Phillip follows me upstairs to my bedroom, the same one my mother used to get ready this morning. Her makeup is scattered on my desk, her veil, which at the last minute she opted out of as too traditional, sits on my chair, the scene disorienting and disarming at the same time. What was supposed to happen and what actually did, so far apart it seems impossible. It was years ago—two different people talking—when my mother promised me that she'd show up.

Phillip and I crawl into my bed, and we each lie on our back, eyes open to the blackness. "Good night," I say.

"Good night," he says.

And then, in my head, one word, an introduction for our baby: *Dad.*

We sleep that way straight through the night, Phillip and I, like two gingerbread men, overcooked and flattened by the weight of the day. Our fingertips almost, almost touching.

The next morning we decide to do this walking. Actually, it is Phillip's idea to stroll around the neighborhood, which is always at its most beautiful in autumn, when the air has just the starting edge of cold, a promise that there will be a winter, and then a spring after that, nature keeping its time, even when you don't want it to. The Harvard students are back from summer break, backpacked and earnest and, at least for the undergrads, experiencing what it's like to be away from home for the first time. They scamper by us in groups on Mass Ave. and punctuate the air with their nervous chatter and occasional outbursts of overblown hilarity.

"Any word from the hospital?" Phillip asks, just to be polite. He must know that if there had been bad news I would have told him already.

"Yup. Dad's coming home today. Everything looks fine."

"Thank God. So what happens now? You think they'll try to get married again?"

"Who knows? My mom said she thinks this whole thing is a sign that they should get hitched. My dad has taken it as a sign that they shouldn't."

"Typical." His voice is imbued with fondness. He's always enjoyed the quirkiness of my parents. So different from his own, who have been quietly and unhappily married for forty years.

At Harvard Square, the punks are out, as always, wearing the uniforms of their rebellion, tattoos and piercings and Mohawks, a uniform that has never changed for as long as I can remember. I wonder if it would break their hearts to learn that they are just like everyone else, and one another, and probably their parents before them.

When we lived in the Back Bay we used to walk here, first across the bridge and then down Memorial Drive along the river, finally turning toward the Square to reward ourselves with cheap beers at the happy hour at John Harvard's. The place had enough of a yuppified air and plenty of B-school students at the bar to make sure we didn't stick out as the lifestyle tourists that we were. My father would sometimes come to meet us, sometimes not, depending on whether he had devoted his weekend to Widener, Harvard's library, which is more beautiful but not nearly as much fun as my new favorite British one at St. Pancras. At the time, Phillip and I were only a handful of years out of college ourselves, and returning to the life of a student felt like a relaxing regression. Sometimes even a necessity.

We wind our way down to the Charles River, where the groups thin out into couples with books but no intention of reading, and families on blankets eating out of Tupperware, and solo bicyclists stopping for a break against a tree. The rowers are out, gliding by, keeping an easy rhythm. I didn't realize how much I missed this particular scene, one I've been a part of since I was a little kid, until I am back here again, listening to the melodic splash of the water, the hissing of the feverish wind. We are not far from the spot where Phillip proposed.

He chooses a patch of grass, and then we sit next to each other, our arms resting on our bent knees.

"I'll start." There is no more room for stalling. We are here, and we need to talk, and no amount of fear is going to keep this conversation from happening. "First of all, I'm sorry."

"For what?" He says it like he's genuinely curious about which of my many sins I've decided to apologize for.

"It wasn't fair how I stayed in London, and I barely even let you know what was going on in my head and why I felt I had to be there. I can't say I'm sorry for being there—I don't know if you'll ever understand that I had to be—but I'm sorry for the way I handled it."

Phillip picks up a twig from the ground and starts to peel off the bark with his fingernail. He looks like he's getting ready to prepare bark soup.

"You know us separating wasn't just about you leaving," he says, his words slow and methodical.

"I know. But I'm sorry anyway."

"None of it matters, does it? We can say all the things we never

324 / Julie Buxbaum

said and go around and around and point fingers—God knows I've done it enough times in my head—but it's not going to get us anywhere. You know what it comes down to?"

I don't answer, because I don't know what it comes down to. I wish it were simple enough to come down to one thing.

"We were put to the biggest test a marriage can be put to. I mean, I never, ever thought, I couldn't imagine, we'd have to go through what we went through, but the saddest part, almost as sad as losing Oliver, is that we failed."

"I know."

"We failed the test, Ellie. The shit hit the fan and we did the opposite of what we were supposed to. We went ahead and lost each other." His voice catches, and he throws his stick as far as it will go. It lands in the water, barely rippling the surface.

The tears begin to build behind my eyes, because for the first time since that horrible day almost two years ago now, Phillip says the exact right thing. We lost Oliver, and then we turned a dead baby into a bat and used him as a weapon to destroy ourselves. I don't know how to respond, so I say what comes into my mind next, a non sequitur, and yet not really. Not a non sequitur at all.

"I'm pregnant. I mean, we're having a baby."

Phillip freezes, and in that moment all the air is sucked out of the universe, and it feels like we are inside, somewhere without oxygen, not by the Charles, not in an old favorite spot where we used to be able to say anything. I feel the baby in there, in a physical way, not a kick or a stirring but just in there, deep inside and attached to me, still growing its cells, increasing its molecular mass, nonetheless.

"That one night? In London?"

"Yes."

He doesn't ask what I expected him to ask next, the worst question imaginable: *Are you sure it's mine?* There's relief, at the very least, in that. After all this, I've still kept a part of my former self intact. I've always been honest.

"Oh. I. I. Are you serious?"

"I'm serious."

"Have you been to a doctor? A good doctor? And what did they say about, you know, last time? Will she be okay?" His voice has risen an octave in panic; he is as scared as I was when, not so long ago, I was breathing in and out of a paper bag.

"She?" Despite myself, despite the weight of the moment, I'm touched that he's already making grand gender leaps.

"Is it a he?"

"I don't know yet. And the doctor said that there is no more or less chance than last time. It's unlikely."

"But what if? I mean, it was unlikely last time too. One in two hundred is still one in two hundred." He puts his head between his knees to catch his breath, and just like that, we have a role reversal. I'm calming him down. I'm the one who will be strong for us.

"She or he is going to be fine. I don't know how, but I just know. We will be fine."

"You almost died the last time."

"I didn't. Not really."

"You lost a lot of blood, and you could have—" His voice breaks, and I see the panic he must have felt on that day, the possibility that he could have walked out of the hospital having lost everything all at once. He had everything to lose too. He always has.

"I didn't and I won't. And this baby won't."

"How many weeks?"

"Thirteen."

"This big," he says, demonstrating the baby's length, as I did for

Sophie. Thumb to pointer finger. Phillip read all the books last time; he loved the books, used to read me random facts out loud.

We sit without talking for a while. I feel relief having said the words; Phillip knows, and now it's real. My tadpole is not a tadpole anymore. My tadpole has graduated to baby. I let Phillip think whatever he's thinking, let him sort through the land mine I have set off in his life. I'll let him wade his way through until he comes out the other end.

"I don't know what to say."

"That's okay. You don't have to say anything just yet." The disappointment squeezes my lungs, makes me feel small and light, a human paper airplane. There was a part of me, larger than I care to admit, that had hoped Phillip would take me in his arms, promise to love me and the baby forever, and press restart on the life we had been living. We'd be a new and improved version of PhillipandEllie, one where we wouldn't be tested and fail. Where we had learned our lessons and applied them, like the straight-A students we once were.

Instead, I can feel his confusion and heavy terror. His reaction identical to mine when my mother pronounced me pregnant. When she couldn't grasp how terrifying the prospect was.

"A baby." Phillip breathes the word.

"Yup."

"We need a specialist. Like a neonatal expert, or a high-risk-pregnancy one, you know? Someone who knows what they're doing. We can't, I can't, I wouldn't survive if, if something happened, to the baby, or to you."

"I'm going to be fine." I motion to my belly. "We're going to be fine. This is not a high-risk pregnancy. I spent the first trimester throwing up, which is supposed to be a good sign, and now I feel great, and . . . I don't know. I just know we're going to be fine. But, you're right, a specialist couldn't hurt."

"I wasn't there."

"What?"

"I wasn't there while you were throwing up. I should have been there."

"You didn't miss much, believe me. It wasn't pretty."

"Still." Phillip grabs my shoulders and turns me to face him. His move is forceful and strong, angry. "Wait a minute. You've known about this for thirteen weeks, and you're just telling me now? Are you serious?"

"I wanted to tell you in person."

"There are these things called planes."

"I'm sorry." Empty words, I know, but I mean them. I *am* sorry. I have chosen me over him every time, and I have to stop doing that. Soon I'll find a way to explain that I needed those three months to get over my fears, to make sure this was real, that the baby was going to stick around. That I needed that time to grow back into me again. That telling him would have somehow made it too real too early. We would have started making plans—of course we would have been presumptuous, we wouldn't have been able to help ourselves— and I couldn't risk that.

I am not sure my explanations matter. It's done.

"For God's sake, Ellie." Phillip gets up off the ground and walks away from me, to the water, so close to the edge he could wet his feet. He just stands there, his hands in tight fists, trying to fight too many emotions at once, sadness and fear and anger and confusion, and maybe excitement too. For too long, he stands like that, show- ing only his back, riding out the carnival in his head.

* * *

"Are you staying here or are you going back to London?" he asks me now, again sitting forearms to knees, about a foot away from me, his eyes bloodshot from tears I have not witnessed.

"Yes. I mean, I'm staying here. I'll visit Sophie as much as I can, but we're having a baby. I want to be here."

"Were you planning on coming home?" He means the house in Sharon, our home. An honest question. Far from an invitation.

"I don't know. I guess it depends." And then my own tears come, because I don't even know what it depends on. More than Phillip taking me back. I realize now that I am as confused as I've always been, that the unburdening of words, of the truth, can't undo the last few years of retreat. I left Phillip and Phillip left me, long before Lucy died, long before he mentioned the D-word in the hotel room, back when our sentences started piling up in corners around the house, like impromptu book stacks, everything that never got spoken or heard or asked about. All the times we turned away while the other was speaking, absorbed in our BlackBerrys, or the television, or a novel; a whole year may have gone by where we barely looked each other in the eyes. How do we get back to something recognizable?

Phillip nods.

"I don't know either." There is only sadness now where anger used to live, in that gaping space between us. There won't be answers today or maybe anytime soon. Too many layers to be unraveled, and poked at, and aired. Too much work for an afternoon like this.

"Must have been a strong swimmer," he says now, and I follow his eyes out to the river, looking for a brave soul in a wet suit, but there isn't one.

"Huh?"

"To have hit the jackpot on that one time? That was wham, bam, thank you, ma'am. I mean, seriously, a strong swimmer." Phillip smiles, all masculinity and pride. "That's a good sign."

"Yeah."

"Wow. I mean, wow." Another smile. This one, my favorite of his: Phillip looks like a little kid the second before clawing into wrapping paper. Pure wonder.

"Yeah. Wow is right."

And then, without asking, he takes his hands and slips them under my sweater, so they are cupped against my belly, warm and surprising. He moves them back and forth, waving hello to our baby.

48

I am sitting at the dining table in my dad's house and Sophie is sitting on her mini-bed, and it's almost like we are in the same room. I want to reach out and touch her hair, tuck the piece that has fallen out of her messy ponytail behind her ear, smooth down the bumpy top. The wonder of Skype, something not so far off from what I dreamed up in my dot-com days. We've been talking for two minutes, and Sophie has already shown me her armpit, the inside of her left nostril, and her tonsils.

"How many days?" she asks.

"Ten."

"I've been meaning to tell you, you left your book here. *What to Expect When You're Expecting.* I've been reading it."

"Soph, I don't think that's appropriate for your age."

"I'm nine now."

"Exactly. You're not allowed to read it until you're at least thirty."

"But it's interesting. Like a science book. Do you have hemorrhoids?"

"Sophie."

"And are you taking folic acid? You better be taking folic acid. I don't want my godsister having brain damage. Next time I see you, she'll be, like, four and a half inches long."

"She, huh? So you think it's going to be a girl."

"Yup. You know what I've been thinking about lately?"

"What?"

"Isn't it weird that what happened to Mummy happened in the same year that you made a new person?"

"Yeah, it is. Kind of reassuring, if you think about it. That good can follow bad."

"We so needed something happy this year."

"We did."

"And I've always wanted to be a big sister."

"Really?"

"Yeah, I used to do all these spells and stuff, but it never happened. And now look. You're having a baby, and I'm going to be a godsister."

"It's almost enough to make you believe in magic."

"Nah, it's not magic. It's biology. I learned all about it from Google."

49

I am sleeping at my father's, but every day, when Phillip comes home from work—hours earlier than I remember him returning when I lived here—I meet him in Sharon, and we sit in our kitchen and discuss our lives over the dinner table we spent months picking out. The house looks only slightly different from how I left it; I haven't realized how ingrained this place is, until I look around and can catalog the minute changes. The pen jar has migrated to the other side of the room; a pile of mail has been set aside for me on the counter instead of in the wicker basket. A new photo of Sophie is on the refrigerator, this year's class photo, with a thank-you note for Phillip's birthday gift. She hadn't told me she sent him one, particularly one that says *WE miss you* with the *WE* triple-underlined. Our wedding photo is still framed in the entryway, which I decide to take as a good sign.

We are on a crash-course diet of confrontation. Fingers pointed, sentences slung like the weapons they are, doors slammed and opened and slammed again. We take turns screaming and fighting and apologizing and comforting, like we are spinning a chore wheel.

Phillip says he wants this baby, he has never wanted anything more, and he'll use words that are new for him, that delight both of us—*fate, miracle, blessing.* Ten minutes later, we flip them over and wallow in the dark edges. What if we don't fix us? The words that are the opposite of *fate* and *miracle* and *blessing* rear up: *accident, mistake.*

"Are we kidding ourselves that we can do this?" Phillip asks me. "This is not the way you're supposed to bring a child into the world."

But we are bringing a child into the world, whether we are supposed to or not.

"I think we can do this," I say.

We talk about Oliver, something we have never done, not really, not in a way that wasn't about the practical: dismantling the nursery, the God damn medical bills, sending the stuff we had bought to Goodwill. Never about what it was like afterward, how we'd both turn away from our neighbors pushing strollers down the street, the horrible mail from the baby-product companies congratulating us on stages our child never got to reach, and that throbbing pain when my milk came in and there was no place for it all to go. The tears or the pain or the milk.

When Phillip saw me crying at the wasted wet circles on my T-shirt or sometimes at nothing at all, he looked away. And when he kept going for both of us—got up in the early hours of the morning and put on a flawless suit and went to work—I looked away, too, like he was doing something wrong. I tell him how much I regret that first flinch in the hospital room, how I lay awake at nights wondering if everything would have been different had I not moved away from his hand.

"It wasn't about the first flinch, Ellie. It was the two years of flinching that came afterward. From both of us."

"I retreated," I say, remembering for a moment that cold paralysis

I felt after we lost Oliver. How any comfort seemed a paltry, empty offering. The way everything and everyone suddenly seemed farther and farther away, like I was looking at them from an airplane window.

"Yeah, and after a while I retreated too." He's talking about this last year of late nights in the office, weekends also. Of us going to bed forgetting to kiss each other good night. Forgetting that there was a reason we had chosen to share a bed—our lives—in the first place. "And then you went and left. Literally. Just dropped everything, and I didn't know what I was supposed to do."

"I know," I say. "I'm sorry."

Our questions pile up, our answers meek in comparison. *Where were you? Why didn't you hear me? What happened to us? Why did you go? How did we get here?* Nothing is clear or clear-cut, except that there is a baby, and it's growing. I almost have a real bump now, and when we are not terrified and angry we are overjoyed.

Seven days later we are not on the other side. We are far from the other side. We don't even know if another side exists yet. Please, let another side exist.

I relish the moments when we forget we are climbing anything at all and we fall back into ourselves.

"How's your arm?" Phillip looks at my limb, takes it in his hands, and turns it over, looking for evidence.

"Totally fine."

"Does it hurt?"

"Nope. As good as new." I flex my fingers, bend my elbow, as if to prove it to both of us, my arm thick and strong and unleashed. I'm amazed by the fact that keeping my bone swaddled into a whole forced it to re-fuse, that the doctors relied solely on the power of proximity. A silent dialogue between bone and bone.

"I'm glad you're okay," Phillip says.

I think about that white line the doctor showed us on the X ray, my breaking point, and wonder if the scar is still visible. Somehow, I think not.

Later, we are on the couch, our heads aching from the brutal rattle of words. We are tired of mountain climbing, of going backward through our marital garbage, of being adults and treating this like there is a problem to be solved. My head is resting on Phillip's shoulder, his hand is on my belly.

"You know how your entire life can change in an instant for the worse? Like when Oliver suddenly stopped kicking or that call about Lucy? Everything changes. But do you think it can work the other way too? One second you think your entire life has gone to shit, and the next you realize that maybe things can be okay? Do you think that can happen?" I ask Phillip now, hoping that the answer is *yes, yes, yes.* That we can just decide to be the happy couple we had always intended to be. We hit restart. Do-over.

"I hope so," Phillip says. He has decided to call in sick tomorrow, to give us more time, to do what, I don't know. Hopefully not to *talk-talk*, hopefully for more of those delicious forgetting moments, when it's just PhillipandEllie in a room together again. When we eat off each other's plate, when one of us washes the dishes and the other dries, when we hold hands, just because our fingers are close.

In some ways, it's like being back in the waiting room. Two futures here, both plausible, where so much hinges on some words. The doctor said *panic*, not *heart*. But he could have said *heart*. I was sure he was going to.

"Let's just try to be us again," I say. "Can we at least try that?

Give it a shot? I mean the old us, the good us." I hold my breath, hoping he sees it, too, the opening of a box in our brains giving ourselves the power to choose. We can go to couple's therapy, for real this time. We can take a retest.

"Okay," he says, and I can see in his eyes he understands what I'm proposing. The new, new PhillipandEllie. "We owe it to ourselves to try. Not even the old us, but the real us again."

He looks at me, and I look back, and there it is: another promise we are making, another vow that we hope this time we will not break.

Phillip leans closer. His hand, my cheek. A soft, careful touch. I feel warm and loved, fragile, too, and I rest my nose in the spot on his neck. The home spot.

I hope I get to stay here.

"You think we can do it?" I ask, my words muffled by his skin.

Phillip doesn't say anything. We are out of real words for the moment. He kisses me instead, tender, a warm blanket of a kiss. A memory, too, the way those kisses used to feel: precious and something to be savored.

His hand, my cheek, again, the slightest hint of touch.

"An eyelash," he says, offering a black half-moon to me on his finger as a gift. "Make a wish."

The baby, first the baby. But there is the real us, too, and Sophie and Greg, and my parents, Claire and Mikey, Lucy, even. I close my eyes, wrap us all into one thing, love and home and home and love, and I say it in my head like a mantra and I blow.

I open my eyes. My eyelash is still stuck to his finger. The wish has gone nowhere at all.

"Try again," he says, and so I do.

Acknowledgments

Thank you first and foremost to my agent, Elaine Koster, for her tireless support, encouragement, and wisdom, and to my editor, Susan Kamil, whose deft hand and insight coaxed this book into existence. I feel so lucky and honored to work with these two fabulous women.

My deepest gratitude to all of the folks at Dial and Random House, and, in particular, Noah Eaker, Nita Taublib, Cynthia Lasky, Kathy Lord, and Theresa Zoro.

Francesca Liversidge and the whole Transworld team, thank you so much for your support.

Special thanks to Chandler Crawford, David Grossman, and Helen Heller.

Thanks also to Mark Haskell Smith for being my trusted and brilliant first reader; Richard Kay for teaching me about the intricacies of the British press; Roger Watts for showing me the actual Secret Garden; the Third Street School in Los Angeles for letting me observe; Halee Hochman for answering a million questions about eight-year-olds; Naomi Goldstein for both the professor's and the psychologist's angle; Lena Greenberg for her encouragement; and Gretchen Holbrook Gerzina's book *The Annotated Secret Garden*, which has been an invaluable resource.

And, of course, this book is, in many ways, a love letter to *The Secret Garden*, and so I'd like to take this opportunity to thank Frances Hodgson Burnett for giving the world her masterpiece, and me countless hours of reading delight. Her book continues to be a respite whenever I need one most.

Much love to all of the Flore clan, of which I am very proud to now officially be a member.

Finally, I wish there were words to express how grateful I feel for the love and support of my three favorite men. To Dad, Josh, and Indy, all of my love and thanks.

About the Author

JULIE BUXBAUM is a graduate of the University of Pennsylvania and Harvard Law School. Her first novel, *The Opposite of Love,* has been translated into eighteen languages, and optioned to film by Twentieth Century Fox. She currently lives in London.